Midnight HEIST

KATHERINE MCINTYRE

HOT TREE PUBLISHING

For information, contact the publisher, Hot Tree Publishing.

www.hottreepublishing.com

Editing: Hot Tree Editing

Cover Designer: BookSmith Design

E-book ISBN: 978-1-922359-54-4

Paperback ISBN: 978-1-922359-53-7

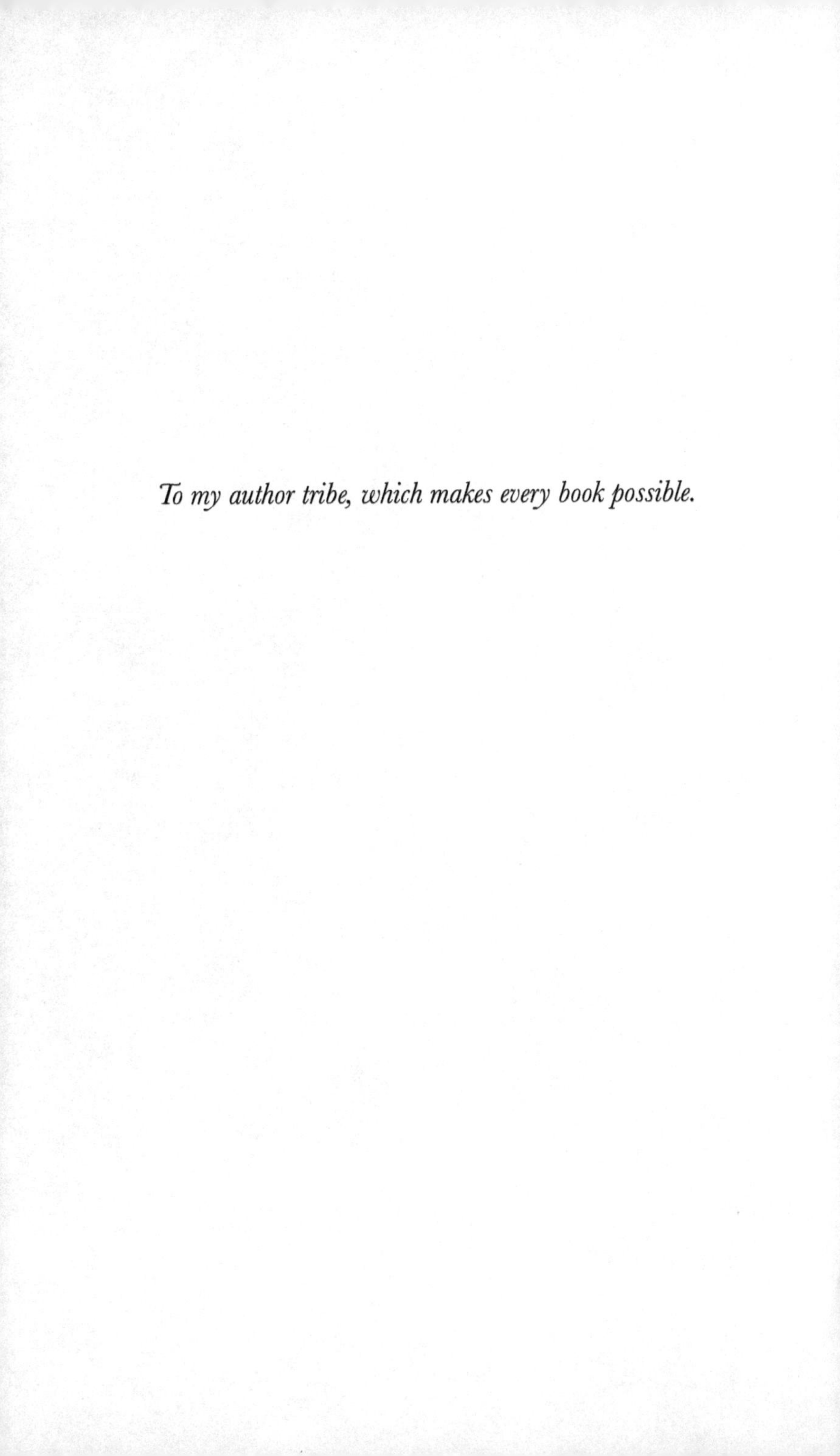

To my author tribe, which makes every book possible.

ONE

Grif Blackmore never did a job on a Tuesday.

The other Outlaws might call him a superstitious fuck, but he didn't give a damn. If he didn't have a code to live by, he wouldn't have much more than a vinegar attitude and too many scars to carry into the next life. Still, said code also meant he got saddled with research duty for their current job, trapped behind their luxury condo's wall of glass overlooking Lower West Side of big, beautiful, and rotting-from-within Chicago.

Static buzzed from the speaker at the main computer rig connected to the group comm in their family room opposite the foyer. Their console sat on the lacquer desk overlooking their spectacular view, a metallic beast Scarlet had assembled when they first set up shop here. Grif might not be on the job, but the others worked out in the field today. He perched in the leather seat. Until each member of his crew had walked in through the door, he wouldn't be able to settle. He tapped his foot to the melody in his head, the cycle of different tempos in constant flux.

His fingers flew across the keyboard as he dug in for more information on Torres Industries. The energy and commodities company was one of the businesses in the Aon Center, a skyscraper tall enough to loom over half of Chicago. After the insider tip he got last week on some of their seedier activities, they'd warranted a look. He knew at least a dozen people who would pay quality cash for the information to torpedo the corporation.

If a company was rich and corrupt, Grif Blackmore would destroy them. Most times, the two went hand in hand anyway. He'd sworn the oath years ago and still upheld it today.

The CEO's image popped up on the screen. Danilo Torres, a guy who looked far too young and attractive to be in charge of such a wide-scale operation. Slender eyebrows and a wide smile accented the soft curves of his face, and he must've inherited the bronzed Filipino skin tone and thick, dark hair from his father, the former head of the company. He'd taken over a mere year ago when Torres Sr. went into retirement. A few more years in the industry, and the big open smile would vanish, replaced by the slick fake sort that circulated around the upper echelons of the big corporations.

Grif had mastered his own game face far earlier than necessary.

He lit his cigarette, taking in a deep drag, and continued to run through the list of the top dogs in the company, most of whom neared retirement age. The nicotine did little to calm him, but he let out the slow exhale anyway. The smoke drifted to the vaulted ceiling. John would be pissed at him for smoking inside again, but he could pin the blame on Tucker. Each one of the Outlaws took their turn sitting out on jobs, but Grif never made a good benchwarmer.

If Luka told him this was a solid lead, he believed the man. Few had earned his trust, a fluid thing, but his top informant maintained a reliability rare in their realm of cutthroats and sellouts. Besides, the man ran a solid joint—Port and Porter was one of the few bastions for his kind that hadn't been outed by the cops at some point. He sucked in another drag and leaned forward to ash into the nearest coffee cup littering the desk. Grif peered inside. Crap, he'd sprinkled ash in a half-filled mug.

"Locksley." John's voice came loud and clear through the speaker. They always spoke through the comms in code names, and the Outlaws had dubbed him Locksley from the moment they heard of his vendetta and resulting mission to steal from the rich and give to the poor.

Grif shot up, his cigarette hanging from the side of his mouth. His shoulders braced for action, even though he sat behind a keyboard, not out in the field. He pressed on the silver comm button beside the console setup.

"What is it, J-man?"

"We're coming in hot. Need you to secure the perimeter."

"Aces. Taking care of the problem as we speak."

Grif didn't roll from his seat, he leapt. He nearly bit his cigarette in half with how tight his jaw clenched. Every damn time. Tuesday was cursed, yet his crew insisted on running jobs that day. He headed down the main hallway to open the door to what most would call a linen closet—but for his Outlaws, this was their personal armory. The crew kept everything in there from Sig Sauers to Barretts, hanging them on the walls, packing them into trunks. Anything they might need on a job was here.

And right now, he needed his trusty Barrett M82.

If Grif was a betting man, he'd place his money on a failed gig. Tails only happened when you fucked up, big-time.

The Sunset Ruby was an ambitious steal, but the owner, Robert Davies, had become one of the most important men in the United States in terms of wealth accumulated. And he'd also left bloodstains over almost every inch of this country. Grif had been tracking the man for years, but he didn't think they were ready to take him on yet.

However, when one of his prized possessions happened to be floating through town and Gangland's finest, Marco Nevarra, hired them to steal the exquisite ruby? They couldn't pass up the chance, damn the risk.

Grif checked over his baby, a beaut of a sniper rifle, and made sure she was locked and loaded. Then he headed farther down the hallway to the back room of their penthouse, the main area where they all hung out. They'd taken a high floor apartment for a reason, one overlooking all angles of the city—their place made for the perfect fortress. Most times, they approached through the back entrance of the building, by way of the network of alleys surrounding this area. Every aspect about their abode had been considered when they picked the spot. Grif strode into the room and set to work cracking the windows open. The brisk air that flooded in carried the razor-blade-cold edge of a Chicago winter wind.

Ash trailed off the end of his cigarette, flecks staining the tan carpet. Alanna would wring his neck for making a mess again. He smudged at them with the edge of his combat boot as he crouched in front of the window, settling in to get a good vantage point.

His sniper rifle rested on the portable mount they kept there. The edge of one of their couches brushed against his thigh every time he shifted, but he didn't have the time to move the damn thing.

The city stretched out before him from their seventh-floor view, a maze of skyscrapers, alleyways, and narrow streets. He searched for any tip-offs— erratic pursuit, or the subtler bystanders who would mill about the area, waiting.

This time of day, businessmen trotted along the sidewalks, clutching tight to their leather briefcases as they hustled to head home from work earlier than the rest of the scabs. Grif spat his spent cigarette out the window and settled into a deeper crouch. He peered through the sight of his Barrett. The main sprawl lay clear of his group of vagabonds. Scarlet worked offsite anyway, and J-man would be blending into the first crowd he found.

Grif searched for his shadows, Tucker and Alanna.

If the masters of stealth had caught tails, they'd well and truly fucked this job sideways.

He tilted the scope a fraction to peer down one of the alleys leading toward their penthouse building, a favorite spot of Alanna's. Flickers of movement snagged his attention as two figures clung close to the layered brick walls, blending in with the afternoon shade.

Bingo.

He backtracked, using the sight of his rifle as he traced farther down the alley to the intersection they'd come from. Three hulking guys in dark blue uniforms strode through the street faster than a local heading home, but not with the frantic hurry of a random on the run. He'd been in this game too long to not pick out hired security. He aimed the muzzle of his Barrett toward them, following their movements as they stormed through the same alley Alanna and Tucker had crossed.

His finger traced the trigger as he waited for a shout, a speed up, any sign he needed to act. Grif preferred avoiding casualties, but he wasn't naïve enough to hesitate.

His heartbeat amped to the thump-thump-thump he'd grown familiar with, and the tense breath caught in his throat. Every time he zeroed in on a target, the waiting began. He didn't bother tracking Alanna and Tucker—the reactions of these guards were all he needed to gauge.

They continued through the alleyway, a bit faster than before. Gravel and dust kicked up where they went. He tensed against the trigger. Any moment.

A drop of sweat crawled down his temple, iced by the breeze filtering through.

Ding. Ding. Ding.

The secret bell they'd installed to warn when

someone approached the apartment went off. The door had fingerprint metrics to make sure only the Outlaws could enter. Grif's gaze didn't leave his marks even as the door creaked and the thump of footprints followed. The sound increased in volume, traveling down the hallway behind him.

"You're going to lord this over Alanna and Tuck for the next century, aren't you," Grif said, not glancing back. Based on the heaviness of the tread, the arrival was none other than their resident con man, John Smith. Grif squinted as he shifted the grip of the Barrett along the padded mount. The security guards continued marching through the alley, straight past their penthouse without even casting a glance to the backlit sign. All too fast, the guards disappeared onto the main streets. Grif caught the glimpse of the uniforms as the guys ducked into the nearest unmarked vehicle that pulled up to the sidewalk.

"Where's Scarlet?" Grif asked.

"She's packing up still," John said. "I told her to take the long way home to avoid any trackers. Alanna and Tuck soaked the heat."

Ding. Ding. Ding.

Their alarm went off, and this time when their front door opened, two sets of footsteps followed. Grif's shoulders relaxed, and he stepped away from the window, pulling the barrel of his rifle inside. John approached to help close the windows. Grif clicked the safety on before shifting the mount aside and leaning his Barrett against the wall. He shook his numbed fingers out, the circulation returning with fiery pinpricks.

"Hey, boss," Alanna approached from the hallway. "We fucked up." The woman was all sharp angles, her plucked eyebrows precise enough to slice, cheekbones like a declaration, and obsidian eyes that bored into him. She wore her typical job gear, a black tank top and leggings, a strap belt around her waist filled with her arsenal of tools, and thick combat boots. She kept her nearly black hair pulled into a tight bun, and a constant frown creased her brow.

"What Alanna is trying to say is the whole thing was a setup," Tuck said, running a hand through his thick umber curls. The wiry guy crossed his arms, wearing a similar all black getup to his partner-in-stealth's. "Fairly certain Nevarra struck a deal with Davies so we'd get handed over on a silver platter."

"What Alanna *said* is we fucked up," she repeated, shooting him a dirty look. "We should've never given Nevarra as much cred as we did. But we're out one Sunset Ruby and owe the mafia a hefty sum."

Grif simmered inside, restraining his curses. He maintained a mask, because someone needed to lead this ragged band of misfits. "Where's the Sunset Ruby?" he asked, trying to suss out the one-two-threes of what had happened. He'd already begun walking down the hall toward the foyer, not questioning that the rest would follow.

"The alarms got tripped independently while they were inside the vault," John interjected, striding alongside him with his hands in his pockets. The man had broad enough shoulders to make an impression but possessed the blue eyes and blond hair to blend, one of the many reasons he was their best con man. "Someone had it out for us from the start. The second the alarms went off, the Sunset Ruby was the first thing evacuated from the exhibit, like they'd been tipped off."

Grif let out an exhale. Black days and bleaker times. He should've anticipated this shit, but they'd all been puppy-dog eager to sink their teeth into quarry from Davies. "So now we owe Nevarra his fee." The mafia head didn't tolerate failure, and a steep fee had been involved in taking this job in the first place.

Ding. Ding. Ding.

Scarlet had arrived. Their resident genderfluid hacker strolled in through the door, her crimson lipstick popping and her silver heels higher than practical. She carried her laptop bag slung on her right side like always.

"Hey Grif," she said, flashing him a dazzler of a grin. "The whole operation went bust."

He scrubbed his palms against his forehead. "Mind explaining what's hilarious then?"

"You missed Tuck faceplant on the floor mid-mission. Priceless stuff. I recorded it for posterity's sake." Scarlet grinned even wider, and several strands of her chin-length hair escaped the bobby pins. Tucker let out a groan. "You can bet I'm going to put that shit on replay. Oh, also, I've got a trace on whoever activated the alarm. We might not catch them today, but we're not going down without a second swing."

"Good job, sweetheart," he said, skimming his fingers through his hair. "For now, we'll work on obtaining the fee to fish us out of trouble with Nevarra."

Looked like the lead on Torres Industries wasn't just part of his vendetta.

This job had become a necessity.

TWO

Dan looked to the door of his office again. Philip Brennerman was fifteen minutes late.

Their CFO and his father's longtime friend had been the one making his transition to CEO of Torres Industries the hardest. The man kept treating him like a kid and refused to respect his time or position. Brennerman's brand of snide comments and chiding remarks made it clear he wanted to spit in his coffee. Dan might've been in charge for a year now, but every day of this job tore away more and more of his hope for humanity. He scanned over the figures on the stack of papers in front of him.

Each time he went through these, he kept finding discrepancies in different accounts. Minor ones, but his brain worked better with numbers than with people. The fluctuations in the reports seemed normal on the surface, but something was too regular about them, too even. The main employees who could influence the financials were all upper management, which meant he needed to conduct his investigation from the top down.

Every creak caused him to glance to the door. He sank into his leather seat, the change of position not shifting the unease in his stomach. One of the changes he'd made in taking over was that he wouldn't allow upper management's abuse of company funds, which his father had let slide in the past. Mostly because Torres Sr. was one of the main participants.

His employees gave the appearance of toeing the line, but truth be told, he didn't trust a soul in this building apart from his sister, Vanessa. Given her ambition and dedication, she should've been the CEO —they both agreed on that—but his pops remained entrenched in old-school misogyny, which meant men running the business. If Dan wanted to continue being a part of the family, he needed to don a suit and join the rest riding the elevator up the Aon Center every day. Forget the mechanical engineering grad studies he'd planned on returning to, or the whole career path he'd tailored in that direction.

He placed the stack of papers on the desk and paced over to the wide windows. This high up, Chicago sprawled out in all her industrial glory. In the distance, Lake Michigan dominated the horizon, glittering like a prized sapphire. This view wasn't worth the price he paid—too busy to keep up with friends, and too high up the food chain to swap stories with coworkers. At the end of the day, he didn't have enough energy to even swipe right on any dates for the indeterminable future.

"Nice to know our illustrious CEO has the time to admire the view." Brennerman appeared in the doorway, his Brooks Brothers suit impeccable, and his gray hair combed to the side and slicked down. The deep grooves along his features might look more distinguished with a stronger mouth, but the man always made up for any hint of softness with the verbal vomit pouring from his lips.

Dan glanced to his trimmed nails, biting back the acerbic response on his tongue. "Jealous, Phil?"

When Dan was growing up, the man had always been Mr. Brennerman, or sir, and every time they interacted, he expected more of the same. Tough. The man's pale blue eyes didn't narrow, but he crossed the room with a heavier stride than necessary.

"We need to discuss last quarter," Brennerman persisted. His eyebrows drew together, and his chiding tone burrowed right beneath Dan's skin. "Your father wouldn't want his business run into the ground, junior."

"My father retired," Dan said, his tone turning icy

as he met Brennerman's gaze. If he showed an ounce of weakness amongst these sociopaths, they'd shred him alive. "This is my business now, so you can either give me the rundown of last quarter's reports without the condescension, or you can leave my office."

He wanted to scream. He was trapped in this glass-and-cream room, dealing with a sea of old, arrogant bastards like this one and forced to maintain a politeness none of them deserved.

Brennerman strode past him to drop another manila packet onto his overfull hickory desk. More paperwork to look over; joy.

"We need more acquisitions," Brennerman said. "I've set Mike and Len on the task to bring new leads in."

Dan arched an eyebrow. Funny how the discrepancies he'd been mulling over had to do with acquisitions. They might be his employees, but Mike and Len were part of Brennerman's over-sixty club, and their loyalty lay with him.

"If we need to meet with more leads, who better to do it than the new face of the company?" Dan countered. "Better to get our new connections used to my leadership style from the outset. Mike and Len are off the job. I'll handle this personally."

To Brennerman's credit, he didn't stomp his feet or shake his fists, but Dan didn't miss the flash of acid in his gaze. Given their CFO's sway with the rest of the senior members of Torres Industries, Dan treaded on rotten floorboards.

"There's better use of your time than tasks to be handled by subordinates," Brennerman began.

Dan flashed his best attempt at a charming smile as he interrupted. "Weren't you mentioning all the free time I had? I might as well do something proactive for the company. Now, while I'm sure we have plenty more to discuss, I have a meeting in five I can't reschedule. We can go over the acquisitions numbers after I've had a chance to rectify the situation."

Brennerman opened his mouth, but Dan strode beside him with a lifted hand to guide the man over to the door. He might not have chosen this Patrick Bateman life, but he refused to be a doormat. Apart from when it came to family, of course, because he'd caved immediately to his father's demands of step up or get cut out—no more family dinners, big shindigs full of relatives he loved. However, if he had to be shackled to Torres Industries for the rest of his days, he'd make damn well sure the upper management didn't continue the illicit activities he suspected his father had been involved in for years.

"We'll meet later in the week," Brennerman insisted even as he headed toward the door. The man scrambled to sink his feet in any mud he could find.

"Sure," Dan said with a tilt of his head. "I'll have

my secretary send you a reminder of the meeting time."

Brennerman's face turned granite as the double meaning sank in. Danilo Torres might not be the same loud, charismatic man as his dad, but he wouldn't let his father's regime walk all over him.

And if Philip Brennerman had involved this company in illegal practices, Dan wouldn't stop following the trail until he tracked each and every problem down and eliminated the source.

THREE

THE TONE OF ANY DAY WAS SET BY THREE THINGS: coffee, bacon, and a plan.

This morning, Grif started out with all three, so he was leagues ahead of last week when they botched the Sunset Ruby job. He leaned back in his seat at the head of the table, chewing on an extra-crunchy piece of bacon—Scarlet always toed the line of charred when he took his turn at breakfast.

Alanna hunched over their nickel-and-glossy black kitchen table in sweats and an exercise bra. Both her palms were wrapped around the mug of chai that spread the aroma of sweet spices throughout the room. "Are you sure you guys don't need backup?"

She buzzed with the tension he understood so well —he always had a tough time sitting behind while the other players executed a job. Not to mention everyone in the Outlaws skated on edge since their failure. The bombed job didn't sit well after the talk with Nevarra went less than aces. The funds they could extract from this Torres Industries job would cover their debt with the mafia, which he wanted resolved ASAP. Besides, taking out another greedy corporation made for an added perk.

"It's a lunch meeting," John said, plunking into the seat next to her with a full plate of eggs, no bacon, because the man was a heathen. "If you're skulking around in the shadows, you'll just be a distraction." He'd been in prep mode, practicing tones and looks in the mirror, on top of his full agenda collating dossiers on each of the major players at Torres Industries.

"The whole point of stealth is not to be noticed or seen," Alanna argued, picking up her fork to jab the tines in his direction. "Your argument's faulty."

"You're too gorgeous to not be noticed," John responded, the smooth talk easy for him. He passed her an exaggerated wink before he dove into his massive plate of scrambled eggs.

Alanna flipped him the middle finger, her gaze bleeding irritation. "That fails to be a valid argument."

Grif took a sip of his pitch-dark coffee before responding. The smooth, hot liquid rolled down his throat, sparking him to life. "The argument isn't necessary, because you've got a different task than tailing us today."

Alanna rolled her eyes. "Building recon, I know, I know. Heaven forbid I do something else for once." Today, Alanna and Tuck would be bringing the blueprints of the Aon Center they'd obtained to match up entrances and exits, as well as marking grip points for any necessary climbs.

He snorted. "You want a different task? Learn a different skill."

Scarlet settled on the opposite side of the table, resting his tablet beside his plate as he scrolled through. The glow of the screen reflected against the thick-framed glasses he wore during down time.

"No stepping on my turf though," he said without looking up. "I've got no interest in the acrobatics you and Tuck do." Scarlet had been at hard work all week with Grif backing him up as they pulled together all of the threads necessary—website, a couple of years of earnings, full board of members—for Neo-National, their mock company.

"Let's get real, Ally dearest," John drawled as he leaned back in his seat, his eggs decimated. "If we put you in charge of the fast talking, every door would close in our face."

Alanna lifted her other middle finger, waving both at the whole table. "The lot of you, assholes. Remind me why I work with you again?"

"Because you're a sucker for cold, hard cash," Scarlet said, offering a bright, earnest grin. No one in the Outlaws could compete with his cheerfulness in the morning—or most times.

Tuck strode into the room on silent feet, his thick hair tousled from sleep. He yawned, covering his mouth with his forearm as he strode over to the stovetop where the remainder of the eggs and bacon waited to be snatched. The carafe of coffee grew perilously low. He loaded his plate in silence and then trundled over to join them at the table. Tuck managed to offer everyone a blink and a nod, but they didn't expect much more until he got some sustenance in him.

Scarlet looked up from his tablet to cast them a glance. Even in his casualwear of a maroon button-down shirt and black fitted jeans, he was an elegant handsome that belonged in front of a camera, not buried behind a screen. "Are you guys rehearsed on your proposition?"

Grif gave him a longer than average look, and Scarlet smiled.

"Well now, we're just Neo-National, a wind energy company looking to expand," John responded, his voice shifting to what Grif dubbed his con man tone. "Torres Industry has such a strong reputation, so we needed to at least try to approach you."

The best conmen adapted to any situation necessary, but he'd worked with enough to know each one developed an individual style. John saved his slick sarcasm for their home base. When he worked out in the field, he tended to project an honest front that wooed people far faster in this cynical age.

Alanna let out a gagging sound. "How anyone falls for your gee-golly tripe is beyond me."

"As opposed to browbeating them with insults?" Tuck asked, pushing his empty plate forward. "Name one member of this squad you don't pick arguments with." Even as he poked at Alanna, Tuck's chocolate eyes gleamed with warmth.

Grif sat back and sipped his coffee. Everyone kept different hours, and once the day began, they'd all be diving into their individual tasks, but he loved these breakfasts with his Outlaws. He still remembered the ones with his parents growing up—dinners and lunches might go by the wayside, but they'd always made time for breakfast. He'd continue the tradition they set, even though they couldn't.

Alanna scowled, her dark eyes alight with her normal brimstone. "I don't fight with Scarlet."

Scarlet raised his hand as he continued to skim through his tablet. "Leave me out of this squabble."

John snorted. "Point made. No one fights with Scar." He rose from his seat and gathered the empty plates, bringing them over to the dishwasher. "But I'll field your barbs all day long, sweetheart."

"Ugh." Alanna rolled her eyes. "Go flirt with a cactus, J. You'll get a better response."

"Can't," he said as he strolled in the direction of his bedroom. "I've got a business lunch to gussy up for."

Grif tipped back his mug to drain the dregs of his coffee before he pushed from the table to follow suit. "Ally and Tuck, I'll be waiting on your report when we return. Scarlet, get ready to field any calls or emails we acquire from the meeting."

Scarlet whistled. "Now get yourself in a suit, bossman."

Grif restrained his grin. He tossed a hand up as he sauntered out of the room. The plans had been laid—now he needed to set them in motion.

Skyscrapers towered on either side of the street, casting severe shadows across the landscape as the cab zoomed forward. Grif leaned back in the seat, his suitcase resting on his lap. His Valentino suit was custom-fit and meant to make an impression, a wool-blend, ink-black masterpiece he donned like a costume. He could play pretend with the best of the high rollers, even though he felt most at home in a hoodie and jogging pants.

When he'd crash landed into the underworld, all

the Krav Maga lessons and heavy training made him the blunt force on operations. After enough blood stained his knuckles, he lost track of whether they'd ever been clean. At least, until he'd siphoned enough funds away to stop working for others and started the Outlaws.

"The meeting today is with Leonard James, one of the heads of acquisitions, right?" Grif murmured out loud, running through the mental Rolodex of facts they'd accumulated for the false front they'd be parading under, one Scarlet alone would be the verifying force on. Thank everything holy for their tech wizard. They'd be sunk without him.

John stretched his hands in front of him, cracking his knuckles. The man had made a transformation from the guy lounging around the kitchen in his sweats, scruff on his chin, and blue eyes lit with the wicked humor they knew him for.

He'd pulled himself together in his typical Dolce and Gabbana navy suit with silver cuff links and a matching tie tack. John had combed his dirty-blond locks to the side like he was headed off for his first day working at the Capitol. He'd shaved, the clean lines highlighting a strong chin, and his eyes brimmed with an honesty the man didn't possess. No matter how many times Grif witnessed the transformation, he always found himself impressed.

"When we meet with the guy, I can take the lead

on the chatter," John said, casting him a glance. "Give you more space on the setup end." His gaze flickered to the hidden earpiece Grif wore, their direct link to Scarlet.

Their resident hacker would be listening in and filtering them any information necessary to justify their front as representatives from Neo-National. Scarlet had formulated a dummy page throughout the week, while he and John compiled the fake docket they'd sent to Torres Industries when requesting this meeting. Any extraneous information that might be dug up on them had been integrated into a variety of doctored news articles, old statements, and false names and faces that all routed to Scarlet.

"You're always better at charming our prospective clients, anyway," Grif responded, tapping his fingers along the shiny surface of his suitcase.

John passed him a look. "Your naturally intimidating demeanor is solid backup—you make me seem even more pleasant and legitimate—but yeah, you're not going to be winning over droves with your glower."

Grif smirked. "I've had a fair amount of success with my glower."

"Sure, maybe with shaking down cronies and the guys you bring to your bedroom, but we're talking the delicate art of business negotiations. That requires a finesse you can't slam your fists into." A hint of rebellion flared in John's gaze, the one bit of himself he let slip past the placid mask he wore.

The cabbie carved through the streets with a fluid ease of someone who'd done this drive in the dark during a helluva blizzard. Grif increased the tempo as he tapped out a beat on top of his briefcase—not from the nerves but the anticipation. In his past life, he could've never imagined the thrill of thieving or how well he'd fit into this life. However, in his past life, he could've never imagined his parents would get murdered as a part of a business maneuver.

Welcome to Chicago.

The cab slowed as they approached the intersection of Michigan and Chicago Ave. A stunning building with a bone-white granite façade appeared more like a museum than the entrance of Penn Luxe, the restaurant they were having their business lunch at. As the cabbie ground to a halt, John leaned up to pass him the fare. Grif stepped out and onto the asphalt. Showtime.

If they wanted a chance at getting inside Torres Industries at the Aon Center, this was step one. From there, the building would have a thousand and one advantages to exploit—they all did if you viewed them with the right eyes.

Penn Luxe was one of those places dripping muted elegance, which of course made this place a flytrap for all the bloated, too-loaded pests in the city.

His nose twitched as they headed to the front door of the joint, all glass. Places like this with their thousands of mirrors and reflective surfaces were prime real estate for narcissists and thieves. Once they stepped through the double glass doors, the cream and black accents assaulted him.

"We're here, Scar," he murmured, alerting him of their arrival.

"Roger that, boss," Scarlet said over the intercom in the semidistracted tone he always had while working. "I'm ready for you."

Grif approached the host stand first. "We have a reservation under Greg Locksley."

The thin waiter at the stand nodded, waving his arm in the direction of the dozens of circular tables spread out across the floor, most of them two or four seaters. "Your friend has already arrived. I'll take you to him."

Grif internally cursed. They hadn't arrived late, or even on time by any measure. They'd arrived early, because the control freak in him always preferred to be the first one to arrive. Showing up after meant he needed to adjust to their established terrain.

"Prep our welcome packet," he murmured, knowing Scarlet listened in. "If all goes well, send it off at the end of the meeting."

"You've got it," Scarlet responded loud and clear through his earpiece. "And Locksley? Have fun."

Grif restrained his snort as he strode behind the waiter who led them toward the back of the room. He searched out the vantage points on instinct. John kept a step or two behind him, his slower pace coming across as less intimidating than Grif's brisk walk.

The rich scent of quality steak lingered in the air, a pleasant orange blossom fragrance floating above it all. They passed the filled tables, but Grif hadn't spotted the older guy they were supposed to be meeting with. He'd checked out the pictures of Leonard James, your average rich sleaze who golfed on the weekends, fucked prostitutes after hours, and then went to church with his family on Sundays.

The waiter slowed and gestured toward a table with two seats open. Grif's eyebrows drew together as his gaze landed on the man waiting for them.

The guy looked decades too young. He appeared closer to his thirties like him, with his black hair slicked back, flawless bronze skin, and a serious, contemplative expression. He was pure professionalism in a gray Burberry suit that highlighted his trim figure, and everything matched from the platinum watch he wore to the tack on his tie. He stood to greet them and offered a blinder of a grin.

The open expression on his face was the innocent sort of hot that punched him in the gut, because Grif Blackmore liked to ruin pretty things. And wreck him, he would. His tongue traveled over the front of his teeth as he scanned the man up and down one more time.

Until it dawned on him why he looked so familiar.

Danilo Torres. They weren't having lunch with some easy-to-schmooze middle manager. The fucking CEO had shown up.

FOUR

Dan had taken over all of Mike and Len's acquisitions meetings for a few weeks, which meant he now perched in a black chair with the cream cushions that matched the rest of this swanky, unnecessary restaurant. Dozens of mirrors glared at him, like he'd entered a carnival attraction, and he couldn't help the residual discomfort he felt in posh places like these.

The discrepancies in the financials remained buried too deep to get a pulse of what went on, so he figured the hands-on approach might offer some tangible leads. Ever since he'd pulled a microscope over the company's earning and spending, Brennerman had been finding more and more excuses to meet with him. Dan took another sip from his coffee with enough milk and sugar to soothe his nerves. As if that could temper out the shitty attitudes of his employees.

Each time he entered the Aon Center and rode the elevator to Torres Industries, he needed to don a set of armor. And ever since Brennerman soured on him, the man had been spinning trouble. Dan didn't need the problems spelled out—he could see them in the furtive glances as he walked through the offices and the murmurs trailing him in the halls. Even the lack of quick response to his emails could be traced to unrest in the upper management.

Dan traced his finger around the rim of the porcelain cup, staring at the tan surface of his coffee. He almost didn't hear the slow thump of approaching footsteps.

For the first time since he started taking over these meetings, Dan was glad of the decision.

The two guys who strode his way were grade A gorgeous. One walked forward with a casual smile and stroll, his easy eyes gleaming. Even in the trim suit he wore, his height and broad shoulders betrayed the solid muscle he hid beneath the layers. However, the first guy might as well have been invisible once he spotted the other one.

The man sucked all the attention from the room with a glower in his ice-blue eyes and a presence that crashed in like an earthquake. Dan had to suck in a sharp breath as he scanned him over. His blond hair was tightly trimmed, his goatee neat in a way that highlighted his sharp chin and cheekbones. Even though he wore a Valentino suit accentuating a lean figure, his corded neck and the way he held himself made it clear he was all cut muscle.

Dan somehow shook some sense into himself, even if his dormant libido had kickstarted at the mere sight of this man who exuded power from his pores. Maybe if he moved like this guy, his employees might step in line.

"Welcome," he said, extending a hand. He flashed a smile, his body a traitor as he stood in front of this gorgeous man. "I stepped in for Leonard."

"What did we do to snare the attention of the CEO of Torres Industries?" the man said, reaching out to shake his hand. Their palms pressed together, and the guy shook with a firm and authoritative grip. If Dan was honest, the intensity made him a little weak in the knees, especially when he caught a whiff of amber and citrus from his cologne. The man stared him down like he wanted to devour him, and Dan was ready and willing to offer himself up.

"So, it seems you already know who I am," Dan said, pulling his hand back before his body betrayed him any more. He hadn't gotten laid in far too long, and it showed. "Now what's your name?"

"Greg Locksley." He flashed a grin that didn't soften his features in the slightest. That gaze could bore right through a person, and his stance screamed intimidation. Why he found that quality so damned attractive made him question his sanity.

"John Smith." The other guy stepped between them to extend his hand. Dan shook and offered a nod before the man continued. "We're thrilled to have the chance to talk to the CEO of Torres. If we had known, we might've sent someone higher up on the food chain than lowly reps like us."

Dan lifted his hand. "That's the exact sort of attitude I'm trying to dispel. The days of Torres Industries as an unapproachable hierarchy are of the past. I'm happy to meet with both of you today. Please, call me Dan."

Greg settled into a seat on the opposite side of the table and placed his suitcase beside him. He cast Dan an appraising look as their eyes met. "Okay, Dan. Then let's sit down and talk." For some reason, his name on those lips felt filthy, and he liked it. Christ, he needed to get his head in the game—every other meeting had been more of the same polite back and forth jabber, but he hadn't met anyone who evoked such a visceral reaction since his first boyfriend.

He returned to his seat as John took the one in the middle. Dan snagged the blue folder he'd brought on Neo-National even though he didn't need a refresher. He'd gone through the papers ahead of time. Their case seemed simple—a small organization looking for the stability of a larger company like his. Some of the others he'd fielded set off his internal alarms, companies that had no reason to be working with them, whether due to their current means or focus. He'd leveled extra questions their way, ones to make them sweat.

He refused to further the corruption rampant in Torres Industries, even if most of Chicago hated him by the end of this.

Dan tipped back his coffee cup again, finishing it as the waiter swung by to get drink orders—iced tea for John and whiskey for Greg.

"While I read the email request for the meeting, I'd like to hear from both of you in person as to why you're approaching Torres Industries," he started, taking control of the situation. "Your company seems to be in good standing, even if it's fairly new."

He leaned back in his seat, prepared to listen. The one thing he'd gotten sick of the most when he'd ascended into the CEO position was the sheer amount of lip service people paid him. Maybe old folks like his dad liked to reside over people like a lord and his peasants, but Dan hated that attitude. He just wanted people to be real with him. In an ideal world, he'd prefer not dealing with them at all, but he had entered the wrong industry for that.

John leaned forward. "We're looking to expand," he began. The man had a straightforward tone rather than the normal slick he'd been dealing with, which somehow set off his warning bells. Maybe it said something for the amount of douchebags he'd been dealing with that a regular response raised his suspicion. John continued, "There are limited avenues we can explore where we're at, and out of the companies we'd been looking to hitch our wagon to, yours has reputation and longevity behind it."

Dan restrained his sigh. He'd been hoping for something refreshing, but the man offered more of the same. "You have to understand, we get thousands of proposals a year. Why would your company be a good acquisition? Given the fact you're new in the field and barely tested, you don't have the permanency other proposals do to be a beneficial addition rather than a drain."

Greg crooked an eyebrow at him, something like surprise flashing in his eyes. Dan maintained his cool, sliding his thumb along the porcelain of his cup. Everyone continued to underestimate him, but he had no problem proving them wrong.

John opened his mouth, but before he could continue, Greg locked eyes with him.

"Because you're new," he said, the blunt words dropping into the air like a bomb. Dan blinked. He hadn't been expecting that response, and neither had John based on the dirty look he flashed his partner.

Dan didn't respond, waiting for Greg to continue.

The man didn't shrink at the silence, though in all honesty, he didn't look like a guy who cowered from anything.

Greg's lips curled in a hint of a grin, and his gaze never faltered. "You said it yourself. You're taking the hands-on approach because you're new to the role and want to establish the direction you're leading the company. If you continue with the older companies like the ones who formed in a different era, you're going to get more of the same attitudes. We might be new and untested, but we're malleable, flexible in a way the other companies wouldn't be."

Well, damn.

John gave his partner another look and shook his head, a grin spreading on his face. "I'd argue with my friend here, but he's making a damn good point."

Dan had half-expected the guy to backtrack rather than defending his coworker, but he admired the solidarity. And he was blown away by Greg—his audacity and his willingness to be candid.

The waiter swung around with their drinks, including a fresh cup of coffee. Dan seized the temporary interruption to collect himself. His immediate impulse was "thank fucking God," but people expected more decorum from the CEO of one of Chicago's heavy-hitter companies. One thing was sure —Greg Locksley was the exact shake-up he'd been looking for.

Dan poured some cream and then placed a few hefty spoonfuls of sugar in. As he stirred, Greg's gaze lingered on him.

"How are you supposed to taste the bitterness under all the sugar and cream?" The teasing note in Greg's voice stroked at Dan's libido. Hell, almost everything this man did made his brain switch to sex.

Dan couldn't help his smile as he lifted the steaming liquid to his lips. "Life's too short and chaotic not to indulge," he responded, his tone coming out more of a purr than intended. He coughed, wishing he could backtrack. Not like he was out at the company. "You've raised a valid point, enough that I'm willing to bring you into the office for a real discussion. Any acquisition has to be approved by the board, but if we nail down some details and everything about your business stacks up, you'll have the full weight of my support behind you."

John offered a grin as he took a sip from his iced tea. "We appreciate you giving us the chance. We know we're newer, but we've reached the point where we either expand on our own or find a company to connect with."

"We're looking forward to working with a company that's looking to move ahead instead of backward," Greg said before taking a swig of whiskey. "I'm guessing this conversation might've gone much differently if we'd been meeting with the original guy?"

Perceptive, perceptive. A wry grin spread on Dan's face as he shook his head. For the first time in far too long, someone got it—got him. "I need allies of my own in shaking up the company," he responded. Around someone like him, the duct tape had been peeled from his mouth, and he could speak at last. "There are plenty in the company who would prefer things stay the way they always were, but unfortunately for them, my father placed me in charge."

Greg's gaze smoldered. "Then I'm looking forward to shaking things up with you."

Dan sucked in a sharp breath. Damn if that wasn't a come-on. He reached into his pocket and pulled out one of his business cards. In the grip of madness, he jotted his cell number on the back. As if someone bolder, braver possessed him, he handed the card right into Greg's open palm.

"Feel free to contact me if you need anything." His gaze locked with Greg's. Based on the faint smile lingering on the man's face, his double meaning landed. His heart sped like he'd taken a hit of cocaine. If he doubted the attraction was mutual, one look from Greg confirmed he wasn't imagining things.

John reached past his partner to crack open the briefcase and pull out one of the folders. "We've got some figures here we didn't include in the initial email, but they should be some help." To his relief, John didn't even glance their way or make any mention of the loaded exchange.

Dan took another sip from his cup, trying to shake himself out of the stupor. He should be interviewing prospective acquisitions, not hitting on them, and sure as hell not handing out his personal number. If his lack of a dating life had seeped into his work, he needed to go on a Tinder spree, a blind date, or something more drastic. Even though he was supposed to be the one in the position of power, in charge, Greg Locksley had flipped him on his head in mere minutes.

His stomach flip-flopped. The idea of Greg ignoring his number to go on his merry way made his nerves simmer, but it paled in comparison to the prospect of what might happen if he called.

FIVE

Grif stared at the toothache-white ceiling of his room. He leaned back against his mattress, his bed a minefield of tousled blankets, World War II memoirs, and the array of lockpicking tools he'd been playing with the night before when he couldn't fall asleep. Tough to catch shut-eye when the liquid running through his veins consisted of 50 percent coffee.

He flipped a quarter into the air. Heads, he'd call Danilo Torres. Tails, he'd keep their relationship strictly professional.

Grif continued to toss the quarter in the air again and again. Once they'd returned to the Outlaws' HQ, he'd ditched the suit for a pair of sweats. They'd secured their in, so the rest of the day's work could be done slacking behind a computer screen. He heaved a sigh. Dan Torres wasn't the musty old jackass he'd expected. The guy seemed earnest and genuine. Plus, he'd watched the guy leave. The way Dan's muscled ass filled out his trim suit could fast turn into a fetish.

Grif snatched the quarter out of the air and smacked it on his arm. Decision made. He tossed the coin to the ground and stretched from the bed to reach for the pocket of his suit jacket, which hung off the chair by his desk. He stretched further, almost teetering off the edge as he snatched his phone.

This was the smart move to make. He'd have an inside angle on the company, and maybe he could even finagle access to his private files. After he indulged in some other private access, that was.

Grif dialed the number and sank back into his bed to stare at a ceiling so pristine he wanted to splatter paint across it. As soon as the phone began to ring, the first pinpricks of adrenaline trickled through his veins, a surefire sign his dick had taken the wheel.

"Hello?" That delicious voice sounded on the other end.

"For all the swanky fixtures and fancy lingo at Penn Luxe, their meals don't do a whole lot to whet an appetite," Grif responded, dragging the tip of his finger along his phone case. He swung his foot back and forth in front of him; *tick-tock, tick-tock.*

"Greg Locksley," Dan responded, a hint of wonder in his tone. Hot damn, he couldn't help but imagine the guy on the other end, all soft brown eyes and bronze skin he wanted to bite. "I wasn't sure if you would call."

"I wasn't sure either." He hadn't lied—game time decision and all.

"Look, I'm sorry. We were at a business meeting—it was inappropriate. I can't be asking out prospective clients." The worry in his tone contradicted every dirty deal whispered about Torres Industries. Grif was dead-on with his reads, and this guy didn't fit amongst the sharks circling for chum in corporate.

"Well, that's an easy solve. I'll ask you," he drawled. "Meet me at Polished Knives tonight. Seven sharp."

"Is that a date, Mr. Locksley?" Dan's tone turned coy, the sound enough to get his blood pumping.

"Well, it's sure as hell not another business meeting," he responded. "See you there, gorgeous." Grif didn't give him the chance to respond, ending the call. He rolled up from the bed and tossed his phone onto the mattress. Time to strip out of these sweats and slide into something suitable. Tonight, he had a date with their mark.

POLISHED KNIVES WAS ONE OF THOSE DARK, SULTRY places with enough glossy surfaces to convince almost anyone that blood hadn't stained them. Grif had been one of the people making the messes back in his beater days. Unlike a lot of the thieves' joints in Chicago that gave off a "fuck right off" vibe, this one managed to blend in with average society.

"Hey, J-Bass." Grif lifted his fingers in salute before striding past the bouncer.

The hulk of a guy leaned against the side wall, his arms crossed and a sketchy look in his eyes. "I know that look in your eye. Don't tell me you're bringing another booty call to this place, G. You're going to give us a bad reputation."

He snorted, following through with a middle finger. "I'll quit when they stop showing up for the slaughter," he called as he sauntered past the backlit bar, all cream, polished obsidian, and pine. The bottles of scotch were on full display, the lights making the amber liquid glow. Black vinyl booths stretched throughout the entire place, and Edison bulbs overhead cast the perfect amount of dim lighting to blend the lines between murky and intimate.

J-man and Scarlet had voiced their complaints at his excursion, but he'd been able to dodge out before Alanna and Tuck returned, saving him from even more reaming out. The only thing he risked was an STD, but he'd brought condoms to solve that. He wouldn't blow their cover, and he'd already established this date wasn't about business.

Grif slipped into the corner booth tucked away in the opposite end of the place, the one he always claimed when he visited Polished Knives. He hated having his back exposed. He sank into the black vinyl booth, and his fingertips skimmed against the wood grain of the pine tables, the variation in the yellowed wood even more distinct with all the shadows begging to dive into the cracks. Within seconds of sitting, Kelly swung over with his normal scotch, neat.

He checked his watch. After getting caught arriving second at lunch, he'd headed out extra early to make sure he showed up first here. All the more time to settle in and decompress. Grif sank into the seat and tipped back the glass. The velvety sip lingered on his tongue even after he swallowed it down.

Couples chatted in the booths all around him, some leaning forward, eyes locked and loaded, while others teetered back with an ease to their conversation suggesting they'd known each other for ages. He already picked out the three underground deals going on, from the quick flash of a gang tattoo on a wrist to the way their hands would brush to their waists where he could guarantee a piece hid.

He'd lifted his glass, ready to take another sip, when his gaze landed on Dan Torres.

The man wore a dark pair of jeans that highlighted

muscular thighs and a thick brown belt Grif couldn't wait to tear off. Dan's ice-blue button-down accented his slender frame, and with the top buttons undone and the sleeves rolled to his elbows, the brief glimpses of his smooth, tan skin enticed. His thick black hair was slicked back, and as he approached, Grif caught the hint of ginger and lime from his cologne. Dan's gaze zeroed in on him, interest flashing in that gaze.

"Do you always roll the dice with your dates?" Dan asked, slipping into the seat opposite him. He began to fidget with his sleeves, as if they weren't already rolled all the way to his elbows. "I never gave you a yes or no—I could've no-showed."

"Instincts," Grif responded, lifting his glass for another sip of scotch. "You seem a decent sort, the kind of guy who'd follow up. And even if you weren't, I'm not opposed to grabbing a glass of scotch at my favorite bar solo."

"Am I that easy to read?" Dan asked, his careful eyebrows drawing together. A grin spread on his lips. "Let's put your instincts to the test. Order a drink for me."

The man was fucking adorable, which was a problem. Where at their business meeting he'd been competent and forthright, even in the five seconds they'd been on this date, Grif noticed the shift. This playfulness, the hesitant flirtation hadn't been there at the meeting, but he enjoyed it like a glass of fifteen-year Glenfiddich.

Grif couldn't help his grin in return. Kelly strolled over, smoothing the black apron she wore with the black tee and equally color-devoid pants. She gave Dan a cursory scan—he wore a Cartier watch with a black band, no obvious piercings, and not a strand of his hair was out of place.

"What'll you have?" Kelly asked, leaning against the side of the booth as she glanced to Dan. His date looked to him.

"Would you mind bringing over an Old Fashioned?" Grif asked. Kelly pursed her lips to try and hide her smirk as she nodded and headed off to the bar.

Dan crooked an eyebrow. "What makes you say Old Fashioned?"

"Bourbon's on the sweeter side, which by the way you massacre your coffee it's clear you like. You're careful about your appearance, meticulous, so no time for extravagant or ridiculous ingredients. Besides, the Old Fashioned is a classic with wide appeal." Grif leaned back, placing his arms on either side of the booth.

"Cheater," Dan responded, the grin reaching his eyes. "Was your next choice a rum and Coke?"

Grif snorted. "You've got way too much class to be a rum and Coke."

A blush darkened Dan's cheeks, and he glanced down at his hands clasped in front of him. Heaven and hell, he was the easiest mark to read on the planet—all his expressions brimmed right on the surface. Grif's stomach twisted with what might have been guilt if he hadn't divorced his conscience and ignored the alimony years ago.

"Business meetings I can do, but this stuff is way out of my depth," Dan confessed. "What are the usual date questions? Hobbies? Favorite dinosaur?" He ran a hand through his hair, casting him a helpless look.

A genuine smile stole Grif's lips before he could help himself. Too damned adorable. "Favorite dinosaur is a new one. I was always a big fan of the allosaurus. I'm not much of a Q and A kind of guy anyway. Relax, this isn't an audition."

"You sure?" Dan's forehead wrinkled. "My dating life has reached prehistoric status, so rusty is putting it mildly."

Grif shook his head. "Big-time CEO like you? I'd assume you'd be up to your ears in dick, pardon my French."

Dan's shoulders relaxed, and amusement gleamed in his dark eyes. "Trouble with one year under your belt at a company like Torres Industries is the learning curve is steep. Shockingly, running a company the right way requires a whole lot of extra legwork."

Grif's gaze traveled to the side of the booth where one of Torres's long legs stretched out. "Looks like it's paying off."

Dan shook his head, the grin widening on his lips. "That was pretty bad. Are you always this shameless?"

Grif shrugged, lifting his scotch to his lips. His gaze snagged on Dan's, and he didn't look away. "Only if I'm interested."

Kelly swung by with the Old Fashioned, and Dan tipped the drink back in seconds. He buzzed like he was way more nervous here. Dan's tongue trailed across his lower lip, and Grif couldn't help but watch. Dan had a mouth made for smiling, and his smooth lips glistened from the liquid. The man was pure temptation in one slender package.

"Damn, you were on the money," he responded, swirling his drink around. "This is delicious. Honestly, your directness is one of the things I like the most about you. Most times there's so much subtle back and forth, and everyone's too afraid to make a move or a declaration. With how demanding the position's been, I just don't have time for that."

"Neither do I." Grif ran his tongue behind his teeth as he tapped his foot on the ground. Maybe this had been a trash plan from the start. He'd expected Dan to be a hot-as-fuck lay, but even in their short back and forth here, he found himself liking the guy.

He could empathize with the way leadership drained like an IV drip—lives rode on his decisions, some of the few he gave a damn about. And already from their brief conversation, he'd drawn several enlightening conclusions about the man.

"How'd you get stuck in the role?" Grif asked.

Dan's eyebrows shot up. "Those are some damned good instincts. Did you do a stint as a detective or something?"

Grif's lips quirked, but he didn't answer. Working card tables, fighting for money, or years of running cons bubbled to the surface, but one word summed up all those responses: survival.

Dan lifted his hands. "All right, all right. First off, from a business standpoint—we're doing fine."

"CEO and prospective left at the business meeting," Grif reminded him. "Right here, we're just Greg and Dan, and I'm curious."

Dan took another swig from his Old Fashioned before he continued, the ice clinking in the glass. "Dad retired, and instead of transferring the position to Vanessa, who's been working for this role her entire life, he decided to drag his oldest son into the business. He's old-school, which is code for being a sexist dick. I was finishing up grad studies to go into a mechanical engineering job, just me and the numbers."

"Instead, you're stuck babysitting a bunch of old dickheads, from the sounds of it," Grif responded. He slammed back the rest of his scotch, hoping the liquid would burn away the rusted knife of regret carving a hold in his chest. This guy didn't deserve to get bled dry, even if the rest of his company made their fortunes at the expense of every Joe, Sally, and Bob.

"Seriously, man, I don't believe in psychics, but you're making me question it." Dan ran his fingers through his hair again. Grif wanted to reach across the table and follow suit, to grip him by the neck and taste the bourbon on those sensual lips. Dan locked eyes with him, curiosity gleaming there. "I'm sitting here complaining though. Tell me more about you."

"What do you want to know?" Grif asked, his brain running through the Rolodex of Greg Locksley.

"Well, hell," Dan said, tapping his fingers on the table. The attraction between them was a static force in the air, and Dan's gaze penetrated right through him. "Forget the number of siblings, net worth bullshit. I want to know what makes Greg Locksley tick. What were your dreams as a kid? What do you want out of life?"

Grif's eyebrows drew together before he could help himself. Window trappings were how he constructed all his aliases, easy character details he could draw upon at any point. However, Dan was a sledgehammer disguised as a too-honest sweetheart who happened to have an ass made for gripping and the type of slim body Grif wanted to bend over and fuck.

He'd learned the old adage early: the best lies drew from truth.

Grif crossed his arms over his chest. "I was a weird kid. No fireman or astronaut for me. I wanted to be a librarian."

Dan's jaw dropped. "No, really? That's so damn adorable."

Grif's lips quirked with his half-smile while he tamped the bitterness like espresso grounds. Stupid dreams of a naïve kid who still had both of his parents. Those got buried the same day they did. "As for what I want out of life, I'm never going to be a picket fence kind of guy. I like my freedom. But I'm all for seeking out the next opportunity; anything to put me in a better position to clear out the mess of double dealings in the corporate life."

The conviction in Dan's eyes as he nodded got his blood pumping a little harder. Rarely did he find folks who had *that* look. The ones he'd met, he'd already scooped up and included in his Outlaws.

Scar and J-man were right. He shouldn't have indulged in the date tonight. Grif tapped the side of his empty glass. He should call it quits now, before this guy managed to scalpel any deeper beneath his surface layers.

"Hey, do you want to get out of here?" Dan

asked, his tone dripping with intent. Grif tapped the side of his glass, once, twice, three times. "My condo's up the street."

Well now, those were the magic words. His libido thrummed to life again, and he shoved all his obnoxious feelings into the sidecar.

"I've got a tab here, so the bill's already paid," Grif said, pushing up from the table. "Lead the way."

SIX

Dan's palms broke into a sweat before they ever left Polished Knives. Greg Locksley stepped inside, and the door to his condo closed with a click. Even here, in Dan's own home, the man dominated the space. It was like he'd invited the Big Bad Wolf in through his front door.

From the second he'd arrived at the bar to find Greg sprawled in the booth waiting for him, he'd wanted to pinch himself. The summer sky eyes had bored into him with the same predatory intent, and even the way he lounged there couldn't hide the sheer power brimming with every move.

Dan flipped on the lights and thanked everything holy he'd had the foresight to clean earlier in the week. The soft glow of his overheads revealed his living room, all tan cushions on the couches and patterned stone half-walls. He didn't miss how Greg's gaze drifted to the black-and-chrome staircase leading to his bedroom. Not like what they both had on their minds was any secret.

Greg shrugged off his fitted leather jacket and slung it over his shoulder in a liquid move. Dan's tongue slipped out to trace his lips before he could help himself. In a thin white T-shirt, the man was carved from enough muscle to make him salivate, and the dim lights of his apartment emphasized the wicked curve of his eyebrows, the bit of stubble grazing a proud chin, and his aquiline nose.

Dan wasn't the type to bring guys back home on the first date, but for Greg Locksley, he made an exception. This man was a lightning strike of coiled sexuality and magnetism, and he'd never felt his libido slam into awareness with this freighter force. Besides, despite the conviction that blazed in Greg's gaze and the blunt way he swung his words around, Dan sensed a savagery to him as difficult to contain as a wildfire.

If he didn't indulge in this now and missed the chance, passing on a night with Greg Locksley was something he'd regret.

Dan reached out to grab the jacket from him and strode with it to his coat closet. He tried to ignore the rich scent of the leather and how he could feel this man's presence suffuse through every inch of his condo, even with his back turned to him.

The door clicked shut, the sound echoing in the intense quiet that descended between them like the hazy, loaded moments before a storm.

"So, I guess this is the point where I offer you a drink," Dan said when he turned around.

Greg loomed, his shadow falling across him as the man stood mere inches away. A feral grin curled his lips. "I'll take you up on the offer," he murmured, sensuality dripping from his lips.

Dan's brow creased as he digested the words. Not like he got the chance to think for long. Greg closed the inches between them with one step forward, then another. Dan moved on instinct, his back thumping against the wall. Greg's arm shot out beside his head, the look in his ice-blue eyes pure wolf.

This wild man pinned Dan against the wall, and he couldn't think of a time his body had last soared with a thrill like this. His cock stiffened from the masculine scent of him, the contained strength of his surrounding muscles, and the gorgeous features that held him spellbound. Dan's mouth dropped open in response, his breaths coming out in short pants.

"Last chance to duck and run, Torres," Greg murmured, his words low and hoarse, like he fought to rope down a twister. "Because I've been wanting to wreck you from the moment I saw your hot-as-sin face."

Fuck, this guy turned him upside down.

"Bring it."

Greg's sensuous mouth curled into a cocky grin, and he leaned forward.

Greg Locksley's kiss wasn't anything as tame as "thrilling." His kiss was the walk up to the cliffs as the sea churned foamy crests below; one step off the edge of such soaring heights guaranteeing destruction. Greg's fingers wove through Dan's hair, and he gripped his nape tight. As he sank his lips over his, he didn't just possess, he devoured. A sinful shudder rolled down Dan's back as he let the sensations glide through him.

He reached out, his fingers trailing over the flimsy fabric of Greg's T-shirt, and he slipped them beneath the hem. When his fingertips touched the scorching heat of that muscled chest, he almost drew them away, as if burned. Greg's lips met his again and again, his tongue slipping in to stroke with a force that left him breathless. Dan settled his hand around the slim black belt looped through Greg's jeans.

Greg closed the space between them, and Dan's back pressed against the cool wall. Those big thighs surrounded him on either side, and as Greg settled around him, the firm length in his jeans brushed against his thigh. Dan's erection throbbed at the contact, and he sank deeper into the kiss. His fingers fumbled as he flicked open the latch on Greg's belt. His cologne formed a heady musk combined with the lingering scent of leather, dizzying his mind almost as much as the rough kisses.

Greg's stubble scraped against his chin, his tongue entering his mouth with thrusts that made him weak in the knees. He bit Greg's lower lip, desperate to feel, to taste, to touch. Precum beaded on the tip of Dan's cock at the way this man descended to claim control, as effortlessly smooth as a sword wielded by a master. Greg tugged at his hair, and a shiver trickled through him at the possessive hold. Everything about being pinned against the wall by this massive, muscled man turned him on in ways he hadn't thought possible.

Dan undid the buttons on Greg's jeans, and he followed with the zipper, the snick audible between their harsh, ragged breaths. Greg's mouth proved an insatiable distraction. His lips brushed against Dan's neck, biting and sucking the sensitive skin. Dan's cock throbbed, and in the haze, he couldn't focus on anything beyond getting the guy's jeans off.

He shoved the fabric down, bringing the waistband of Greg's CKs and jeans to his knees in one go. His hand glided over Greg's cock, which was thick and long enough that Dan couldn't help his moan.

"See something you like?" Greg murmured against his mouth, and he pressed his palm over Dan's to glide his hand up and down his erection, once, twice. The smooth feel of the velvet skin against his palm caused hunger to coil tighter inside him.

"Very much," Dan responded, his voice a throaty, foreign thing. He slipped out of Greg's grip and lowered to the ground. He wanted to breach the defensive walls this gorgeous man hid behind, to sneak past the gates. Dan already spun undone from the mere whisper of what Greg had offered.

His knees hit the oak floor, and he hadn't even leaned forward before Greg's fingers wove through his hair. All the time and effort he spent on his appearance, trying to fit into this posh and polished world he'd never planned on entering, and this man dropped in, cracking him wide open the moment they met. Greg's grip tightened on his hair, the dose of pleasure-pain shooting straight to his toes.

Dan reached out to trail his palm along those smooth, thick thighs, all muscle and light blond hair. The bumps and knots of scars marked them the whole way down. He leaned forward, bracing his other hand on his thigh as he licked the tip of Greg's dick. The salty taste of his precum spread across his tongue, and the musky scent of his cock had Dan's own aching.

He wrapped his lips around Greg's erection before he took the whole length in his mouth. The man let out a guttural grunt, and his thighs tensed. Greg rocked his hips forward, and together, they found a rhythm that he lost himself in. Dan stroked his tongue along the base of Greg's cock, unable to help the way his throat tightened. This man made him so hot, skin flushed and his mind spinning in a delirious whirl. If the guy even stroked his length, he was liable to explode on the spot.

Greg rocked into him with enough power to his thrusts that the tip of his cock hit the back of his throat. Dan took all of him in, fueled by a hunger that had been growing ever since they'd met. He'd been in long-term relationships with guys and never learned their bodies the way he instinctively understood Greg's. His thighs squeezed tight, and Dan sucked harder. He needed to bring him over the edge.

"Heaven and hell, you're fucking sexy," Greg panted as he yanked on Dan's hair. "But I'd rather come inside you."

Greg stepped back to draw his cock out of Dan's mouth. Dan's tongue traced his lips before he could help himself. Greg reached down and offered a hand up, and Dan rose on shaky legs. His cock throbbed with a deafening demand, need squeezing him tighter and tighter.

Greg toed off his boots, and a second later, his jeans hit the floor. Dan reached out to tug at the hem of his shirt. The man winked before he slung the flimsy fabric up and over. It hit the floor a moment later, leaving all six foot four of this massive man bare. Dan couldn't help but gape. This wasn't the body of your average office worker, or even a guy who hit the gym every day. Ridges of cut muscle, the raised skin of countless scars, and the readiness to his frame brought his mind to bare-knuckle boxers or underground fighters.

"Your turn," Greg purred in his ear as his fingers worked the buttons on his shirt.

Dan's cock strained the fabric of his jeans. He was so hard right now, his erection might punch right through the seams. Greg's fingers moved fast, but Dan couldn't look away from that intense gaze. The man saw all of him without even trying, like he could peer past to peek at his inner thoughts, his fears, his worries. Even fully clothed, he felt utterly stripped down.

Greg undid the final button of his shirt, and Dan shrugged it off his shoulders. Dan's palms skated the surface of Greg's muscular arms, running across the ridges and firm lines.

Any other time he'd tried the one-night stand thing, his insecurities had risen to the surface—how he wished he packed on more muscle, how he hated the way the part in his hair fell, even his bony ankles —but Greg's appreciative gaze melted all the concerns away.

Greg grabbed Dan's belt and gave a hard yank. Dan stumbled from the tug, and by the time Greg's mouth crashed against his again, his belt had hit the floor with a clank. Greg shoved his jeans down with enough force to send him careening into his arms. The man caught him with no effort, those strong arms bracing him. His chest pressed against the firm wall of Greg Locksley, but the moment their cocks brushed against each other, his mind near blanked. The silken feel of Greg's against his was too much euphoria too fast.

Greg kissed him, the rough stubble scraping against his chin again, and then the man wrapped a hand around his cock and began to pump. Fuck, that felt so good he might blow on the spot. Dan let out a low moan, his hands gripping defined hips that trailed in a V toward Greg's heavy, thick cock. Their legs tangled together, and he continued to kiss him back, surrendering to the volcanic force of this man.

"God, I need you inside me now," he breathed, the ache unbearable with the way Greg stroked up and down his shaft. Dan reached up to skim his hands through the flaxen hair of the guy who towered over him like some Michelangelo. Something tender flashed in that sultry gaze, and Dan's heart sped a little faster.

"And to think, I didn't even have to ask you to beg," Greg murmured against his lips. "I want to ride you so fucking hard. I came prepared."

Three magic words. This had been a done deal the moment he slipped his number into Greg's hand. Dan could have melted in those arms as Greg wrapped them around his waist. Greg leaned down to grab something from his jeans pocket before he guided them away from the wall and into the living room. They stepped toward his coffee table, and his palms broke into a sweat in anticipation.

"Bend over, sweetheart." Greg's voice held a command he didn't dare defy, but the silky way he said the words was the smooth glide of butter over toast. Dan leaned against his polished mahogany table and braced his palms against the surface. Greg's hands settled around his hips, and Dan thrust his ass back, not giving a damn how needy he seemed. He wanted that cock buried in him so badly, he couldn't see straight.

Greg's palm glided over the slope of his ass, and Dan sucked in a sharp breath in anticipation. The cap snapped, and a moment later, the travel-sized lube clattered onto the coffee table. Greg's thumb brushed over his asshole, and Dan's knees almost buckled on the spot. Greg teased around the hole with small, maddening circles before sliding a cool, slick finger inside. He pumped one in, and then followed with a second. Dan's breaths came out hard as his cock throbbed from how damn good that felt.

Dan glanced over his shoulder, a pert grin rising to his lips. "Thought I said I wanted your fucking cock," he snarked.

Greg's palm cracked down on his ass a second later as he thrust his fingers in harder. "Brat."

Something coiled tight inside him. Whether it was the hunger reaching a roar he couldn't deny or the ease he'd felt around Greg from the second they met, he'd been searching for this feeling for far too long. The rip of the foil packet followed. Greg nudged the head of his cock against Dan's entrance, and all other thoughts vanished from his mind. He eased in, inch by thick inch, taking his time as he alternated between forward motion and retreat until desperate words leapt to Dan's lips.

Then Greg sank his full length inside him, causing the breath to leave his throat.

Dan saw sparks, and a curse slipped past his lips. The man filled him utterly, his large, smooth length perfect inside. Greg began to rock behind him, and all Dan could do was grip the table, his palms growing slicker by the moment. Greg's hands wrapped tight around his hips, bracing him there. He couldn't explain why he trusted that touch implicitly, or how he knew that for all the snarl and power behind those movements, the man wouldn't dare hurt him.

Greg began at a slow roll, each glide inward making his cock stiffer. Fuck, he wouldn't last long. When he started ramming in harder, that was when need pounded through his entire body, more intensely than a steamy shower after an exhausting day. Greg leaned over, pinning him to the table. His taut nipples grazed against Dan's back, and his hands pressed onto the table beside his. Greg thrust with enough force to radiate through Dan's whole body.

"You feel so fucking good, gorgeous," Greg purred in his ear, the throaty sound of his deep voice so hot. His cock throbbed, and then Greg's hand wrapped around it. He continued to thrust inside him, but those strokes of Greg's palm against his cock sent him tumbling over the edge. Dan swore as his vision blanked. His hands curled onto the table as heat spurted from inside him. He emptied out, cum splattering on the smooth mahogany surface.

Dan let out a ragged breath, the force of the orgasm still radiating through him. It pulsed in waves, each one threatening to drag him under all over again. Greg hadn't stopped thrusting. His grip tightened on his hips, and his nails bit into Dan's skin with a delicious sting that brought him back down to earth. Sweat pricked on Dan's forehead, and his knees threatened to buckle. Greg's hold on his hips alone kept him upright.

Greg glided all the way in again, hard enough that Dan almost slid forward on the table. His cock stiffened inside him, and a moment later, Dan could feel the pulse of his orgasm as he came. Greg leaned over him, their sweat-slicked skin glued together as the cycle of their heavy breaths cut through the loaded quiet of his condo. When Greg finally went limp inside him, he pulled out and took a seat on the edge of his coffee table, the massive man testing the weight of his expensive furniture.

Though, after the way he'd just come, Greg could break anything he liked.

Dan's chest heaved as he took a seat on the other side, not trusting his legs to hold him upright. Sweat beaded his forehead, slicked his backside, and several droplets glided down his chest. Greg glanced at him, inches away, and reached forward to sweep his fingers across Dan's thigh. In the moment, the tender touch meant everything.

The man was breathtaking, the ice in his eyes melting and the shadows suffusing the defined edges of his features. With his golden strands mussed and his shoulders rising with his breaths, Greg no longer seemed remote, but tangible in a way that enhanced his sexiness. The effects of the orgasm radiated through him, traveling down his legs, and his skin grew tender where Greg's stubble had raked across it.

Dan's lips quirked as he shot Greg a glance. "You don't mess around, do you? I haven't had sex like that in forever."

Greg crooked an eyebrow at him. "What gave you the impression this was finished?" Those fingers gripped tight along his thigh with a possessive hold. "We've got all night."

SEVEN

Grif's eyes snapped open.

A glacial sweat coated his skin, an aftereffect of the nightmares that always haunted his sleep. He glanced up—strange ceiling, not his. He was rolling up and onto his feet by the time he realized he'd never left Dan's condo. To his relief, the inky hues of night coated all the pristine surfaces of this place. The moon cast her steady beams through the windows, spilling silver like it didn't cost a cent.

Dan slept on his side. The soft light of the early hours turned his dark lashes even darker and accentuated the curve of those plush lips. Like this, the guy radiated innocence, even after the filthy things they'd gotten up to. Grif had taken plenty of guys to bed before, but few of them were as responsive and intuitive as Dan. The chemistry between them was rare, something that couldn't be concocted in a lab.

Except, he hadn't just arrived for an unforgettable night. The Outlaws would take turns gouging him with the contents of their armory if he didn't root around for some extra intel—and that's if he didn't flay himself first. Grif ignored the lurch inside his chest and snagged his clothes from the bedroom floor where he'd dragged them before he and Dan had passed out. Another rule broken, but he hadn't been able to resist when Dan tugged him into that inviting bed and offered a sweet-as-sin smile.

Grif ran a hand through his hair in an attempt to clear his head. He needed to forget the delicious ache in his muscles from all the exertion they'd gotten up to last night and the nail indents in his thighs from when Dan got enthusiastic. Intel. Right. What he really needed to do was start rummaging through the guy's stuff before the daylight hours hit.

He skimmed his fingers along the smooth surface of Dan's desk on the opposite side of the room. Everything from binders tucked in the side shelf to the pens in their proper holder was precise, neat. His skin prickled—he'd been stealing for a long time, but rarely did he feel like a thief.

Grif tugged open the drawers, slowly, so they didn't make a squeak. Folders stacked up inside the top drawer, and he plucked them out to skim, one by one. With the minimal lighting, he couldn't decipher many of the words, but he'd worked in trickier conditions. He couldn't risk busting out his phone and waking up Dan. Figures and equations dominated the pages he stared at—not financials, business reports, or anything he'd expect from Torres Industries.

Stacks and stacks of blueprints filled the manila folders. Of course. Dan Torres had been in grad studies for mechanical engineering before his father plucked him out and shoved him into the CEO role at Torres Industries. The guilt that wrenched his stomach was a new something he didn't like. If the meeting had been with the garden variety of old rich asshole with a not-so-secret god complex, Grif would've been pumped and primed to smite him down.

He knelt to reach the bottom drawers, but more of the same filled them—stacks of grad school papers and an array of drawing tools and rulers. His skin itched with awareness. At any moment, Dan could stir, and he'd get caught. Grif might be able to silver tongue his way out of this or brush off his rummaging as curiosity, but heaven and hell, he didn't want to.

The drawers weren't of any use to him, nor was anything in the bedroom. Even still, the elegant gray lamps, the evenly spaced jade carvings, and the way the files were all marked and categorized reminded Grif of Danilo Torres. The man's mark was all over this condo, a mixture of sleek and geek that charmed him without even trying.

He strode over to the doorway, patting himself down for his keys and wallet.

Grif paused to chance one more look in Dan's direction. The man slept soundly, his shoulders rising and falling with even regularity. A couple of strands of his thick black hair drifted over his forehead, and Grif's fingers itched to brush them out of the way. Dan was all smooth features, a rounded nose, those velvet lips, and an ass he could spend hours worshipping. The covers lay halfway off him, exposing the delicious tan skin he'd tasted all last night. Grif's heart stumbled, and the rising warmth in his chest was something he needed to splash cold water over pronto.

He turned away and took the first steps toward the living room. Last night, they'd been so busy fucking against the coffee table, he hadn't been able to scope out the place much. Most of the condo looked pristine, from the not-a-crumb couches to the books on the shelves suspended against the wall, an array of thrillers and non-fiction—textbooks on mechanical engineering. However, Grif wasn't searching for those. His gaze snared on the lone briefcase leaning against the far wall.

Bingo.

He crouched on the cream rug and scanned over

the three-dial lock on the top of the briefcase. Those locks were easier to pop than a balloon. He wiped his hands on his pants to reduce the oil and then pressed his thumb against the side latch. With his other hand, he rolled through the combinations. The numbers scrolled through under his careful motions, one after another at increasing speed. The slight tick-tick-tick sound echoed in the hushed silence of night that stained this room.

His skin prickled with the cinnamon sweep of awareness and a smattering of guilt. The combination clicked, and the side latch gave way. Grif opened the case, careful to not disrupt the contents as he peered inside. More folders—except he could guarantee this wasn't any engineering research. Grif tugged out the nearest manila folder and began to skim the contents. Financial figures. This. He'd been searching for this.

He snapped a couple of pictures of the sheets, one after another. They came out dark, but he'd be able to tweak the brightness at the penthouse. More than paranoia, guilt sat him down and reamed him out as he placed everything back into order and clipped the case shut again. Except, guilt wouldn't pay off Nevarra, and hell, he couldn't even afford distractions. He'd sworn his life to taking down corrupt corporations like this one, like so many others. Like the one that got his parents killed.

Grif sucked in a deep breath.

I've got some news for you. Take a seat, Griffin.

His muscles tensed on instinct at the memory of the soft scrape of his aunt Helen's voice. The sensation of falling, falling, falling had stretched from that moment until the day he'd started the Outlaws and they'd moved into their penthouse. Ever since then, he'd begun placing one tile after another beneath his feet until he found himself on solid ground once more.

Time to get out of this place before those tiles cracked and his foundation got snatched from beneath him. Dan Torres had a fucking gorgeous body, a winsome face, and a honeysuckle sweetness to him, but if Grif didn't chew him up and spit him out, it was only a matter of time before the industry would.

Grif moved the briefcase back in place and rose to his feet. He'd gotten what he came for.

***

GRIF HADN'T EVEN CHEWED THROUGH HIS FIRST PIECE of bacon when the rage parade, i.e. Alanna, descended.

"So, while we dangled from stories up to get you the access points of the Aon Center, you were busy sticking your dick in the enemy?" Alanna marched in, her eyes flashing and her ponytail swinging with the tick-tock of a pendulum. Sounded like John and Scarlet had broken the news.

Grif swallowed the piece of bacon and lifted his coffee to his lips, taking a scorching sip before responding. The pause infuriated her more, like he'd known it would.

"What's to say I wasn't on a recon mission myself?" he responded, keeping his tone level as he plucked his phone from his pocket. After he'd left Dan Torres's condo, he'd gone for a three-in-the-morning jog to clear his head, the brisk Chicago wind the bracing punishment he needed to combat the warm and fuzzies. Instead of catching another couple of hours of shut-eye, Grif had set to prepping breakfast, since it was his turn anyway.

"Because you're a grade A hoe, boss," Tuck muttered, slumping into the seat beside him like spilled Jell-O.

Scarlet sauntered into the room with his laptop in tow, delivering an arch look Grif probably deserved. As much as he might've gotten some intel plucked from the CEO's personal briefcase, he was lying to them and himself in his proclamations of a loftier reason. Truth was, Dan Torres had a stunning face, a muscular ass, and for a few brief moments, his moans had sounded like salvation.

"Well, this grade A hoe got himself some photos

of the Torres Industries financials Dan stowed away in his briefcase."

"So, a thief too," John rumbled behind him. The big man strode over to the coffee maker and began to pour. Grif snorted in response. Like that couldn't describe all of them.

"Don't think that makes your bump and grind with our mark all aces, Grif," Alanna growled as she stomped over to the counter and loaded up on bacon and eggs. Pieces of egg sailed through the air with her erratic movements. "You could've spilled some trivial detail to tip him over into thinking we're not who we say we are."

"Trust me, there wasn't a lot of talk going on," Grif responded, unable to resist the grin that quirked his mouth. The tip of his tongue traveled over his canine. He might've regretted the talk they had—jobs were far easier when the mark remained a blank journal, and their time together had already filled several pages. But the way they'd come together offered the pulse-pounding relief he'd been reaching for ever since the Sunset Ruby heist went tits up.

Scarlet shook his head and settled into the seat at the opposite end of the table, his laptop precariously balanced in one hand and a cup of coffee in the other. He wasn't much of a breakfast person, at most having a piece of toast with his first of about fifteen coffees for the day. "Send those snaps over to me, boss. We'll see what we can do with them."

Even though the edge of judgement gleamed in Scarlet's gaze, he settled into professional mode, like they all did. The laptop cracked open, and the screen glowed against his glasses.

"Already done," Grif said, slamming back the rest of his coffee. Scarlet's fingers flew across the keypad, the sound colliding with the loud chewing from Tuck as he worked on his plate of eggs. Alanna plucked sausages from the pan and chewed them there, leaning against the counter.

"Well, while you were off fucking the enemy, we found our entry points," she said, chewing with her mouth open because it annoyed the rest of the crew.

John strode over and placed a hand beneath her chin, pushing her mouth closed. A nuclear bomb might as well have gone off. A brief silence descended on the room, followed by Alanna's right hook speeding toward John's jaw like the L whipping around a bend. The man wasn't just a smooth talker though. Her fist thudded against his palm with a smack that resounded through the room.

"Kids, stop fighting and eat your breakfast," Grif droned, challenge sparking in his gaze. Alanna opened her mouth again, the protest guaranteed to follow. However, John swept past her to take a seat opposite Grif at the table and plunk his mug of coffee down. As much grief as the guy had given him the night before, John cared about results, a currency they both understood.

"These are older financial records," Scarlet said, his utter lack of concern for their chaos managing to rein everyone in on the spot.

"Why would he be toting around older financial records for the company?" Tuck asked, tapping the tines of his fork against his empty plate. Now that he'd gotten food in his system, the dead-fish look in his eyes vanished, replaced by a hazy one. Tuck would never be considered a morning person.

Grif tapped his fingers on the smooth lacquer tabletop as he chewed on the information. He hadn't missed the way Dan talked about the people in his company, or the way he'd mentioned running things the "right" way. Apparently, this new CEO wasn't oblivious, and he didn't seem to be joining Dick Harrington or Charles Weatherby to putt on the green while they stole from their own companies. However, with the debt he and the Outlaws owed to the Chicago mob, they weren't in the position to be stepping away from a guaranteed score.

"He's newer to the company, so these might be the discrepancies we're looking for," Grif suggested, ignoring the scalpel slice to his insides as he directed his crew. If Dan Torres was anyone else, Grif might be tempted to sway the clever bastard to work with them. Someone with a bright, mechanical mind like his would be an asset to their criminal enterprises, and he rarely met anyone with the same zeal to change corruption for the better.

However, Dan Torres was their mark, and Grif needed to get his Outlaws out of their current quagmire.

"I'll isolate the dates in my searches," Scarlet said, tapping the thick black frames of his glasses before his fingers clacked over the keys again. "We'll see if we can pinpoint the exact spot before our next rendezvous."

"Our meeting with Torres Industries is on Wednesday," John said. "Dan's assistant reached out to me yesterday, and we set everything up. Think you can keep it in your pants that long?"

As if on cue, his phone began to vibrate on the table. Five pairs of eyes bored into the burner.

"You know that now you've baited the fish, you've got to keep him on the reel, right? No tossing the phone in the trash like usual," John continued. "At least until the end of the job."

Scarlet's quirked eyebrow delivered the same amount of "told ya so."

Grif withheld his sigh and lifted the phone. "Yes, yes. Keep up the charade. I'll play the distraction."

"Poor baby," Alanna drawled through another open mouth full of the sausage she shunted down.

"Heaven forbid you have to keep in touch with one of your booty calls."

Grif pushed himself up from the table and headed off to his room before any of them got another crack in. Even though he could've checked the message with the rest of the crew around, he didn't want them peeking over his shoulder. Like he could even hope for privacy after he'd fucked the CEO of the company they'd targeted.

Tuck let out a low whistle as he left with a "go get him" that ensured Grif made the right decision. Once he slipped into the hallway, he checked the text.

Had a great time last night. Too bad you weren't here for another round this morning.

The simple message had him sporting a semi. He'd left Dan sprawled out in bed, his ebony strands askew and his arm curled into the rumpled spot where Grif had been. Goddamn if the idea of wrapping his lips around that morning wood didn't appeal. The second Grif stepped inside his room and shut the door, he palmed his length and gave it a couple of strokes. He leaned against the door and stared at the caulk-white ceiling.

Right, he needed to respond. This was first steps on the moon territory after his normal hit-it-and-quit-its, but they weren't planning their job until the following week, so he had the whole span to keep Dan interested. After the frag bomb of passion that had detonated last night, it wouldn't be difficult. He shot off a return text.

Maybe I like being a tease. You'll just have to be patient until next time.

Grif stroked his cock another couple of times, trying to smother the memories of the sound of Dan's moans, as sweet as Maker's Mark, or the way those velvet lips felt around his erection. The man made an impression, even without trying.

His phone began to buzz again, this time with a call.

Unknown number.

Grif pushed up from his slouch against the door, his muscles tightening on instinct. The lazy indulgence of his thoughts shattered like a golf club through a windshield.

"Hello?" he answered.

"Grif Blackmore." The sleazy, dulcet tones of Marco Nevarra. Joy. "I was promised a fee for the failed job, and your crew has yet to deliver."

"We agreed on a time and date already," Grif responded, his tone flat. Nevarra might be able to place a few calls to crush them, since he not only had dozens of crews stationed through the city but more connections than a telephone network. Still, the man respected strength. "Leaving me love notes won't get your date pushed up further. The job might've botched, but we're good for the money."

"If you're good for the money, then pay up now," Nevarra said with the shaken soda tone of a grade A asshole used to getting his way.

"Careful, man," Grif purred. "Don't want to sound desperate for the cash."

Nevarra responded with a growl. "Two weeks from now. If you're not prompt on the payment, we'll start picking off your Outlaws."

Grif's stomach dropped, and he gripped the phone a little tighter. Threaten him, cut him, beat him, and he'd just laugh and spit in their faces, but his Outlaws were the one thing on this earth he gave a damn about. And Nevarra wasn't fucking around. He'd seen the bloated bodies floating in the Chicago River, the hit squads patrolling through the back alleys, and the alternating thumps of fists and final cries as Nevarra's men beat the payment out of the poor saps who didn't deliver.

"You'll have your cash in hand by then," Grif responded at last. Not bothering to wait for another threat, he ended the call.

Grif tossed his phone to thud onto the bed and let out a low curse. They couldn't afford to screw this job up. Dan Torres was wet-dream worthy and honest in a way that Grif wished he could still remember, but two weeks from now, Torres Industries would be tanked.

EIGHT

Dan never dreaded Mondays until he started working for Torres Industries. Week after week he faced stiff suits, fluorescent lights, and bandying delicate words with blowhards. And after his first successful date in far too long, nothing doused an afterglow like a meeting with Phil Brennerman.

"See you at the board luncheon later," Dan called to Phil's fast retreating form. He didn't budge from his desk, and once his door clicked shut, Dan slumped into the leather chair. A moment's peace was too much to ask for. The man had marched in, face blotchy red like he'd choked on a ghost pepper, after Dan had met with new companies on his own. So, today he had the task of convincing Phil and his cronies on the board to take a chance on them. With the recycled arguments and fights, he'd begun to feel like Tantalus.

Dan's nose twitched. The man needed to lay off the aftershave—his entire office stank like a lumberjack's cabin every time Phil Brennerman visited. He heaved a sigh and reached forward to press the line on his phone and typed the number on his keypad. If he had to face these bastards at lunch, he needed backup, pronto. The call went through, and a click sounded.

"Leo, you have a free moment?" Dan asked, staring at the ceiling and wishing each interaction with his coworkers didn't require another maneuver on the chess board.

"Define free," Leo's chipper tone responded, "since I pretty much consider every day trapped in this nine to five the opposite of."

"Is this the way you talk to all your bosses, or am I just special?" Dan tapped the phone, unable to help his grin. If he didn't have Leo and Vanessa, he would've run off to become the worst monk ever after the first week.

"If your ego so badly needs to be stroked, I'll tell you you're special," Leo drawled in a way that always veered toward flirty. Not like that would ever happen. When they'd met back in college, they tried going on a date at the local bowling alley, and after five frames they realized they made better friends than lovers.

Dan's stomach curled at the thought of the last guy he'd taken back to his house. Christ, he didn't know how he was supposed to look Greg in the eye without his face erupting in flames at their upcoming meeting. Not after the filthy things Greg had whispered in Dan's ear, the way he'd gripped his hips, and how they'd fucked so hard he could feel it the next day.

"Danny-boy, did I lose you?" Leo said, his wry voice snapping Dan to the present.

"Come up to my office," he responded. "I need your help with something private."

"The words every guy wants to hear." Suggestion dripped from Leo's tone, and he hung up with a click.

Dan snorted and pushed up from his chair. He'd been staring at the same stack of papers until the numbers and letters had begun to blur into squiggles. No matter how many times he scanned the patterns in the financials and despite the fact none of them led anywhere illegal, he couldn't shake the feeling in his gut. Something shadier than Chicago's alleys was going on around here, something either his father hadn't deigned to clue him in on or the old man hadn't known about. Either way, he refused to ignore the rust threatening to corrode the entire engine of this company. If the top management were skimming funds or abusing the company money, hell, any infraction, Dan would stop them.

A knock sounded on the door, drawing his attention. Vanessa leaned against the frame, emanating the power and poise he wished he felt right now. No one would mistake them for anything but siblings with their thick black hair, sepia skin, and the same rounded chin as their father. However, while he'd inherited their mother's softer eyes, his sister possessed the Machiavellian gaze of their father.

"You look like you caught someone dancing on our lola's grave." Vanessa strode in without being invited, her heels grazing against the thin carpet as she approached. His sister wore an impeccable Armani suit with the perfect accents of delicate rose gold earrings and a slender chain around her neck, the epitome of feminine power.

"Meeting with Phil Brennerman." Dan made a disgusted sound in the back of his throat to follow. "You know, if I knew I was going to get stuck wrangling the old bastard, I wouldn't have been nearly as polite to him when we were kids."

Vanessa snorted and perched on the edge of his desk. "Right, like that wouldn't have ended with your ass beat. Pops is as much of a stubborn dinosaur as the rest of these guys."

Dan heaved a sigh. "I know. If I could somehow step aside to work for you instead of running this Hindenburg, you know I would, Nessa. I'm just trying to avoid getting disowned by the family."

Vanessa swung her legs back and forth as she glanced out to the window. "Please, like I'd want to run this nasty-ass lemon party. Way more fun to watch you sweat, little brother."

Even as she said the words, he couldn't miss the edge of yearning she always tried to hide. Vanessa was a fighter, but practicality dominated for her, unlike him. He'd spent most of their childhood daydreaming, his mind puffing up like cumulus clouds. No matter how high his office in the Aon Center stretched, he felt further from those azure skies than ever before.

"Don't suppose you got any information from the employees about what our board's been up to?" Dan asked, casting her a sidelong glance.

Vanessa swung her legs back and forth again before glancing back. "Please, like they'll talk to a Torres. We've got to get someone besides your IT boyfriend on our side."

Dan rolled his eyes. "Leo's a friend, nothing more."

Same couldn't be said about Greg, who was dominating his thoughts far too much for a one-night stand.

"You could at least do me the favor of getting a boyfriend," Vanessa responded with a wry grin. "Dad will be so pissed, he'll lay off me about finding a man and pumping out grandbabies."

"Hard pass there." He and his father maintained a whole lot of radio silence on the subject of Dan's preferences, because Torres Sr. followed Don't Ask, Don't Tell to a T. "I'll stick to my crusade of uprooting whatever shady shit the members of this company are up to. Can't wage a war on both fronts."

"About that," Vanessa said, hopping from her perch on his desk to land on the floor, heels and all. When she leaned in, the serious glint in her dark eyes had his veins buzzing. That look always meant trouble. "I've got some suspicions I wanted to talk to you about."

"Knock, knock," Leo called from the door as he strode in, not bothering to actually knock. The guy was lanky, all limbs like an oak tree in fall, yet he moved with unexpected grace. His black-rimmed glasses kept sliding down his long nose, and he quirked an eyebrow at the two of them when he came to a halt in front of Dan's desk. "Oh look, the gang's all here."

"Have you heard of professional boundaries, Barnes?" Vanessa asked, her hands on her hips. "This is the head of the company, and I'm on the board."

Leo's thick eyebrows drew together. "Am I supposed to bow or something? I've been to one too many house parties with you crazy Torres kids to observe the strict norms of corporate hierarchy."

"I asked him to come up here," Dan said,

smacking a stuffed folder onto his desk. "I need some serious ammunition before the board meeting at lunch if I have a hope or a prayer of any of the acquisitions I vetted getting approved. Chances are, Brennerman and his yes-men will shoot them all down. But I don't trust any of the people they'd bring in."

"You're right not to," Vanessa said, her tone as sharp as a cat's claws. "For what it's worth, I support what you're doing, little bro. Dad might've been fine with rampant corruption, and knowing him, he was probably just as involved. But if we're supposed to keep this company going, that means running the place our way."

Dan reached out to squeeze Vanessa's hand. The further into this mess he walked, the less he recognized the terrain. He was standing alone in the middle of a barren field, throat aching as he screamed to be heard. Nessa reaffirmed the reason he started doing this investigation in the first place. If Dad wanted to put Dan in charge, then in another year, this company wouldn't operate under the Good Ol' Boys rules any longer. Vanessa squeezed back, passing him an affectionate look.

"So, you brought me in because you want me to what?" Leo asked, his eyes dancing as he straightened his glasses. He knew exactly what Dan would be asking him—the man's expertise lay in computers, beyond running their IT department.

"I could scan over these financials until my eyes bleed, but apart from establishing some suspicious patterns, I haven't been able to find any fine-print proof of wrongdoing. I can't bring my gut instinct and sneaking suspicions to the board. If I want to oust Brennerman and whoever else is in on this, I need irrefutable evidence. Any acquisitions in the past, and any future ones need screening as well." Dan pushed up from his desk and stalked back and forth. The adrenaline pumped through his veins, swirling around all those worries.

"Right, so you want my special expertise." Leo leaned against the desk, a wry grin on his lips. In Leo's off time, the man spent his nights as Polonius, an unrepentant hacker, pushing the limits on all of the "challenges" that cropped up. Once he found something that twisted his brain into constrictor knots, he rarely let it go.

"If you wouldn't mind," Dan responded, casting him a glance. Leo shook his head and stared at the ceiling, his green eyes losing focus—which meant his brain had started whirring like an exhaust fan with the new project. "You'll be compensated."

Leo gave him an arch look. "Don't patronize me with all the cash you flash around, Torres. You knew the moment you brought this up I'd be interested."

"The man keeps his office under close watch or locked at all times he isn't in it. My father's former ruling on privacy for the higher ups is currently kicking my ass, so if you could patch together a reason to at least get in and snoop…" Dan glanced up to Leo who nodded, an amused grin on his face.

"What can I do, Danny?" Vanessa asked. Her gaze kept flicking to the door, still open a crack, like any minute she expected someone to march on through. The same paranoia buzzed through his veins —they worked around hundreds of people and couldn't trust a single one of them.

"Help me stall them at the board meeting today." Dan slipped his hands into his pockets, unable to stop the jitters running through him. What they talked about would shake through the whole corporation, and guaranteed, darker days would come. "They're going to try and stonewall these new acquisitions since they didn't have a hand in them. If I can't push them through, I at least need to fight to keep them in the ring."

"You've got whatever you need," Vanessa said, stalking over to the door. She pushed it shut with a click and turned around to face them. Her voice lowered, and a chill raced down Dan's spine. "I've been doing some digging on my own."

Whatever digging his sister had done, it sounded more like she'd tugged out skeletons, not worms.

"Hope you've been more successful than me," Dan said. "All I've reaped is more angry meetings with our board members."

Leo shuddered. "Don't know how you deal with all those people."

Dan raised an eyebrow. "Aren't you the head of IT?"

Leo snagged a pen from his desk and twirled it between his fingers. "Exactly. None of us do any face-to-face talks."

Vanessa clapped her palms on the surface of his desk, commanding their attention. "This plan of ours needs to stay between us three, you got that?" She let out a sigh and tugged at a strand of hair that had slipped out of her bun. She always straightened her appearance when nerves rode her. "I looked into some of the people who had been fired from the company—I was searching for any situations involving the higher-ups and what our recourse might be."

Dan stopped midstride and he turned to face her, hands in his pockets. "What did you find, Nessa?"

Her eyebrows drew together. "You want to talk unsettling patterns? More than a couple of our ex-employees have disappeared. We're talking never showed up for work and six weeks later were found dead in Lake Michigan."

His temperature plummeted. He didn't like a lot

of things about his father—the sexist, homophobic comments topping the list. However, the man had raised him, never raised a fist to him, and made sure he was well taken care of. Any time he thought about ditching this position and braving the family Cold War to follow, he knew his father wouldn't be the only one he would disappoint. The rest of the extended family's response would be crushing, and Dan loved his mom enough to deal with this bullshit.

However, would his own dad condone murder?

"And you think someone here might be involved?" he asked, unable to ask the real question reflected in her eyes.

"If there's large sums of money being skimmed off the top or moved around, then things could get ugly, fast." Vanessa unbuttoned her collar, and a moment later she rebuttoned it again, her fingers moving with restless energy.

Dan, on the other hand, planted his feet, glued to the ground like he'd been bolted into place. His date over the weekend felt sepia-toned and faded, like some memory from earlier times, as if he'd aged a century this morning alone.

"And here I thought I'd get bored working corporate," Leo drawled as he spun the pen around again. "You Torreses know how to keep things interesting."

Dan skimmed his fingers through his hair as he let

out a sigh. He met Vanessa's eyes and nodded. "You keep following your lead on that. And Leo, you follow the financials. I think it's time I had a talk with my father."

NINE

After Nevarra's phone call had simmered in the back of his mind all day, there was no place Grif wanted to be more than out in the field. He'd rather feel productive than jump rope, run laps in the streets, or scan the intel he'd nabbed for the thousandth time while he waited for the meeting at Torres Industries.

He flexed his gloved hands again as he strode through the streets with Alanna. Tuck enjoyed a well-deserved break while the mouthier of the duo showed him the spots they'd located. In this part of the city, the monoliths dominated the terrain, their inky shadows the perfect breeding ground for beatdowns and blood splatters.

Grif tapped his fingers along the side of his thigh, his arm brushing against the handle of one of the six different knives he kept on his person most times. The solid weight of his Glock rested in his hidden holster, something he never left the penthouse without, though he often switched locations.

"What's got you surlier than normal, boss?" Alanna asked. Her ponytail whipped back and forth with the jaunty way she walked. In her black hoodie and fleece leggings that clung to her muscular legs, she didn't look too out of place. They both attempted to blend with street casual for this foray rather than outfitting for intense climbs.

"Lincoln Zoo's in mourning—they lost Sparky the penguin today," he commented as they strode down the street. Despite Alanna's height—at least a foot shorter—she managed to keep pace with him.

"Well, bully for the Lincoln Zoo, but I wasn't asking about them," Alanna continued with all the tact of a knockout punch.

Grif sniffed. "Maybe I was attached to Sparky."

Alanna snorted.

They strode through a stretch of trees that broke through the dominating asphalt and concrete littering this section of the city. The feeble elms stood a couple of feet taller than he did. Like everything and everyone in Chicago, they fought hard to survive.

"Since you're playing the evasion game, I'm going to slice right through the bullshit. How fucked are we from the failed job?" Alanna asked. The shadows sharpened her dark eyes, her elegant nose, and her defined lips. The shadows stained her skin purple.

Grif's stomach twisted. His Outlaws were the sort of loyal he didn't deserve. Except, he couldn't just open his mouth without the cascade of shame tumbling out. They shouldn't have gotten themselves into this mess in the first place. He should've known they were trying to leap a skyscraper with targeting Robert Davies. He should've kept them from going on the stupid Sunset Ruby heist.

If he hadn't been glazed over and hungry for the chance to stick it to Davies, maybe he would've. Grif tugged a cigarette from his pack and followed through with the Zippo. As of late, he made a lot of bad calls, thinking with his heart not his smarts. He sucked back the first drag from his cigarette and let the smoke filter through his lips. The nicotine was a hollow kiss of relief.

"Nevarra's calling and making empty threats," he mentioned, tapping the stray ash from the end of his cigarette. He couldn't look her way, not while the shame burned through him like this. "He gave us two weeks, and we'll pay up in two weeks."

"In other words, we can't fuck up this job." Alanna reached out and flicked him in the side. "I know we messed up the Sunset Ruby heist, but this should be as easy as first position, Locksley."

"Considering I never took ballet, first position might not be a breeze," he shot back.

"Five-year-olds can do it," Alanna responded, keeping pace, her strides fast and furious.

Grif arched an eyebrow, looking her way. "You know better than to taunt the gods of chance like that. You're just asking for trouble now."

"Don't want things to get boring," Alanna responded, strolling ahead of him as she tipped her head up to look ahead.

The Aon Center loomed over them alongside the other skyscrapers of this stretch. A street trailed down the side with its arched, marked covering, in case folks didn't know who owned this block. The white monstrosity gleamed in the spotlights marking it out, part of the difficulty they'd have if they needed to make a fast exit or any sort of high-up extraction. The sight of these buildings never failed to summon memories, and with the sheer number of skyscrapers throughout Chicago, he was a masochist for staying.

His neck prickled the closer they got to the building. A few quick rounds were all they needed. However, his gaze strayed and stuck to the repair vehicle camped out on the side of the road, headlights switched off. Alanna mumbled some directions he should've been paying attention to, but his focus lasered in on the van. Two figures sat in the front seat.

As much as they tried to stay inconspicuous, the way their silhouettes shifted tipped them off.

"Careful," Grif murmured, keeping his voice low. "I don't think we're the only ones scoping out this building."

Alanna's pace slowed, but to her credit she didn't gape in the direction of the van. His Outlaws were better than that. They'd been heading that way in the first place, so any quick-step detour now would seem suspicious. Grif's hands slipped to his waistband, and his palm rested on the handle of his pistol.

The closer they got to the van, the more the prickle of awareness grew stronger. Guaranteed, whoever sat in there watched them approach. Grif took another drag from his cigarette before casting a glance to Alanna. She gave the slightest nod and continued down the sidewalk a step or two ahead. The shadow of the Aon Center fell over them, blocking out the natural light of the moon that mingled with the streetlights. Grif tapped more ash on the sidewalk while he glanced to the Aon Center, as if he didn't have the guys in the van in his peripheral.

Whatever these guys waited around here for, their loitering couldn't spell good news for the Outlaws. Coincidence was for innocents and suckers.

"So where are these routes I'm supposed to be looking at?" Grif asked, feigning casual conversation as they stepped closer and closer. The folks in the van could get up to whatever hinky business they wanted to as long as they weren't planning a heist on Torres Industries.

Alanna looked to the Center and her gaze trailed to the higher floors. Of course, Torres Industries would have to be near the top—maybe even the fiftieth or sixtieth floors. Then she scanned back to the midsection. That was the best escape route.

The stares of whoever sat in the van bore down on him, their scrutiny like the whisper of fall breezes, causing leaves to skitter and goose bumps to rise.

Closer. Close enough if he glanced to the left, he'd be staring right at whoever looked out the windows. Grif's fingers brushed against the handle of his Glock again. Almost past them, and then they could finish the walkthrough and cut a scenic retreat along the Riverfront.

The creak of a door tipped him off.

When the van doors flew open, Grif bolted. The two guys who'd been sitting idle in the van leapt out. His Glock was out of his waistband by the time he moved another pace forward. A glimpse of the fuckers was all he needed. The broad-shouldered pipsqueak with the scowl was a new arrival, but he recognized the sallow face, skeletal cheekbones, and sour eyes of Roger Doncaster.

He didn't need the flash of the heat they packed to know he and Alanna were made.

"Long time no see, Doncaster," he called before vaulting onto the raised walls around the bike racks. A terrace surrounded the Aon Center on this side, featuring concrete interlays, rows of trees, and pathways for pedestrians. He planned on taking full advantage. Grif palmed his pistol in one hand, but he lifted his middle finger with the other. Alanna raced past him, sailing across the narrow walkway.

"Should've figured Outlaw scum would be sniffing around here," Doncaster called from the sidewalk, the safety of his pistol clicking off.

"Let's be real, Donny," Grif shouted back as he continued to race across the surface of the raised wall. "You can't get your own job if your life depended on it. Like always, you're begging for scraps."

Pipsqueak let out a low growl.

"Left." Grif gave the command as they reached the end of the raised walls. To the right lay the path closer to the entrance, while the left held the terrace, tiers of manicured shrubs, and dainty little trees about to get riddled with bullets. Alanna hurtled toward the trees, blurring with the sort of speed that got her nicknamed the Shadow in the first place. With his height and heft, he could never blend like that, but he sure as hell could duck. His feet slammed onto the mulch, spraying pieces as he slipped behind the first elm.

After he'd entered the Chicago underworld in his late teens and picked a king's share of fights, Grif had learned a valuable lesson. Getting shot at couldn't be taught in textbooks. However, face enough assholes with anger problems and Rugers, and eventually the lessons stuck. A subtle current in the air, thick like the volts of a Taser, danced through. Tension smeared the space between them.

The first bullet zipped through the air. Pipsqueak blew his load early.

Grif ducked behind the row of spindly elms, his fingers grazing the bark of the tree he used for cover. The bullet whizzed a foot behind him, sailing through the air until it thudded against the building. He didn't stop to inspect. Doncaster and Pipsqueak still raced along the sidewalk, trying to keep up with them. Grif sailed past the first, the second, and the third maple in the lineup. Alanna wove in zigzags around them, so short she couldn't be spotted beyond the thick shrubs on the second level.

If Doncaster was on the scene, Luka must have spilled the details. He'd promised Grif this job belonged to him alone, and he'd worked with the guy for so long he'd started taking him on his word. Fool mistake. Only a matter of time before the universe doled the haymaker punch, reminding him that at the end of the day, no one could be trusted.

Black days and bleaker times.

Grif heard the stutter of the footsteps from farther behind him, and he ducked. Based on the source of the sound, they'd abandoned the sidewalk and decided to follow them directly.

Another bullet zipped by, this one burying inside the last maple he'd raced past. Splinters of bark spattered out in every direction. A second followed suit, close enough the breeze ruffled his sleeve. His breath snagged in his throat. Pipsqueak might be shoddy on his aim, but Doncaster wasn't.

The walkway up ahead stretched to the opposite end of the Aon Center before hitting the highway, where the lineup of flags rippled in the icy breeze. Alanna threaded from tree to tree like she was sewing a quilt. Shadow had switched from mere pursuit to full-on parkour, vaulting over railings to land onto the next rail, and from there, her feet barely hit the ground before she looped around the next set of manicured shrubs.

His slow ass would have to play distraction.

Grif crouched behind the last elm in the lineup, his finger on the trigger of his Glock. He set his sights on Pipsqueak, who raced ahead of Doncaster, his pistol arm wavering around like the town drunk. The two of them cut down the center line of the path between the trees, shrubs, and elevated concrete.

Bang, bang, motherfucker.

Grif squeezed the trigger, but he didn't wait for

the shot to land. The next of Doncaster's bullets zipped toward him, death on the breeze.

It tunneled into the ground beside him. The breath he'd been holding escaped, but his feet moved before his mind connected.

Alanna had reached the road. She sailed across the intersection, her ponytail trailing behind her like the flags she'd just bypassed. She moved like a blur, whipping between the cars stopped at the light. A drop of sweat trickled down his neck, freezing there as he raced, faster, faster. His heart thundered to the point he couldn't hear anything else. The opposite light flicked from green to yellow. Any minute, and he'd be stuck on this side with Doncaster and his shitty lackey.

Time to soar.

Grif vaulted forward, his rubber soles inches above the concrete as he bounded across the remaining sidewalk. He lunged onto the crosswalk. Not fast enough. One of the cars stuck out ahead of the pack, a little Fiat. Grif's calves tensed as he sprang ahead. His shoes slammed onto the hood for one second, two.

Grif pushed off to sail through the air, flying over the remaining stretch of crosswalk.

Horns blared behind him.

The light turned green. The cars squealed as they surged forward.

He chanced a single glance back. Doncaster and his lackey stood on the opposite side of the crosswalk, the full force of Chicago traffic rushing between them. Even with their pistols hidden behind their backs, they wouldn't hesitate to shoot if given the chance. Grif didn't plan on offering one.

Grif caught sight of Alanna's disappearing form and bolted to the split in the streets at the left, following her. One of the large walkways narrowed and wove between two more buildings, which would give them cover. Grif bounded off the ledges surrounding the mulched trees, using the leverage to soar faster across the pavement. The wind rifled through his hair, and the icy breeze stung his cheeks as he raced along the path. The shadows swept in to devour him the moment he got close to the looming buildings.

He glanced back. The light had just turned red.

Grif ran after Alanna so fast his calves burned. This should've been a quick job, an easy job. As of late, though, Lady Luck had decided to spin them around and spit in their faces, so of course Doncaster was involved. He disappeared past the two buildings, which placed him out of view from the road. Up ahead, Alanna darted into the first alley past the towers to the right. He swerved to follow her, and together, they plunged into the maze of side streets that comprised Chicago proper.

Grif closed the door to his bedroom, and his shoulders finally relaxed.

The rest of the Outlaws had lobbed questions like hand grenades when he and Alanna burst through the front door, shoulders heaving and dripping with sweat. He had just lifted a hand, muttered "Doncaster," and headed for his room. Before the rest of the crew started dumping their opinions on him, he needed to run some damage control. This job should've been aces. Luka should've been someone they could trust after all those years of loyalty. However, once the job got leaked to other sources, their easy payday evaporated like gasoline on the concrete in the middle of summer.

Grif peeled off his shirt, which stuck to his skin with the sheer amount of sweat after their parkour adventure through Chicago central. He flung the sopping fabric to the floor and kicked off his pants a moment later. He flopped into his bed and shot off a single-word text to Luka: *Doncaster*. It was the only one the bastard deserved.

The sweat began to dry in a thin film across his skin, and Grif ran a hand through his sodden hair. He needed a fucking shower. Heaven and hell, after the past couple of days, he needed a lobotomy.

His phone buzzed, and he glanced at the screen, expecting some form of roundabout from Luka.

Nope, Dan-goddamn-Torres.

Dan: Long fucking day. Can't help but wish I was in your bed rather than here.

Grif swallowed hard. He could empathize with the sentiment. He'd much rather be hot and sweaty from a couple rounds with Dan Torres rather than from running through Chicago and getting shot at. Instead, he lay here trying to dodge a headache determined to descend.

The thought of the gorgeous guy made his cock stiffen from memories of the way he'd thrust into that tight ass and the desperate moans that followed. As much as Dan might've let him take the lead in the bedroom, whenever they texted, his honesty steered Grif in a way he wasn't used to. If he weren't such a vet at lying to himself, he might even admit he liked it.

Grif: Long fucking day here too. Might not have you in my bed, but at least I'll get to see that sexy ass on Wednesday.

The simple admission unlocked something inside him. As much as he loved his Outlaws, he always held back—a leader couldn't bitch about every problem that cropped up or their confidence in his ability would be shaken. And as much as Alanna, Scarlet, J-man, and Tuck sank their lion claws in and tried to peel past skin to take some of the burden, the subtle pressure of expectation remained. He would provide the answers, because he had to.

Dan Torres didn't have any expectations from him. They were bitching about their shitty days, and for fuck's sake, that felt… nice. Hell, it felt gayer than sticking his dick in the guy. They'd been texting the past couple of days, and every interaction charmed him more. Each single time Dan Torres's name flashed on his phone, relief caressed him like a tender touch, and he loathed the weak way he craved it like he'd been starving.

Dan: Thanks, now I'm hard again. I don't know how I'm supposed to face you at the meeting without blushing.

A grin spread on his lips, and warmth brushed across his chest like molten caramel.

Grif: Just keep thinking of all the filthy things I want to do to you. Guaranteed to help.

Grif stared at his blank ceiling, trying to ignore the stutter-start of his heart. He'd come in from a long run and a huge mess, so of course his heart would be racing like it drove in the Indy 500. Not like that explained the honeyed way heat coursed through his veins, tingling down to his fingers and toes. His simple conversation with Dan somehow leached away some of the pounding necessity of his problems and cast them off the shore like broken shells to sink into the ocean.

Nevarra might be growling at his door, and Doncaster breathing down his neck, but the biggest danger he faced was Dan Torres.

TEN

THE SUN FLICKERED ACROSS DAN'S WINDSHIELD, brightening the patches of green grass that tried to bloom in early spring. The parade of gorgeous, quasi-Victorian houses flashed by in shades of powder blue, lavender, and creamy yellow as he slowed at an all-too-familiar street, one he pulled into at least once a week for family dinner. Even though he'd moved to the city years ago, he'd grown up in the suburbs, first in Harvey until Dad had made it big and started Torres Industries. From there, they'd ended up in the opposite area, Clarendon Hills.

This might be his childhood home, but he'd always felt more natural on the streets of Harvey than he did amidst the cliquish communities here. He wheeled his Audi onto the winding drive, the gorgeous houses with their sprawling lawns and manicured shrubs rising up to greet him. The Torres house stood at the end of the lane, the two-car garage, dozens of framed windows, and the rounded entryway with its very own turret the reason he'd declared this place a castle from the day they'd moved in.

He and Vanessa still came over for Sunday dinner every week, the drive so comfortable he barely thought it over. This week's dinner got rescheduled to Tuesday due to Aunt Darna needing a ride to the airport. After his talk with Nessa at the office, his veins buzzed. He and his father had clashed over decisions any time he tried to follow his own path or act any different from the son Torres Sr. pictured.

Leo had told him to ditch the family judgement years ago, especially when his dad strong-armed him into running the company, and sometimes, he was tempted. He pulled into the driveway and turned off the engine.

The idea of a future without the family he'd grown up with caused his stomach to dive deep into Lake Michigan and never surface. Dan couldn't imagine sitting alone in his condo on Sunday evenings, knowing Mama was making adobo and lumpia and Vanessa was sitting on the sofa with their black lab, Rufus. Dad always had some random story to share from the Wall Street Journal, the gruff, low tone a comfort. Dan's stomach twisted. He knew his view of his family was skewed and Dad either ignored or participated in dirty dealings within his company. But what Vanessa had uncovered—potential murder? None of them could step back from that line.

And Leo's most recent attempt to dig had him unnerved. Leo had managed to transmit a virus to Brennerman's computer, one that he got called in to take care of. However, there wasn't much he could do about digging into the files Brennerman kept on the local network the senior partners used while the man himself skulked around behind him. The one thing that had come out of it was Leo's discovery of the locked safe underneath the man's desk, a high enough grade one to ping their internal alarms.

Dan loped up the concrete steps leading to the polished oak door. He didn't bother to knock, just grabbed the wrought iron handle and stepped inside. The rich scents of kare kare wafted his way, notes of peanut and garlic strong in the air. His stomach rumbled despite the way his insides twisted in a dozen tight knots.

Vanessa's voice filtered in from the kitchen in the far back of the house as he walked through the sunny room. The apricot beams poured across the polished hardwood. He stepped into the foyer and kicked off his shoes right by the door, where the others had been neatly set. Dan couldn't help but run a hand through his hair to comb through his strands again.

"About time you showed up," his dad's voice rumbled from the other room.

Dan sucked in a deep breath as he bypassed the white banister leading upstairs and entered the living room—at least, the main one they used. Dad sat on the plum sofa along the back wall, his glasses perched on the edge of his nose as he skimmed over a newspaper. A stack of other papers rested on the coffee table in front of him. Even post-retirement, Dad kept vigilant about his investments—which of course included him and Nessa.

Wrinkles sharpened his father's features, the deep grooves giving him a distinguished air that fit the loafers-and-sweaters look his father swept into upon retirement. He entered the cloud of his father's sandalwood aftershave and took a seat on the couch beside him. Dan hunched forward, elbows digging into his thighs to keep from fidgeting.

"Phil Brennerman called me last week," Dad mentioned, his tone careful in a trap Dan knew better than to fall for.

The words jumped to his tongue, how Phil Brennerman was a pain in his ass, how the man had been throwing tantrums from the day he took over the company. Dan swallowed them back. He needed to control his temper.

"What's Phil Brennerman bothering an old retired

guy like you about?" Dan asked, forcing levity into his voice.

"He's got some concerns with how you're running the business," Dad said, staring at the text on his newspaper rather than him. Oh, screw that guy. What grown-ass man needed to tattle to his father?

Dan shrugged. "Well, new regime, new procedures. If we don't adapt to modern times, the business will ultimately fail. You always taught me that, Pops." He emphasized his last statement, daring his father to challenge him.

His father's eyebrows drew together, and he folded the newspaper onto his lap, which meant a lecture would follow. "I trust you, son. I know you want what's best for the company. However, Phil Brennerman's been at the business for a lot longer than you. He's got knowledge on the inner workings of the business you don't, and I think you need to take that into account before brushing him off."

Dan's stomach dropped. Even though the scents of the meal cooking in the other room had made him salivate a second ago, he couldn't find his appetite now. Sure, his dad was a control freak and he expected the interrogations, but asking him to defer to Brennerman? Why bother putting him in charge of the company?

The obvious answer smacked him in the face, the one he'd tried to dodge around for a while now, and the one that had become brighter than the lights at Wrigley Field.

"If there's some inner knowledge I don't have, I think it's an essential part of being able to run the company," Dan insisted, attempting to argue with his father. Truth be told, he wanted to run far from whatever his father and the board had mired themselves in. "You wanted me as CEO of this company, so if I'm to keep Torres Industries growing, I'm going to need every tool in my arsenal. Care to share why our CFO has his own top-notch safe in his office?"

His dad's dark eyes flickered with guilt, and the lines around his eyes softened with an expression Dan knew all too well. Regret. The sight socked him in the stomach. A couple of years ago, he wouldn't have been able to bluff around his father for shit, but learning a false face had become a survival mechanism at Torres Industries.

"People have their roles in the company for a reason, Nilo. Sometimes it's better to just stay out of certain things. How do you think I lasted as long as I did? Corporate dealings aren't for the faint of heart."

The affection in his father's voice and the old nickname on his lips was like glass hitting the hardwood. The closed-door response was the exact one he feared, the closest his father would ever come to an admission of guilt.

His father's gaze bored into him. "Tell me you'll

let Phil do what he needs to do. The two of you can achieve a working peace, I believe it. He's just a bit stubborn and old-fashioned, not unlike your old father."

Dan's smile frayed around the edges. He barely held back the bile. Out of everyone, he'd hoped he could trust his family. That this remained a safe haven, not another war-torn battlefield like his work had become. However, the pressure behind his father's statement and the intent in his eyes made the reason his father wanted him as CEO clear.

Dad might've retired, but not by choice—the man would've kept working until he prepared his own funeral arrangements, but he thought retiring looked best for the company. And Dan had always been the pliable son, adjustable, because he hated to fight with his family.

He'd be the shitty bobble-head nodding yes while Phil Brennerman and his crew continued to rake in a fortune and abuse company funds at the expense of their workers. Dad never expected him to push back against the corruption within Torres Industries, because he'd never pushed back against him growing up.

Whether it was never bringing his boyfriends home to meet the family.

Whether it was attending every Mother's Day, graduation, and reunion with the extended family, even though he had to brace himself for the homo-phobic comments that sometimes slipped out from his uncles.

Whether it was dropping out of the graduate work in mechanical engineering he loved to assume a role in a company that made him nauseous.

"Yeah," Dan forced out, the words tasting tart on his tongue. "Phil can do his thing. I'll focus on working around him."

Lie. Lie. Lie.

His father nodded, his fingers skimming across the newspaper as he pulled the pages up again like a protective shield. Like it would kill him to talk with his son for a little longer than five minutes.

"My Danilo." Mom's voice sounded from the kitchen entryway. "You snuck in so quietly. Come, give me a hug." His mother wiped her hands down on the apron she wore, covered in stains from the kare kare he smelled. Her thick black ringlets were pulled back in a bun, and she wore maroon lipstick like always, even when she wasn't going out for the day. Her eyes crinkled with warmth that on a normal day filled him with sunlight.

Right now, a heat wave could sizzle through Chicago, and he wouldn't feel an ounce of it.

Dan pushed himself from his seat on the couch, ignoring the sweat pricking his palms. He made himself smile, even though the motion felt like slices carved onto a wooden doll. He moved on reflex toward his mother, striding across the room to throw his arms around her in a hug. She smelled like flour and spice, but even with the way she clutched him tight, the numbness had already spread to his fingertips.

"Good to see you, Mama," Dan murmured into her soft hair. "The food smells amazing. I can't wait to dig in." Did she know what his father was involved in? Or did he prefer to keep her ignorant too? His stomach clenched.

Vanessa stepped in behind Mom, her jeans covered in flour and her hair pulled into a low ponytail. This was the sister he knew, so different from the Armani-clad professional who thundered into the board meetings with her barbed words and icy stare. Her dark eyes met his, and the ground dropped beneath him like he'd stepped into a sinkhole.

He caught the question in the tilt of her head. However, he couldn't bring himself to reveal the truth, even if she'd be pissed at him for lying. Vanessa and Dad were a fractured thing glued together by his and Mom's efforts alone—this would shatter them. Maybe he was weak for clinging to these weekly dinners, to this family that strained at the seams with secrets, but right now, they were all he had.

Dan jerked his head "no." He couldn't cut

Vanessa out of their trio, but he could at least protect her from this.

Vanessa's lips pressed tight together, the relief crystalizing in her eyes. "About time you got here, little bro. What took you so long?"

"Got lost in the mirror," he responded automatically. "You know how I like to primp." Even as he said the words, he could feel his father's gaze bearing down on him with the familiar censure any time he indulged in behaviors considered less than "masculine." He swallowed hard and pulled away from Mom, placing a hand on her shoulder, anxious to get through the family dinner as fast as possible. The longer he had to stare at his father, the more the coals in his chest would flare, and the closer he'd come to breaking.

"Do you need help with the dishes?" he asked. Dan looked his mom in the eye, hoping to find answers there like he had as a kid. Her eyes crinkled with her smile, causing the faulty spark plugs in his heart to ignite once more. His father might be involved, but his mother couldn't have been. "Let me go get the table set."

He took the excuse to step into the kitchen, away from the rest of the family. The pressure built inside him like he'd lost his regulator and hurtled toward implosion. He wanted to run out of the house and drive long and far into the night until it was just him, the open highway, and the twinkling lights of the city.

If he were being honest with himself, he wanted Greg Locksley in his condo again and a repeat of that night. His life had narrowed into a black hole of late, one that had been sucking him under more and more, and the date, that night, had become the one bright spot.

Tomorrow. He'd see him tomorrow.

Dan tugged out the dishes, the porcelain clinking, and then grabbed the silverware with a jangle. He took one breath, two, drawing in the scent of his mother's cooking, the kare kare he grew up with. He just needed to survive dinner first.

ELEVEN

Today needed to go right. No room for mistakes.

Which, given the Outlaws' current streak of luck, meant they'd end up with the building burning down around them while Alanna hurled insults, Tuck attempted a leap from sixty stories high, and Scarlet took up knitting.

Grif straightened his tie and stepped out of his room at last.

John already waited by the door, clad in a sharp gray Burberry suit and a liar's smile. "About time you came out of there. Gussying up for the meeting with your new lover?"

"Ass." Grif shot him a deadeye stare. He'd earned the ribbing, sure, but what crept under his skin was the fact he'd spent at least a little longer in front of the mirror than normal, tweaking the product in his hair.

"Ass is what you'll be getting if you have another secret rendezvous with Danilo Torres," John cracked back, his blue eyes dancing.

"Why do I tolerate the lot of you, again?" Grif asked, lifting an eyebrow. "Let's be real, nothing stays secret here with this group of busybodies."

Scarlet's heels clicked as she approached behind him. "You'd be lonely without us, boss." She flashed him a grin, the white of her teeth even brighter against her carmine lips. "And, don't worry, we won't spill to your new beau how long you spent on that look."

Grif groaned. "Et tu, Scar? We're going to set the stage for our heist, not so I can take Dan Torres over his office table." He strode up beside John, trying to ignore how his cock woke to life at the thought of fucking that gorgeous man in his own office.

"With your lack of shame, I wouldn't be surprised." Scarlet passed them to crack the door open. Her pixie-cut hair was slicked back with a bit of product, and she wore a fitted Tom Ford pantsuit that clung to her slender body. "What are you lot waiting around for? We've got a business to infiltrate."

John shook his head, a grin on his lips as he followed Scarlet out the door. Grif grabbed the handle and glanced back inside, but Tuck and Alanna were still crashed out this early on a Wednesday morning. His stomach twisted, and his nerves whistled like a pot of tea, but whether it was Nevarra's threats, adrenaline from the upcoming heist, or the idea of seeing Dan again, he couldn't tell. He just knew they couldn't fuck this up.

He closed the door and locked it behind him before he jogged down the steps to catch up with John and Scarlet.

THE AON CENTER LOOMED AHEAD, TALL ENOUGH TO make an impression even surrounded by all those giants. Today was typical Chicago weather, the clouds coated in silver as they crowded the cobalt skies. Blustery breezes caused McDonald's wrappers to skitter across the ground and crushed foam coffee cups to tumble around and snag under tires.

Their cab driver wasn't the talking type, the partition closed and his gaze forward. Exactly what they preferred.

"Comms are working?" Scarlet asked, tapping at her ear.

He heard her loud and clear, not just because she sat beside him but through the earbud nestled in place. While he and John chatted up Dan Torres, Scarlet would be working her magic on the computers in the offices. She'd brought her arsenal of extraction tools for direct hardwire access to the information in these computers. A pro had handled the encryption of Torres Industries electronic info, which meant if they wanted to nab this intel, they needed an in-person removal.

"Based on the files we've looked through, I'm thinking we might need to pay a visit to the CFO," John murmured, cracking open his briefcase to cause some noise around his statement.

"First stop will be the CEO's office," Scarlet reminded them. "If I have time, I'll try the CFO's, but if he's in his office, I won't have much of an excuse or reason to lure him out. That's on the two of you."

Grif ran a hand through his hair. "I'm pretty sure the CEO's not guilty of much, with his one-man attempt to clear the company of corruption."

John cocked an eyebrow. "Because you're definitely an impartial party."

Grif's lips thinned. "Yeah, I am. Because you can bet if he's involved, I won't hesitate to bury him." His heart thudded hard enough to punch through his rib cage. He didn't have to force the conviction in his tone, because he'd lived and breathed his mission from the day his parents died. No matter how much he'd come to like Dan Torres in their brief interactions, everyone betrayed, and everyone lied. He had survived on reading people as best he could, but he wasn't infallible.

Luka served as a reminder of that. Turncoat shit hadn't responded to his text.

"Touché, boss," John said, lifting his hands. He donned his gee-golly disarming smile, nothing like the wisecracking swindler he knew. Grif had his Outlaws. No one else could be trusted, because no one else had earned it. And today needed to go off perfectly, the sound check before their after-hours rock show. The days were ticking down to the payment due date, and Nevarra wouldn't be forgiving on an extension.

The cab screeched to a halt by the streets he had vaulted through the other night while Doncaster and his scum tried and failed to play Pin the Bullet on the Outlaw's Skull.

"Both of you are on the comm," Scarlet reinforced, her hazel eyes flashing with insistence. "If anything changes, report in." He didn't question why she reminded them again and again. Their resident hacker didn't often step into the field, so this was as uncomfortable for her as a trip to the Chicago Theater was for him.

Grif reached out to rest a hand on her shoulder. "We'll be keeping a close watch on the situation. If anything happens or anyone gets too inquisitive with you, don't hesitate to disappear. We'll catch up."

She shot him a grateful look, those moss-brown eyes softening. "Thanks, boss."

He cracked a grin. "This is an easy retrieval. The sort of job we could sleepwalk through, so leave the worrying to me." He squeezed her shoulder one more time before letting go.

John rapped on the partition and paid the driver while they slipped out to the sidewalk. This place looked different in broad daylight with the crowds of suits strolling across the pavement, the honks of the cars passing by, and the low murmur of chatter permeating through every crack and seam of this city. Grif slipped a hand in his right pocket and strode forward to the entrance. The triangular frame of the Aon Center's entryway beckoned, all dark steel and glittering glass.

Scarlet's heels clicked behind him, and John's Clarks barely made a whisper on the concrete even though he could feel the man's solid presence.

Once he stepped through the doors, his skin began to crawl. He might live in a city of skyscrapers and shit, but the polished marble tiles, the recessed lighting above, and the sheer number of reflective surfaces reminded him far too much of his parents' company. Once upon a time, that might've brought him comfort, but once upon a time, he'd been a stupid kid.

Grif strode forward, chin up and gaze focused on

the elevator at the far end. Hushed tones filtered through this bright, spacious place, accented by the occasional manicured shrub or plant that looked out of place in this cold, sterile building. On one end of the room, escalators headed downstairs to the lower floors, while accent tables and a manned help desk took up a different corner. Torres Industries claimed a cushy spot on the upper floors, so he approached the chrome elevators on the opposite side.

Every step they made reverberated through this open, sunlit building, and every word echoed.

"Here's your guest pass," John said, handing him the key card that'd been priority shipped to the hotel they were "staying at" while in town. Scarlet had copied one for herself, and their plan today consisted of getting the intel to make themselves upgrades for their break-in next week.

The neon numbers flashed above the elevator as the ding-ding-ding echoed around them. Grif tapped the side of his leg again and again while they waited, the silence descending between them. The elevator settled on their floor, and those doors slid open with a soft click. Showtime.

Grif strode in and leaned against the mirrored panels at the back of the elevator. They'd gotten lucky enough for a solo ride up, but with the way cameras monitored everything here, he didn't trust open conversation. Scarlet pressed in the floor number for

Torres Industries, the doors closed, and the elevator lurched up. Sweat pricked his palms, and he stared at the ceiling, hoping the sight would soothe the edge. It didn't.

Elevators sparked a primal fear response—they had from the time he rode up them thousands of times to his parents' business as a kid. Back then, they'd helped him breathe through the distress until he could put on as good of a game face as anyone, a trick that he'd used to con poker tables when he descended to the criminal underworld.

"Did you hear about Sparky the penguin?" John asked, staring at his nails.

"Yeah, the little guy bit it the other day," Grif responded, glancing from one recording device to the next. "Damn tragedy."

Scarlet crossed her arms as she fixed the two of them with a stare. "Really? The two of you barely blink at the half dozen shootings that happen on the daily here, but Sparky the penguin gets a mournful mention?"

"This is Chicago, babe. Shooting's just a casual way of saying hi," Grif drawled.

Scarlet rolled her eyes and lifted her middle finger at him. "This is why I never leave my house."

"They're throwing Sparky a parade," John responded, a faint grin on his lips.

"That's because he was a national treasure," Grif

added, not bothering to hide his smile. He loved his Outlaws with every last broken piece inside him.

"Fuck both of you," Scarlet responded, transferring her glare to the elevator doors, which miraculously hadn't opened yet. The numbers ticked up, higher, higher, higher, as did Grif's adrenaline levels.

The elevator car settled into place at the floor for Torres Industries, and the doors clicked open. Grif's tongue dried, but he swallowed his resolve anyway and stepped off. Greg Locksley of Neo-National had arrived.

The marble walls gleamed under the amber lighting, almost blinding when paired with the polished floors. Black lettering and an arrow indicated the direction of Torres Industries to the right, and Grif set a fast pace, his footsteps echoing across the polished tile. Scarlet slowed hers—she wouldn't be entering with them, instead arriving as one of the newer employees in the system. Ideally, she should've arrived separately, but Scarlet didn't often do in-person ops—better to settle her nerves beforehand.

"See you in an hour," Grif whispered into the comm. He reached the double glass doors and gripped the cool metal handle. He yanked it open, the scents of toner and ink and dry-cleaned suits blasting him in the face when he stepped inside. Those bright lights glared down like a cop's Streamlight, but he ignored them and strode straight to the front desk, where a woman sat on the phone.

She glanced to them and offered a nod. He flashed his badge and mouthed "Meeting." The woman offered a polite smile and lifted a clipboard, pen attached to sign in. Grif snagged it and began scribbling out their essentials. John stood next to him, equipped with his briefcase and a friendly smile. A click-click-click sounded as Scarlet strode in behind him, acting like she worked here.

The woman hung up the phone the same time he handed the clipboard back. She skimmed their form and looked up to him. "Mr. Torres is finishing up a meeting right now, but there's a waiting area right by his office. I'll show you there."

John tipped his fingers at her in salute, and she led them past the front desk to head deeper into the building. Grif strode through the hall, different rooms opening into seas of flimsy-as-cardboard cubicles. Other, smaller offices featured wide windows and solo desks, making the hierarchy clear. He absorbed the details as he went, one of the rooms clearly IT by the volume of computers and people wearing headsets. The marketing department contained fewer cubicles, and more people strode around the room, half of them on cell phones.

The end of the long corridor opened into the waiting room.

"Take a seat here," the woman from the desk gestured before she left, heading back through the hall. The place featured a wide-windowed overlook of the city as well as the typical lineup of chairs and copies of *Forbes*, *Harvard Business Review*, and *Consumer Reports* stacked on the glass tables. Grif's fingers tap-tap-tapped at his leg. He loped over to one of the seats and sprawled out. He'd worn a different Valentino suit today, this one a similar gray wool-blend to John's. His gaze flicked to the closed office door.

Dan Torres waited behind there, and he couldn't deny the way his adrenaline pulsed at the thought. Whether it was the hot fucking night in his condo or the stream of texts since then, somehow the man had infiltrated his thoughts. Time to regain control of the situation.

"So, we're signing the fancy documents today," John commented, tapping at the briefcase.

"That's the hope," he responded, then lowering his voice to a murmur. "How are you doing, Scar?"

The comm buzzed in his ear. "So far, no one's given me a second glance. Exactly the way I like it."

"We'll be heading into the meeting in a minute, so it'll be some radio silence on our end. Don't hesitate to comm in if you need us."

"We can't bank our business on hope, Greg," John said in his normal register, as if Grif wasn't having a whispered convo on the side. Smart move—he'd already caught the probing eye of at least a dozen security cams along their way up, ones that would need to be disabled when they broke in. Either that or rerouted to old footage. That's where Scarlet would come in.

"Which is why we won't take no for an answer," Grif said, his gaze on the door. The scuff of footsteps sounded from inside, which meant the meeting was wrapping up. He perked up, leaning forward. John's gaze zeroed in on him, and his lips curled in amusement.

The door creaked open, and Dan Torres stepped out first.

His skin gleamed copper with a healthy glow, and his thick black hair was combed to the side, meticulous as always. His tailored charcoal suit showcased a lithe body Grif couldn't get enough of. Even now, his libido kickstarted to life at the mere sight of the guy.

Dan looked up at him, and when their eyes met, his dark brown ones softened, crinkling around the edges with an honesty that made Grif feel as sleazy as the corporate assholes he targeted. He cracked a wolfish grin, gripping the edges of the chair he sprawled out in. His gaze traveled from head to toe and back again before he met Dan's eyes. A flush broke out on the CEO's cheeks, one that made him even more delicious.

Dan stepped to the side and gestured for the person behind him to pass.

A woman strode past him, her black stilettos clicking on the tile. Her curls were pinned back, her thin red lips like knife slashes, and the black-and-white polka dot dress she wore nothing short of professional. Her gaze landed on him, and a knowing smile lit her eyes.

Betty Kirklees was already on the scene, the Bonnie to Roger Doncaster's Clyde.

Oh, fuck.

TWELVE

From the moment he'd woken up, today had been better than most. A little because the sun peeked out past the clouds, casting some of the golden glow in through the windows, but a lot because Greg Locksley was coming into the office for the Neo-National meeting.

He ushered Betty Lancaster out. He'd agreed to a meeting with the prospective client, but she felt as phony as an Instagram celeb. Not that he'd gotten a pass from the board to sign on any new companies. Out of all the newer acquisitions, he only wanted to fight for a few, and Neo-National topped his list. Mostly because they'd been the most forthright with him, but maybe a little because their rep looked like a Viking god and was scorching in bed.

Dan stepped through the door to spot John and

Greg lounging in the chairs while they waited for him. Greg's ice-blue stare landed on him, and the heat in his eyes that followed coursed down to his toes.

The man knocked the breath from him on sight alone, like the first time they'd met. Today, Greg had combed his blond hair back, putting his angular jaw on full display. His muscled body strained the seams of the suit he wore, a gray color that made his sky eyes pop. He hadn't been sure if the man was a lucid dream, but here he stood again, emanating power like he'd been plucked from an MMA match. The man would be a natural leader, with the confidence of his movements and the arrogance in his stare.

When Greg scanned him up and down, Dan needed to suppress the memory of how easily he'd pinned him down over his own coffee table. He'd felt the flex of those muscles, the power behind the man, and one taste hadn't been enough.

"Thank you, Ms. Lancaster," Dan called as she strode away. Good riddance. He'd entertained the preliminary meeting, but there wouldn't be a follow-up. Betty slowed her steps as she walked by John and Greg, her gaze lingering on them. Not like he could blame her—the two guys were gorgeous. They stared right on back with a challenge in their gaze hinting familiarity. Not surprising. The corporate world was cutthroat, and reps tended to know one another.

"Neo-National, you're up," he said, his heart fluttering faster than a hummingbird's wings. Christ in heaven, he needed to be the CEO of Torres Industries here, not some teenager nursing a crush. "Good to see you again, John." He nodded to the broad-shouldered guy who strode toward him. "Greg." The man's name died on his lips as Greg Locksley walked his way.

John offered a handshake, even though Dan couldn't miss the twinkle in his eyes. Chances were, he knew about his and Greg's rendezvous. Dan wanted to groan. All his attempts at being professional had careened out the window like a crumpled wrapper once he gave Greg Locksley his personal number. Great job he was doing at running Torres Industries right now. Not only had he started waging war against his own board, but he'd also given them ample fodder to undermine him.

"Funny meeting you here," Greg said, his callused palm meeting his in a touch far too intimate to be considered a handshake. When their skin grazed, the shock rolled through him like thermal radiation. That sort of chemistry couldn't be faked, or even developed over time. The mere scent of his aftershave made his knees weak; amber and notes of aged oak. From the moment he'd met Greg Locksley, the attraction between them had been as vast and powerful as Lake Michigan, and even what should've been a one-night stand hadn't gotten the man out of his system.

"Almost like we named a time and place," Dan responded, somehow maintaining his cool, even with his hormones dancing the bachata.

"Tell me you've got good news for us," John said, swinging his briefcase back and forth. "I know it's been a few days since the lunch meeting, but we hoped to be able to move forward sooner rather than later."

During the conversation after the meeting, Phil and Len's citrus-sour faces had gotten redder and redder while they argued with Vanessa, who responded to each furious claim with a winter chill. He'd let everyone squabble their frustrations out, and then he'd postponed the vote. Until he had solid evidence, Dan wouldn't be able to get a board majority on his side.

Leo had met with him throughout the week, setting him up in all his techie glory with every countermeasure to track the goings-on in this company.

"I've got news, but I'll need a little more time for the full partnership. My board isn't thrilled with new blood," Dan started, and then glanced to the open waiting area. They could take this meeting in his office, but he'd been feeling twitchier there lately, like he was being watched. Either the nerves were getting the best of him, or his own employees had bugged him. Given the seedy shit his father had inferred he should stay out of, he wouldn't be shocked by the latter.

Dan tilted his head toward the hallway. "We've got a private meeting room we can use. Follow me."

He slipped into his office and snagged the stack of papers he'd left on the edge of his desk. A letter of intent was in there, one he planned on having Neo-National look over while he worked on convincing the board. Greg skimmed his fingers through his hair while he waited by the doorway, tucking a few strands behind his ear.

Goddamn, Dan needed to stop drooling over the man for a half second and slip into business mode. Hard to do when the guy's mere proximity shook him up like a bottle of prosecco. Dan strode out of the office, Greg keeping pace with him while John waited in the hallway.

"You look fucking delicious," Greg murmured, his gravelly tone so low only he could hear.

Well, professionalism could jettison out the window. Dan's cheeks flushed, and the tone traveled straight to his cock. Fun thing, doing a business meeting with a hard-on. Though, already, Greg Locksley had made the morning a hell of a lot more pleasurable than his year-long slog through the Badlands here.

"Do you have to be so distracting?" Dan shot back as they reached the hall. He scratched his neck, trying to collect his composure from where it had dribbled onto the floor.

Greg's grin widened, a wolfish, hungry look in his eyes. Of course. Despite the man's placid surface, Greg Locksley was all passion, whether he delivered bedroom eyes or poignant speeches. Either way, the man drew him in like a magnet.

"So, what does the board have to say about us?" Greg asked, switching to business with a whiplash-inducing speed. "I'm sure we were a tough sell, what with the new approach you're taking and all."

Dan glanced down the corridor, hoping none of those members would be walking his way any time soon. Guaranteed, if they spotted him bringing Neo-National in for a meeting, someone would try to edge their way in. The scent of whatever off-brand Lysol the cleaning staff used worked its way under his skin, and he half wanted to sneak in at night to replace the supplies. Yet, the problem wasn't the scent, but this place.

"Let's talk in the meeting room," Dan said, realizing both John and Greg watched him, waiting for an answer. Instead of continuing, he led them down the hall, his gaze narrowing on the handle. Great strategy with new clients: act like a paranoid creep in the place he was supposed to be running. He sucked in a deep breath to compose himself, which snagged in his throat after he caught the intensity of

Greg's stare. Apparently, he failed at one-night stands.

Greg had been clear from the start—he wasn't a picket fence kinda guy, and Dan? Well, he couldn't even take a walk in the park without getting attached to a puppy. The hookup had been a bad, bad plan.

Dan reached for the handle and ushered them inside.

The meeting room was bright and spacious, with fluorescent lights beaming up top and a modern rectangular table with an open center lined by dozens of chairs. The white dry-erase board graced the opposite side of the room, perfect for the too-many presentations they cycled through daily. A slender black table lined the back wall, accompanied by a Keurig, a filled pitcher of water, and a mess load of Coffee-Mate powder, straws, and sugar packets. Dan had come to loathe this room.

The door clicked as it closed behind the pair from Neo-National, and Dan took a seat at the table.

Greg settled right in beside him, his presence dominating so much of the room it blotted out some of the shitty board meetings. Some.

"Not to be the worst," John said from behind them. Dan swiveled to face where he stood by the door with his palm on the handle. "But do you mind telling me where the restroom is?"

"You are the worst, John," Greg drawled

beside him.

"Down the corridor and to the left," Dan said, jabbing a thumb in that direction. "We can wait for you to get back."

The door swung open and shut again, leaving Dan alone in a room with Greg Locksley.

Greg leaned back in the seat, his powerful body eclipsing the flimsy boardroom chairs. A slow, lazy grin rolled over his face, and his electric blues heated like halogen bulbs. Even in the trim suit and with his hair slicked back like polished perfection, the man bore too many scars to look anything but dangerous.

"Well hello, sexy," he drawled, locking eyes with Dan. "Dress like that for me?"

Dan arched an eyebrow, an amused grin rising to his lips. In here, with just the two of them, the trappings melted away, even in the middle of Torres Industries on the top of the Aon Center. "You mean the clothes I wear to work every day? Try a little harder."

Greg's lip quirked with amusement. "I'm a little distracted. Can't focus while that sweet body of yours is begging to get bent over this table."

Thank fuck he wasn't standing, because his knees trembled at the idea of a repeat. "That's exactly how I want my board members to find me," he shot back. "Braced on a table with another guy balls deep in my ass."

Greg snorted. "I mean, if that's your kink, I'm not shaming." He clasped his hands behind his neck, placing his tree-trunk arms on full display.

"Please, I prefer a more private setting," Dan said, scratching his nape. He chanced a glance up to meet Greg's eyes. "Your shitty week get any better?"

"This is the highlight." Greg's gaze scanned over his lips, fixating there. Dan licked them; too, too dry. The guy evaded his questions, but he seemed to operate on reflex. Whatever pain hid in the depths of those glacier blues was the sort most folks didn't air out in the open.

"Yeah, this is all that's tiding me over too," Dan admitted, even though he hated the prickle of vulnerability that swept across his arms after. When his dad started Torres Industries, he had taken years to build the company before they'd moved to the Aon Center at the height of their success. This building was nothing like the old one, with the lights that flickered in an off-tempo, the cozy cubicles, and the *Miami Vice* teal and pink décor.

The Aon Center was the real deal, all cold professionalism and sharp and cutthroat in a way he could never compete with. Dad believed that to be true too.

Greg reached forward and placed a palm on his thigh, the heat drawing Dan's attention. "You're made of stronger stuff than you think, Torres."

Dan bit his lip at the comment, not wanting to let

on how much Greg's words meant. How they settled in his bones right when he'd been feeling like he'd wither away. He wanted to kiss him so badly. The heat from his hand on his thigh, the amber aftershave, and the mere proximity of Greg Locksley scrambled his brains, making him forget he was in Torres Industries and they weren't two steps away from a bedroom.

Greg leaned in a little closer, and Dan's lips parted on instinct.

Inches away, Greg's hot breath puffed against his lips, and Dan shivered. Snared in his gaze, he couldn't look away.

Just one taste.

Greg closed the distance to brush his lips against Dan's. He almost moaned in response at the zephyr touch, at the sweep of those sensuous lips as he deepened the kiss. All the adrenaline from before crashed down again like a lightning strike to earth. Dan couldn't resist this man. Greg tasted like tobacco, like coffee, and he wanted more.

The door handle jangled.

Dan jerked his head away, his back slamming against the seat. Greg leaned back into his seat, the only sign they'd just been locking lips the gentle heave of his shoulders.

"Sorry I took so long," John announced as he entered. "Anyone tell you this place is a maze?"

"All the time," Dan said, a little too fast as he tried

to catch his breath. Business mode. Right. "So, if you're ready, let's dive right into the nuts and bolts of this."

John settled into the other seat beside him, which came as a relief. He didn't think he could look Greg square in the eye right now with the hard-on throbbing beneath his slacks. John lifted his briefcase onto the table and cracked it open, pulling out a stack of papers.

"I brought the other verifications you asked for last time," he said. "Figured they'd be important if we're signing anything."

"About that," Dan said, the knot tight in his chest. "We're working on passing new additions with the board, but I'd like for you to get the process started. I brought letter of intent papers for Neo-National to review and sign, and with any hope, we'll be able to get you on board by the end of the week."

He nudged his own stacks of papers, one in John's direction, and the other to Greg. Locksley leaned back in the seat, fingertips skating the table and a cool-crispness in his eyes that was pure business, switching back on a hair-trigger like they hadn't just been kissing. Even though the scorch of Greg's kiss would fade from his lips, his words would linger far longer.

Dan was so fucked.

THIRTEEN

GRIF HAD ALMOST FORGOTTEN HE WAS HERE ON A JOB. Dan Torres with his easy blushes, rock-solid body, and vulnerable eyes swirled his mind like a late-night summer run through the city.

At least, until his comm buzzed.

"Boss," Scarlet's voice came in loud and clear, and he couldn't dismiss the note of panic. "We've got trouble."

They'd circumnavigated the first obstacle when John snuck to the "bathroom" to make sure the coast was clear for Scarlet to place a bug in Dan's office. Which left Grif to sit there in front of a gorgeous, genuine man and lie to his face. In all his time thieving, he'd never felt filthier. John had given Scarlet the all clear and headed to the conference room. During the negotiations, it had been radio silence from Scarlet's end, which was always a good thing. She didn't indulge in a lot of idle chatter, unlike Alanna who he needed to mute half the time on the comms.

"Phil Brennerman and Len James are lurking outside of Dan's door in the waiting area. They already knocked twice and tried to peek in." The panic in Scarlet's voice flared into a living thing, but Greg couldn't respond. Dan was wrapping up with their meeting.

"So, if you don't mind grabbing the signatures from your higher ups, then we can work on getting you guys into the company as soon as possible," Dan explained, pointing to the spots he'd marked with an X to sign. Unfortunately, all his hard work meant nothing, because Neo-National would vanish the day after they found the blackmail info on one of these damn consoles. His bet was Brennerman's.

John met his gaze. He'd heard Scarlet's plea loud and clear.

Dan's gaze lingered on him, and Grif took the lead, extending a hand. "Pleasure doing business with you, Torres." He added a wink so the comment didn't feel too impersonal, even though he had been fighting a hard-on ever since they'd locked lips. He hadn't meant to—he was supposed to distract Dan while John slipped away, but the man was like a neat glass of scotch—he couldn't help but take a sip. Dan pressed his palm against his, and that didn't help his erection in the slightest. Neither did the danger, if he was being honest.

"*Guys.*" Scarlet's voice sounded through the comm. "They're rattling the door handle again."

They shook, but the handshake lingered a second or two longer than appropriate. Dan's seeking gaze when he looked into his eyes caused his guts to churn like a food processor.

"To the two of you as well," Dan continued when he pulled away at last. "Take your time on the letter of intent, get all the approvals you need from higher up. I'll be contacting you in a week or so to set up the final meeting so we can get your company on board." Dan pushed himself from the seat, and judging by the way he tilted his head, he planned on escorting them straight to the front office.

The opposite direction from Scarlet.

Grif reached into his pocket and furrowed his brow in a concerted effort, the movements a bit exaggerated. "Sorry to be a pain," he said. "I think my keys might've slipped out of my pocket. Do you mind if I check the waiting room?"

Dan blinked in surprise, but he nodded and headed for the door. "I'll take you there. I'm heading in that direction anyway."

John slapped a hand on Grif's back, the flash in his gaze clear. "Good job, buddy." He cast a glance to

Dan. "I promise, his ineptness isn't a reflection of our company."

"Like you haven't lost your keys before," Grif muttered, playing into John's teasing. The amusement in Dan's eyes did stupid things to Grif's insides.

"It's a common mistake," Dan agreed, his gaze soft. They walked inches apart, and Grif couldn't help but count every single one. The kiss had failed to slake his thirst—instead, he only grew hungrier for another night with this man, and another. His body hadn't staged a full-blown revolution like this in years.

They strolled down the corridor, and Grif kept his hand in his pocket on his keys to make sure they didn't jingle. The play was a cheap pickpocket trick, but the more important thing would be getting Scarlet out of Dan's office without getting caught. He prayed she had gotten the information she needed from his computer before the two disruptions came calling.

The bright windows of the waiting room peeked into view, dappled rays causing the marble tiles to gleam. As they rounded the corner into the waiting room, Phil Brennerman and Len James both peered into the window of Dan's office, which Scarlet must've locked with the way they rattled the handle.

Dan coughed into his hand.

Both men nearly leapt out of their shoes.

"Go, Scar," Grif whispered. "John and I will create the distraction."

"Getting tired of waiting for me?" Dan gave them the out, even though his raised eyebrows and simmering gaze told a different story. Brennerman and Calvados stepped away from the door, cutting the distance between them fast.

Not far enough. The wide-open waiting room didn't have anywhere to hide, a square box filled with chairs on one side and Impressionist paintings lining the far wall that led to the door of Dan's office. At minimum, they'd need to lure them to the chairs.

Grif stalked around one side of the room while John took the other, both pretending to search for his keys. They were just waiting.

"You've been gone from your office for a while now, and we needed to discuss some things," Brennerman responded, his voice as smooth as motor oil, as if he hadn't been caught snooping.

"Then learn to do what everyone else in this office does and set an appointment. I had a meeting with these gentlemen from Neo-National." Dan's tone grew brisk and cutting, nothing like the warm, spun-sugar glimpses he got of the man.

"Ready," Scarlet said over the comms.

Distraction time.

Grif reached down. In a fluid motion he dropped his keys and snatched them back up. They jangled as he slipped them into his pocket.

"Looks like I found them," he said, loud enough

to draw the trio's stare. The door to the office cracked open, and Scarlet would attempt to slip out, which meant they needed full attention on them. Grif strode up to the trio. John made his way across the room with his focus zeroed in on Brennerman.

"Mighty fine to meet the two of you." John extended a hand, drawing the stares of both Len and Phil. "Don't suppose we've had the pleasure yet. I'm John Smith. I know, boring name; blame my parents. We're here to represent Neo-National."

Dan's gaze strayed. Grif leaned in, close enough he snared his attention.

"These the guys we were supposed to be meeting with?" he murmured under his breath, low enough only Dan could hear. He nodded, even as his lips flattened with his clear disapproval of them. Grif's skin prickled, and a drop of sweat crawled down his neck as he searched for Scar in his peripheral.

She'd cracked the door open a little bit wider, but no path existed that wouldn't plaster her against the pale white walls. He needed to get them moving in a different direction.

A loud laugh from John split through the room, drawing everyone's attention.

John clapped a hand over Brennerman's again, ever the charmer. The man played Clark Kent in the city far too well, even though no one who knew the guy would believe his aw-shucks routine for a moment.

"I suppose it's best we head out," Grif said, slipping his hands in his pockets. "We've taken up plenty of your time already."

"Why don't the three of us escort them to the front," Dan suggested, a subtle pressure in his voice that Grif had never heard during their exchanges. Brennerman glared at him, but he and his crony still wore that sheepish air of "I've been caught" around them like a knitted shawl. Dan led the way toward the corridor, and Grif chanced a glance back behind them as the rest of the entourage shifted forward.

Scarlet slipped out from the office, but she moved at a caterpillar's pace along the far wall, each movement measured to not draw attention.

They strolled down the corridor at a brisk clip, Dan's ease and camaraderie vanishing in the wake of the two new arrivals. Apparently, these were the old fogies who made his life a nightmare. Grif's skin crawled like he'd been shocked out of sleep at three in the morning. Any moment, they might look back and spot Scar.

Their footsteps echoed as they got closer and closer to the end of the hallway where the front room of the office spilled into the cubicle farm. Grif glanced back again.

Scarlet had reached the corridor. She trailed paces

behind them, ducking her head as she leafed through papers on the clipboard she'd brought, pretending to look busy. Oh, thank fuck.

Dan stopped in front of the door and turned to face him.

"Well, we'll let you guys get back to your business," Grif said, offering Dan another handshake.

He stared into those dark eyes one last time, memorizing the flash of tenderness there, the heat from his slender palm, and the genuine smile on his lush lips that had felt perfect locked against his. If any of this was real, they were an office romance in the making, but Grif hadn't been cut out for a simple life since the tender age of sixteen. He drew in one last inhale of Dan's lime and coconut fragrance, and then those seconds ended. They each pulled their hands away.

"Looking forward to hearing from you soon," Grif added even as the lie dried bitter on his tongue.

That meeting was the last time he'd ever see Dan Torres.

GRIF TORE THROUGH HALF OF HIS BOTTLE OF Jameson, yet the guilt still lingered.

He leaned back in the seat at the kitchen table of the penthouse, returned to his comfortable running pants and a gray tee. The only suit he'd be getting into in the near future was a bodysuit for the infiltration of Torres Industries, coming up stat. He slammed the empty bottle back onto the counter, the thwack echoing through the room. Alanna and Scarlet had decided they'd earned a night out at Berlin to dance their stress away. The escape would be good for Scar. She still walked on sandpaper after that close call.

Not like they'd expected two of the board members to be lurking around their boss's office. If the CFO hadn't been in his crosshairs already, the man had just cemented his position as target numero uno when they made the extraction.

John and Tuck were on Doncaster patrol. With their enemies scouting the building too, they needed to cut off any attempts before their heist. Two more days.

Which left him with an empty house, an empty bottle, and an empty heart.

His phone buzzed, and he wanted to ignore it. He'd need to start weaning off the communications with Dan—no cold ghosting, but he couldn't keep indulging in the flirty texts. Not when each one sliced another cut into his already covered arms. He scanned the wire and pine shelves of their booze rack, but he wasn't in a quiet enough mood for gin, and vodka just made him meaner.

Fuck it, he'd drink coffee. The idea of going to

Polished Knives was scrapped, after he'd ruined the joint by taking his mark there. When had he gotten to be such a careless idiot? He ran ops better than this. Grif always worked more like a spider spinning a web, watching from a noticeable distance as his enemies got themselves tangled up. Yet ever since the botched Nevarra job, he and the Outlaws had been sloppier than ever. Luck hadn't just abandoned them, it had lobbed them off Swallow Cliff.

Grif hopped up and strode over to the coffee maker, tugging his grinder and beans from the overhead shelf. Within seconds, the beans were ground, and the rich scent wafted his way while his machine sputtered to life. Numbness clung to his fingertips, but the bottle of Jameson hadn't done the trick to douse the nerves, because his heart still fucking hurt.

And when he hurt, that was when the memories encroached.

The first night alone, every creak of the floorboards, every scratch of the tree branches against the siding had made him think they were still here. Any moment, the door would creak open, and Mom or Dad would pop their heads in, Dad with a random fact he learned on NPR, and Mom with her doe-eyed concern, always remembering to check in.

Well, lah-dee-fucking-dah, a stroll down memory lane was what he had lined up on this shit-eater of a day.

Grif flexed his fingers and poured himself a cup of joe. The steam was hot enough to scald, but his numbed hands didn't feel shit right now. He always froze over like this every time he let his mind drift to the past. Parts of him ceased to work, like something integral had died with them. Grif tugged out his phone and skimmed over his texts.

The twist of bitterness on the rocks turned to disgust when he realized Luka had sent the texts.

Luka: On the ropes.

Luka: 1935.

Luka: Eagle.

Great. Code. Exactly what would make this night more riveting. He dragged his cup of coffee over to the table in time to hear the front door slam open.

"Bleeding," John barked, the sound carrying from the entrance.

Grif rolled into action, bolting down the opposite corridor to the shared bathroom. Their overstuffed first aid box was wedged right beside the toilet. Grif tossed it open, snagging the gauze, disinfectant, and a needle and thread. He crossed through the corridor in loping strides, making the turn to the left to reach the foyer.

John crouched beside Tuck, who gripped tight to his ankle. Black days and bleaker nights.

Grif slammed to his knees in front of them, the supplies tumbling from his arms and onto the floor.

He scanned for the wet spot in the fabric. He didn't have to look hard—Tuck's fingers were soaked in blood.

"Bullet?" Grif asked. Tuck nodded, his jaw clenched tight enough to see the strain. "Grab a hot towel and water." He didn't bother looking at John. The man was already slipping toward the kitchen by the time the command arrived.

"Keep holding tight to your leg," Grif ordered. Tuck nodded and clung tight to the spot as Grif snagged out his knife and placed a hefty slash through his pants. He cleared the fabric off the leg in the span of seconds and tossed his pocketknife to the floor.

John dropped to the ground beside him, some water sloshing from a filled bowl. Grif reached out to grab the wet towel before he offered it, and he started cleaning out the wound.

"Eyes on my pretty face, Tuck," Grif said while he worked, moving the man's hands from his ankle to press the wet towel to the wound. Tuck's eyes honed in on him with all his might, his skin shades paler than normal—blood always made the guy queasy. Based on the busted skin, the bullet had grazed, not buried itself. The wound was right above the Achilles, so hopefully he hadn't sustained tendon damage. After spending so much time in underground fights, Grif had gotten real good at home patch-ups.

"Mind explaining to me what happened?" Grif

asked while he made a one-hand grab for the disinfectant, fumbling with the cap, and then splashing the liquid onto the open wound.

"Fuckshit. You're a bastard," Tuck swore, reaching for his leg. Grif batted his hands off. With the way the wound was frayed rather than pierced through, gauze should do the trick rather than a stitch job.

"Doncaster's out for blood, that's what," John muttered, wringing out the wet towel into the water. "The man had set patrols on the streets around Aon Center. Any infiltration's going to mean getting past those bastards too."

"Lady Luck's just knocking us down and spitting in our face at this point," Grif responded as he placed a swath of gauze on the spot and began to bind the wound. Tuck's skin grew sallower, but he forced down deep breaths like a champ while he zoned out. He must be bobbing along on the currents of the pain at this point.

"Ever since the stupid Sunset Ruby heist," John murmured, his voice low.

"Agreed. I made a bad call on that one," Grif said, even as his chest squeezed tight.

John's hand clapped onto Grif's shoulder. "We made a bad call. We're the Outlaws, not Locksley's Merry Men."

Grif tied off the bandage and glanced to John. He

clapped a hand over his. The resolve that had been so elusive tonight settled back over him like slipping on a trusted pair of Everlast gloves. He'd chosen each of these individuals—John, Scar, Alanna, and Tuck—all wildly different, and yet each of them had inked their mark on him deeper than any tattoo. The world was full of traitorous scum, but he and his Outlaws were cleaning it up, one heist at a time.

And in five days' time, they'd hit the Aon Center.

FOURTEEN

THE GLIMPSE OF SUNLIGHT BROUGHT BY GREG'S VISIT
got doused in charcoal clouds and torrential downpours with the way the rest of Dan's week had shaped
out. Truth be told, any morning in this building would
probably be a bad one. He had yet another board
meeting, as if they needed to argue with each other
for the fiftieth time this week.

Today, he needed to convince the board to again
postpone the vote on the new acquisitions. If they
pushed for the vote today, the response would be no.
Dan glanced to the clock again, hating the glare of
the numbers as they ticked closer and closer to yet
another confrontation, another push against a
company that didn't want him here in the first place.
Vanessa and Leo were the sole things keeping him in
the game at this point.

That, and maybe a certain stunner of a blond who had captured his attention.

Dan stood, smoothing the wrinkles out of his dress shirt before he slipped his suit jacket back on. Phil and his cronies would seize upon any perceived flaw, whether it was the new policies he tried to introduce or the way he parted his hair. His heart twisted hard at the memories of a mere year ago when he'd been making pennies in comparison, but he'd been innovating, working on projects that mattered. He missed those days more than he missed the old pond from their first house. However, the idea of getting excised from his family scared him just enough to keep slogging through.

The merciless city stared at him through the window. The peaks were so familiar, the breadth of the landscape, the sprawling blue of Lake Michigan a gorgeous that pierced his heart. The view of the city from here summed up everything about this business —cutting, grandiose, and filled with more corruption than could ever be cleansed.

Based on the reports Vanessa kept digging up too, the connections between the deaths of former employees had his alarm bells clanging. This didn't just seem to be average corporate corruption. If someone working for the company was tied to this? They were wading into far more dangerous waters than he could've ever imagined, far out of their depth.

Dan strode to the door. Time to get to this meeting.

———

Two hours. They'd been in this stupid room for two hours bickering like they were back in kindergarten and didn't want to drink the apple juice. The scribbles he'd made of potential growth from the new companies had been viewed with glazed-over eyes. He'd spent hours collating the research and forming the charts, but the reception was the forehead to a brick wall—same as always.

His skin itched as he sat at the head of the table, gazing across the room at the twelve dour faces staring back at him, apart from Vanessa's. She took the opposite end of the table.

"We have to look at what's fiscally responsible," Phil Brennerman said, pointing to the paper in front of him. "A lot of these companies you've brought to the table are new and untested. They could fast turn into a money drain for us, and based on the terms of contract, we'd bear the weight."

Dan hated him. He hated him and his perfect arguments and counters to everything he proposed.

The man had been doing this for years and years longer than him; he understood that. Yet sitting at another of these stifling, noxious meetings while Brennerman swayed the entire team to his side delivered another blow to the stomach when he'd already suffered a dozen. When he dropped into the company, he had been determined to make a difference here, but each day he butted heads with his CFO chipped away at his resolve until he'd soon be reduced to mere gravel.

"We also can't stop acquisitions," Dan countered. "It would be irresponsible to not continue the company's growth."

"Agreed," Phil said, his sharp blue eyes flicking his way. "However, there are plenty of viable options out there to acquire that wouldn't be as much of a risk."

Again, the man with his relentless undermining.

Dan forced his temper back, keeping his palms flat on the table.

"The two of you have been rehashing the same points for the past hour," Rita said, one of the few people in the room who didn't make his hackles rise. "We should just put this up for a vote."

Dan glanced to Vanessa on the other end of the table, hoping the pleading in his eyes flashed clear to her. However, his sister sat there looking like she'd seen Medusa, her lips tight as she met his gaze. He needed someone besides him to argue this, and she wasn't stepping in with an assist.

His gut sank like a stone. A couple of the other board members voiced their agreement on bringing it to a vote, Brennerman just as enthusiastic.

No one recommended postponing the vote, not even Vanessa, which meant he faced off against the rest of his company alone. Again.

Dan's palms broke into a sweat as those stares all turned to him. Of course, as CEO he needed to weigh in. "Let's vote on it," he acquiesced. At least then, he might stand a chance of swaying anyone to his side instead of appearing intractable.

He shot Vanessa a pointed stare, but she averted her gaze. They'd talked last night about this, and Vanessa had been on his side. She'd been swearing up and down about the old cronies in this company and stringing together colorful lines that would've gotten their asses beat back in the day. Had Dad said something to her too?

"Everyone in favor of abstaining from acquiring these companies and starting the process over?" Dan said, even as the words pained him. He stared out at the faces in front of him, all familiar from the year he'd spent working by their sides.

Phil Brennerman led the charge by raising his hand. "Aye."

Eight more popped up as his hope crashed like dominoes. Rita kept her hand down, as did Jeremy. Niles wavered for a moment but put his hand up.

"Anyone else?" Dan asked, even as his heart sank to his feet. Having to break this news to Neo-National would be miserable.

Vanessa's hand rose. She didn't look at him. His stomach lurched, but he sucked in a breath to stay steady. Out of everyone, she had been just as adamant about stopping Brennerman. He counted on two people to have his back in this company: Leo and Nessa.

She hadn't just run him over—she'd switched to reverse and backed up too.

Dad must've said something. There had to be a reason.

All those stares zeroed in on him. Shit, they were waiting on him to continue.

"Majority rules," he pronounced. "We'll abstain from acquiring the companies and start the process from scratch." God above, he hated this place. Dan's chest ached, and all he wanted to do was slam his fist into a wall, flip this behemoth of a conference table, and talk to Vanessa in private.

"The meeting's adjourned," Dan finished. "We'll continue this at a later date."

As if he'd shouted fire, every member of the

board rose from their seats in a clatter of metal squeals against the floor. The thump-thump-thump of his pulse pounded louder and louder. Nessa had been one of the only reasons he hadn't walked away, the big sister who he had always trailed after like a puppy. His legs were already carrying him toward her.

She hunched over, gathering the last of her things to bolt like the rest of them. *Not gonna happen.* He refused to postpone this talk.

Vanessa looked up when he stopped to stand in front of her. Her dark brown eyes bled guilt, as did the firm slash of her mouth.

"Vanessa Angelica Torres," Dan started, his tone low enough she alone could hear.

Her eyes widened, and she took a step away.

A hand tapped his shoulder. "Dan, might I have a word?"

The voice sent a wave of nausea rolling right through him, a Pavlovian response at this point. He bit back his rage. "Sure. We'll catch up later, Vanessa." He cast her a careful glance she was quick to avoid. She all but bolted out of the room, leaving him with Phil Brennerman.

"Hope you're not feeling sore about the vote," Phil started in a manufactured conciliatory tone. "I tried to warn you ahead of time about how big of a risk the acquisitions would be. I know you're coming in heavy because you want to make your mark here, but the board isn't used to movers and shakers."

Uh-huh. Dan didn't buy the sympathetic bullshit for a second. A caring mask might twist Phil's features now, but those eyes were doling out hefty doses of strychnine. He leaned against the table, placing his fingertips on the surface. Today had been long enough already and he needed to drink.

"We're fine, Phil. Though I hope you don't think this means Len is back on the case. I still want to field our newest acquisitions, since they'll be reflecting on my name. Not my father's." Sure, baiting Brennerman wasn't the best idea, but Dan lost his last fuck during the meeting.

Phil's gaze darkened even as his smile remained radiant. "Actually, Len is going to need to be back on the case." He ran a hand through his hair, ducking his head as he stared at the ground. "We need someone with years of experience in acquisitions bringing new partners in," he murmured, his voice low with an edge that frayed at Dan's nerves. He opened his mouth to argue.

"You know," Brennerman continued, "there are a lot of temptations that crop up in acquisitions, which is why it's so important to have someone who's experienced on the job. The last thing we would want is a scandal. Higher ups taking advantage of clients, getting intimate with them in supply closets, copy rooms… hell, even this boardroom."

Dan's fingers numbed. Oh, fuck.

Oh, he knew. He knew about Greg Locksley and the way they'd locked lips in the boardroom yesterday. Dan had been so worried about Brennerman bugging his office that he never even considered the boardroom. Not like he stood a chance at finding proof—if Brennerman was bringing up the threat now, the man would've covered his tracks.

"So," Brennerman continued, his gaze skimming over his pared nails. "I'm sure you can understand why we need Len to be in acquisitions again while you stick to more important tasks."

Dan's stomach lurched. He'd been spiraling before, but this shoved him right off a high-rise with no parachute. Words gummed in his mouth even though he needed to respond, now. *Focus, Torres.* He leaned a little harder against the table, trying not to sag.

"All clear," he responded, his own voice sounding foreign. "Len can resume his responsibilities."

"Good on you, son," Brennerman said, clapping a hand on his shoulder before he stalked off to leave the boardroom. It wasn't until the door clicked shut that the shakes descended. He'd been so stupid. He indulged in a lapse when he couldn't afford one, not when the people in this place were an infection waiting to spread. Now he'd failed to bring Neo-National on board, probably for good, and Brennerman had blackmail on him.

His stomach lurched, and nausea rolled through him in a sinuous wave. Everything spiraled out of his control, and he couldn't even begin to sketch out a blueprint of how to fix this mess. He was screwed. His sister backed out on him, Brennerman threatened to out him, which would sever things between him and Dad, and he didn't know how he would approach his acquisitions to tell them he'd failed. How he'd face Greg. Hell, his job could be on the line too.

Dan pushed off from the boardroom table. He needed to get to his office.

He floated through the hallway, the sounds muted compared to the turbine roar in his mind. His feet barely touched the ground as he drifted toward the office that had become a prison.

Dan stepped into the waiting room where Leo paced back and forth. His lanky friend's eyebrows furrowed, and he pursed his lips. Because of course, more problems had to arise. The exhaustion stole him in one staggering sweep, like hours ticked away waiting in a hospital.

"Hey, Leo," Dan called to get his attention.

His friend's head snapped up, and he looked at him, his blue eyes framed by his black-rimmed glasses more serious than ever. "We need to talk."

Dan didn't bother responding, just offered a nod and led the way to his office. He slumped into his seat, falling apart like he'd been slow cooked. Whatever Leo wanted to level at him couldn't hit as hard as all the other problems.

Leo spread his palms over the table. "We need to talk about Neo-National."

FIFTEEN

BY THE TIME GRIF AND HIS OUTLAWS SORTED through the files Scarlet had isolated from the hard lines at Torres Industries, a few things had been clarified.

1. Dan Torres had no involvement in anything shady, based on his computer history, which Grif felt a significant amount of relief about. If anything, the man seemed as dedicated as they were to stomping out that sort of corruption.
2. Phil Brennerman, the CFO, was who they needed to target. Every discrepancy when traced to the source had been managed by him, and if anyone in the building held the rest of the incriminating files, he did. Only

problem was that while the computers were connected via intranet, most of the higher-ups had private servers under the sorts of firewalls that would require an in-person extraction of the data.

3. According to the notes Dan kept on his computer, Phil Brennerman's office had a high-tech safe in it which his father had told him to leave alone. Scarlet had peered into the man's office, enough to catch a glimpse of the make and model. They had their target.

Grif had stared at so many screens and reports today, he'd smoked through a pack and was ready to break the seal on another. No matter how many times he tried to close the tabs his mind kept opening on Dan, all he could think about was the way he ducked his head when he blushed, far too often, and how somehow, those gentle eyes pierced right through his defenses. Not like Grif could keep anything that pure in his life anyway. Everyone who entered his periphery ended up hurt or dead, and only his stubborn-as-fuck Outlaws clung on despite the odds.

"Tuck, you better not slow me down," Alanna called to him from the couch. They all sat in the living room, Alanna draped on the cushions like a starfish. Tuck hunkered down on the floor with his busted leg up on a pillow, and Scarlet curled into a chair with his laptop. John walked in and out of the room, too restless to do much else, with a frequency that made his skin vibrate. Grif's ass had started to ache from sitting on the floor in front of the coffee table for far too long.

"If you can't do this job, sit out," Grif warned. "Better to have one man less on the field than a hindrance."

"Anyone ever tell you your bedside manner is pure honey?" Tuck responded, casting him a half-lidded look. "Because it's not." Even so, Tuck's gaze softened, because he understood. Grif wouldn't put any of them in danger he didn't believe they could walk out from. His Outlaws were more precious than any take.

"What are you talking about?" John drawled, his eyes twinkling. "Our boss is all dulcet tones and sweet whispers. To our marks, at least."

For fuck's sake. They wouldn't be giving this one up any time in the next century. And Dan hadn't texted him all day, which shouldn't have sat like battery acid in his stomach. Grif pushed up from the coffee table, his limbs creaking with the effort. His hand slipped to his phone, but nothing new.

The last text was the one from Luka the night before, a puzzle he had yet to sit and solve in full.

He'd figured out the first piece—he met Luka

back in his fighting ring days. On the ropes meant cornered on the defensive. Luka's excuse at least.

"Instead of sticking your noses into my illustrious sex life, I've got a better riddle for you," Grif said, pacing across the tan carpet.

Alanna threw a middle finger up. "Fuck riddles. They're stupid."

"Astonishingly helpful, darling," Grif drawled as he strode over to the window to catch a glimpse of the city. Already, the sun reached an apex, the midday blaze gilding the towers of concrete and steel. Scarlet slid forward in his seat, adjusting his glasses at the mention of a riddle. "Luka sent me a coded message last night. He got backed into a corner, which is why the fucker sold our job out, but I'm stuck on Eagle and 1935."

Except the date niggled in the back of his mind like a missed meal. They both had to be relevant things, but his brain kept skipping over the missing thought.

"We can rule out the Roman Empire," John drawled. "Don't take Luka for much of a buff. It's got to be underground related."

"1935," Scarlet said, his voice echoing around the room. "I saw that on a file recently—within the last month. I just can't place the date."

Grif gripped onto the window ledge and stared out the window. The blue skies mocked him as he spun worn tires in the mud over what should've been simple. If Scarlet remembered the number from the past month, chances were, it came from a job, one they'd gotten from Luka.

1935, 1935. Luka wouldn't be referring to the crash of the USS Macon, or the New Deal. Had they stolen any artifacts in the past month?

Or failed to steal.

"The Sunset Ruby," Grif said, the words leaping from his lips. "He was trying to tell us something about the last mission. If he wasn't attempting to make amends, Luka would've never responded."

"Well now, I'm all ears for some new information," Scarlet said, running a hand through his dark hair. "I've been trying to trace everything related to the case, and it's all locked up tight."

"Don't suppose it's coincidence Marco Nevarra used to be a part of the Crimson Eagles," Tuck commented, his voice light like the mention wasn't a locked and loaded bullet.

Because of course Marco Nevarra had been the one who screwed them in the Sunset Ruby heist. But they couldn't prove their innocence for shit, and the Chicago mafia would utilize every tool in their workman's belt in the process. If he didn't pay up, one by one his Outlaws would be left floating in the Chicago River.

"And we still owe that fucker money, even after he

set us up?" Alanna asked, kicking the end of the couch. "I knew the bastard was a turncoat."

Grif swallowed hard, his nails digging into the window ledge. He wished he could offer up some magic solution, that he had a quick fix to nail a "screw you" to Nevarra's skull. However, they couldn't afford to make a public enemy of the Chicago mafia, not if they wanted to stay upright and breathing the sludge they called air around here. No matter what underhanded shit Nevarra had pulled, at the end of the day, the Outlaws owed money.

Their debt would be paid, or blood would be shed.

John let out a low whistle. "Did I miss the point where we got cursed or jinxed? Because damn."

"Curse of the Sunset Ruby," Scarlet responded, his tone gentle compared to the acid-wash of the others. "Obviously we blame this mess on the old artifact."

A genuine grin slipped to Grif's lips as he met his eyes. "Definitely the Sunset Ruby's fault. Look, I'm not going to lie to you guys—this situation's miserable." He could feel their gazes press on him, each of his Outlaws paying rapt attention to the garbage he spewed. But leading didn't revolve around believing in himself, it meant believing in the people he surrounded himself with—and his Outlaws were the best.

"Our backs are to the mats, and there's a KO punch speeding our way," he continued. "But the Torres Industries job is lined up and ready to go off in days, and we put in the steps, did the work. We'll get the payday and never do a job for Marco Nevarra again. And if Doncaster or Kirklees shows up, we'll shoot them in the fucking face."

"If it wasn't a little dangerous, this wouldn't be any fun." A feline grin rose on Alanna's lips.

"Hear, hear," Tuck said, saluting with his mug of coffee.

"Let's rob the reaper another day, Outlaws," Grif called to them, the thump, thump, thump of his heartbeat rising. Alanna let out a hoot and John a loud whistle. Every member of his crew stared back at him, unwavering. A deadly quiet settled over them, the slow, sinuous thrum in the air, the sting of the breeze, and that fresh hit of ozone before the lightning struck. All of this could blow up in their faces.

They'd keep fighting anyway.

The buzz of Grif's phone sliced through the hush.

SIXTEEN

"What about Neo-National?"

Dan might as well have been sitting in a Tilt-A-Whirl with the way the room started spinning. He sucked in a sharp breath to focus on Leo, who closed the office door behind them.

Leo wouldn't stop pacing, and the shup-shup-shup of his shoes to carpet drove him nuts. Dan wanted to stick his foot out to trip the guy just to get him to quit it. But with the way the exhaustion barrel-rolled into him, the most he could manage was a tap to his desk to get Leo to look front and center.

"You asked me to work my brand of magic on the acquisitions," Leo started. If Dan hadn't already been feeling queasy, that would've slammed the nausea right into him. "And I started noticing some familiar patterns with the Neo-National account—the way they were set up kept pinging my radar, so I delved into the website development and started hacking into their databases. A certain signature was marked all over it, one I recognized."

Leo stopped pacing and jammed his hands into his pockets. "It doesn't hurt I've been a fan of Scarlet's finesse in hacking for years, so I've dissected their patterns and style for ages. In fact, I consider Scarlet's work a big influence on my own."

Dan's eyebrows drew together. "So, you're saying someone hacked into their files?" He'd wasted all his brainpower on the meeting, and Leo kept rambling, which made drawing sense from his statements like plucking strands from a carpet.

"Here, move out of the way," Leo said, stalking behind the desk and crouching in front of Dan's computer. Leo's fingers flew across the keyboard, the clack, clack, clack of the keys the sole sound in the room. He'd already started entering in code, turning Dan's console into an unfamiliar landscape. "So," Leo continued, the glare of the screen reflected on his glasses. "Remember how I installed a keylogger on your computer? A day ago, either you developed advanced computing skills and dove into some deep company files, or someone else was hacking into your computer."

Brennerman and Len had been skulking around that day, but he didn't think the two of them possessed a scrap of computer knowledge between them.

Leo let out an annoyed hiss as he shot Dan a look. "Are you still not connecting the dots?"

"Not when you're leveling a bunch of hacker babble at me," Dan shot back. He didn't even have the energy to get defensive, since Leo was the one person in this company who hadn't screwed him over.

Leo rifled a hand through his chestnut hair and let out a sigh. "So, like I was saying, each hacker has a signature style. And Scarlet's code, their footprint, stomped all over your computer, deep digs into the financials of our company. The time stamp can't be a coincidence, because it was the same time as your meeting with Neo-National."

Dan hadn't wanted to go there. The moment Leo said there was a problem with Neo-National, he'd felt a tickle in the back of his brain, like half a refrain of a song he once knew. Like maybe he'd always known something didn't feel right. Yet when Greg had entered the room, Dan's sense and reason didn't just saunter out the door—it bolted. Hell, if last week someone had told him he'd lock lips with anyone in the boardroom, he'd call them insane.

Yet he had. Greg Locksley hadn't just been a dropped bomb of lust and pheromones. He had been the first guy to cause the broken tinder in his chest to spark after too many lonely nights and failed dates.

Dan might make bad decisions. He might bend when he should stand tall, like he had done too, too many times. But he'd always been able to read people, a little too well. The first night together at their date, he'd seen something real in those eyes, a conviction that gave him hope.

Leo straightened. "What I'm trying to tell you is that Neo-National doesn't exist. A pro hacker fabricated the company, and the average corporation would get hoodwinked and never know the difference. But they dug into some top-secret company stuff. They also happened to be in the same rabbit hole we've been diving down, all revolving around our favorite CFO."

Dan's mind roared.

The ground abandoned him—he may as well not even be sitting with the way he tipped down, down, down. Fuck, he'd been chasing after Brennerman for bringing shady people into the company, and he'd been no better. Dan prided himself on integrity, yet he'd welcomed con men in with open arms.

Leo leaned against the side of the desk and crossed his arms, looking like an Ent from Lord of the Rings with his long, lean limbs. The man's blue eyes filled with clouds as he stared into the wall behind them, his lips pursed like he ran through equations.

Meanwhile, Dan attempted to gasp for breath, a

burnt-plastic scent gripping the back of his throat and the loathing threatening to drag him under.

Leo cast him a glance. "So, what do you want to do, boss?"

The question hung in the air between them. Dan forced himself to take another breath. Even as his mind screamed, as his soul rioted, as his hopes crashed and burned into wreckage, he forced himself to process the facts. Pretend. Pretend these were equations he dealt with in his engineering days, not the purgatory of corporate dealings he'd gotten thrust into.

Neo-National didn't exist, and if they were hacking into their databases, they probably searched for a way to sabotage Torres Industries. Whether a rival company hired these guys or they were independent operators, they were more dangerous than a blown engine. Problem was, even if he increased security, Greg and John had already gotten files from them. Who knew what information they had access to?

Dan scrolled through his phone, the mere sight of Greg's flirty texts driving a stake right through his heart.

The texts.

"Leo." Dan looked up. "How difficult is it to trace a text?"

"Whose?" Leo asked, snagging the phone.

"Greg Locksley," Dan responded, even as he cringed at the idea of Leo skimming over the X-rated texts they'd sent. How stupid had he been, to believe the guy might be interested in him?

Leo took on that hyper focused look as he pulled his personal laptop from the briefcase he always lugged around with him. Once the screen booted on, Leo punched a couple of things into his keyboard before switching to Dan's phone.

"What you're asking is child's play. The cops can trace regular phones in thirty damn seconds, and even if this guy is using a burner, the GPS can't be so readily disabled. You want location, right? Are you thinking of tracking this guy down?" The edge in his voice was warranted—if these guys were a big enough setup to pull this level of subterfuge, chances were, the shit they were involved in was darker than a citywide power outage.

Dan didn't know what he wanted though. Whether he would track them down and bring them to justice or look Greg in the eyes and ask why.

"If we can narrow down a location, it might be leverage enough for a meetup. I'll make the situation right, somehow." The words tumbled from his lips even though he strode forward in the dark, fumbling for any path to follow.

Leo brought his laptop onto Dan's desk, and Dan pushed himself up from the chair to give the guy full access. Even though his legs wobbled and he still couldn't feel the floor beneath him, Dan somehow managed to stay upright. Leo slid into the spot and began typing away.

He started to pace, even though the numbness had filtered through his limbs like morphine without the relief. Back and forth, back and forth across the floor while Leo zoned in on his hacker work. The screen gleamed against his glasses as that intense look overtook him that meant he was fully immersed. Dan almost didn't want to look on the off chance that this pitch went wild. That Leo wasn't able to find what he said he could.

He wasn't sure if minutes passed or hours before Leo looked up from his laptop and gestured him over. "I'm closing in on the location of the texts."

Dan leaned over his shoulder, trying to ignore the way his mind screamed. Leo pulled up a map, and multiple coordinates cropped up at once. Most were scattered throughout town, all public areas, but many clustered in another spot, a private residence.

"On the Park is a building of luxury penthouses," Leo mused. "Good security, private place."

"Meaning he may have texted me from his home base," Dan responded, the words not sinking in past his skin. He'd grown so numb, someone could throw him through a woodchipper and he wouldn't feel the blades.

"Fool move on his part," Leo responded. "What do you want to do with the information, Danny?" His friend had been focusing hard on the computer screen, so when he whipped toward him, those cerulean eyes landing on him, Dan took a step back. Leo's gaze softened, and he reached out to squeeze Dan's hand.

He could barely feel the touch. Everything swirled around louder and louder until the temptation to crash through the window and embrace oblivion beckoned with too strong a lure. Dan tried to swallow, but his mouth had grown dry.

"I'm sorry, man," Leo said, casting an awkward glance to the table. "I know it's been awhile since you trusted anyone… like that."

Dan offered a shrug, as if that could communicate the depth of how he hadn't just tripped today, he'd plummeted. "What can we do? All I've got is this information, potentially blood on this company's hands, and zero people I can trust."

Leo met his eyes and nodded, the understanding a current there. He was the exception—their friendship had become "hide a body" solid over the years. "Whatever you choose, I'll stick by you."

Dan sucked in a shaky breath, as if he might stand a chance at clearing his head.

He could let go. Let Brennerman win, let Neo-National do whatever nightmare they attempted, and go along for the miserable ride. Fuck, he hated caring. He hated the fact that at the end of the day, he gave a damn about the corruption his name got tied to. He hated that even though he was pissed at his father and Vanessa right now, he didn't want to ruin them either.

"I'm making the call," Dan said. "Time to find out who Greg Locksley really is."

SEVENTEEN

GRIF PICKED UP THE PHONE THE MOMENT DAN Torres's name flashed across the screen. He crashed onto the couch Alanna sprawled out on, leaning back until she moved her leg.

"Hey there," he drawled, unable to keep the desire out of his voice. Their last encounter left him wanting, even though he should be forgetting about the man. "Is this business or pleasure?"

"Neither," Dan responded, his voice strained and serious in a way that had Grif leaning forward. His warning bells started clanging louder than those in the towers at Notre Dame.

"Well then, what's the surprise phone call about?" he continued, trying to get a pulse on the situation. "Not like I'm complaining. It's good to hear your voice."

"Just… stop," Dan said, his voice tight, pained even. Grif's blood dropped to polar vortex temps. *Oh, fuck.* "I know everything, Greg. Like that's even your name. Look, I've got to protect myself here and my company. We can either discuss this like civilized folks and come to an arrangement, or I can send the cops to On the Park with a hot tip."

Black days and bleaker times. He could feel the stares of his Outlaws press down on him. Dan Torres knew. Somehow, he knew they weren't who they said they were, that Neo-National was a front. Somehow, they'd traced them to here. His grip tightened around his cell phone. Unless he had his own Scarlet on his team, there should've been no way. Only another hacker would recognize her code, and they'd done nothing to tip him off. Except, Grif had been careless, texting him in the late hours when his mind wandered. Hell, sleeping with him in the first place had meant he needed to keep hold of the burner he was supposed to ditch.

Dan Torres made him foolish like he hadn't been since he was a kid.

"Let's talk. You name the time and place," he said, knowing he'd screwed over his Outlaws. A bottle of whiskey wouldn't suffice tonight—no amount of alcohol could scourge away this shame. He'd gotten sloppy, and at the end of the day, he could only blame himself.

"Six tonight, Kaylee's Diner."

Before Grif could respond, the call ended with a click. His tongue dried as he lowered the phone and looked up.

"What's going on, boss?" Alanna asked, nudging him in the side with her foot. She already prepared an attack with her tone. The rest of their stares bored into him, Tuck's cautious, John's reproachful, and Scar's with a pity that made him choke on his self-loathing.

"We've been made," he admitted. He'd fucked up big time, and the one thing he could do was confront his mistake and find a way out of this. All of this. Of Dan Torres finding their location and of Nevarra's men breathing down their neck for a payment the backstabbing asshole didn't deserve. "I'm meeting with him in a few hours to sort this whole mess out. I'll fix it."

Somehow.

THE NEON WHITE SIGN OF KAYLEE'S DINER STOOD out in the distance. Night had fallen, and with it brought the cavalcade of streetlamps to fight the velvety darkness. Grif always felt more comfortable in the dark, but for once, he brimmed with nerves.

They'd spent the last few hours hatching the game

plan to sway Torres Industries' CEO to their side. Between the fact that Dan was pulled out of a master's degree to take his father's role, something he'd discussed with Grif in their conversations, and the resistance he'd been meeting on every board decision since he took charge, the idea of swaying him was plausible. What would require prowess was the rest of his plan, but Grif wouldn't hesitate to pull out every tool in his arsenal.

Alanna and John stomped behind him, alternating between silence and insults he deserved. Grif soaked their jabs in, remaining quiet. He resisted the urge to run his hands through his hair or tweak his appearance. Unlike the swank suits from before, he wore a pair of beat-up Levi's, a plain white shirt, and his worn leather jacket. Even though this meet-up was the furthest thing from a date, getting to see Dan Torres again had him keyed, and hell if he knew whether that stemmed from attraction or nerves.

"With the way you're scowling at each other, no one's going to buy you're a couple," Grif commented.

Alanna crossed her arms over her chest. "Yet with the way you fucked our mark after the first meeting, everyone would buy that the two of you were. Your dick got us into this mess, so your dick better get us out of it."

"She's not wrong," John added, slipping his hands into his pockets as he strolled ahead of them. Unlike

Grif, John still dressed like a charmer in slacks and a blue button-down. He cast a look to him. "I don't care if you've got to take him in the bathroom or fuck on the goddamn table to get him compliant, but we're only a few days away from this heist. Our entire operation isn't going down like this."

Grif sucked in a sharp breath. They were right. Yet they hadn't heard the strain in Dan's voice or the pulse of hurt there. As much as the guy was a hot piece of ass, their connection had lasted even after the fireworks burst and continued through the random texts, the constant check-ins. Heaven and hell, this was the longest he'd kept up with any guy he'd taken to bed—a whole damn week.

"I'll get us out of this," he confirmed as he stalked up the sloping ramp. He skimmed his palm against the cold metal railing while he approached the front door. They were screwed in seven different ways, but he couldn't do anything about the mistakes that had happened. All Grif could do was keep moving forward and find a damn way out of this.

He reached the glass double doors and cast a glance to Alanna and John who glowered at him.

"I'll make it right," Grif said. "I promise."

Alanna met his gaze. "You know the alternative."

That was one he hadn't wanted to fathom, where Dan Torres took a fall outside of the diner—severe enough to incapacitate him, if not cause some permanent damage. Nothing he hadn't done before. Nothing he wouldn't do again. His palms broke into a sweat, and he tried to squeeze out the image of those eyes, soft, hopeful like fresh earth in the spring.

He strode through the door, knowing John and Alanna waited behind to make their own entrance. The air conditioning prickled his skin once he stepped inside, and the fluorescents beamed down on him. Peach lamps decorated the place, casting a glow against the bone-white walls. Glossy black counters lined the far side, each of the tables featuring the same veneer.

He scoped out the diner—he'd arrived early to find the best vantage point.

Except Dan Torres had gotten here first. Again.

The sight of the man socked him in the stomach.

Dan sat in one of the booths, his shoulders hunched and his thick eyebrows furrowed. He'd rolled the sleeves of his gray button-down to the elbows, showcasing those corded forearms and delicious bronze skin. His raven hair was askew for once, like he'd run his fingers through it a dozen times. The haunted look in Dan's eyes stopped him; it was one he recognized all too well. One that descended every time he remembered the day he got the news.

Dan looked at him, and his gaze darkened. All the kindness leached out.

He'd known. He'd known he'd wreck this

gorgeous man, but knowing that and witnessing the flames lick up the frame were different.

Grif walked up to him and thrust his hand out. He would only get one chance, which meant there was no room for error. If he failed to execute, Alanna and John would.

"The name's Grif Blackmore," he said, waiting for Dan to accept his hand. His stomach committed a full-on revolt at the disappointment in those eyes and the pain that broadcast in his tightened mouth.

Dan slipped a hand in his, the skin to skin contact sending a jolt of electricity through him. "So, Greg Locksley?"

Reluctantly, Grif let go and slid into the booth on the opposite side. "The alias I go by on jobs."

"Who hired you?" Dan asked. The weariness in his tone bled out on the table. A waitress swung by with a cup of coffee Dan nabbed at once, setting to work polluting it with creamers and enough sugar to swim in.

"Coffee for me." He caught the waitress's eye before she darted off, then switched his focus back to Dan. This was where he laid the truth out on the table and gambled. Dan had responded well to what he'd perceived as honesty before—the approach just needed to work a second time. Given the access Dan would have to the company and the insider knowledge, he'd be able to fill in the missing gaps to their current plan. "No one hired us, per se. We're an independent enterprise."

"So, thieves," Dan said, taking a sip from his coffee. The monotone from the guy who had been so expressive before near slayed him.

"Me and my Outlaws hunt out corrupt corporations and we steal from them. Most of our take ends up funneled to the people they hurt, or people who need the help." The familiar resolve settled over him, the one that always descended when he spoke about the society they sought to change. "Torres Industries is a drop in the pond—there are so many corrupt corporations who've bulldozed communities and devastated families. I swore when they ruined mine, I would never let injustice like that go unpunished again."

His heart thundered in his chest as the nerves faded away like a distant dream. The conviction always managed to cleanse away the fear, even as he stacked up sins by the hundreds. Either Dan understood his mission, or he'd misread the man. This was the platform he always landed on when his fool's heart took the wheel.

Dan arched an eyebrow. "Outlaws who steal from the rich and give to the poor? What are you, Robin Hood?"

Grif's lips tilted with a half-smile. "That's why my Outlaws dubbed me Locksley. Based on what we've seen though, you're not involved in skimming funds from the company."

"No shit," Dan said, his fingers running through his hair as he sank forward, elbows pressing hard onto the tabletop. Damn, his pouty lip looked biteable, and Grif needed to get his head out of the gutter, because this was not the time or place. Though, he couldn't help how John's jab seized his brain, because the idea of taking Dan Torres over this table was the stuff wet dreams were made from. Especially with the helpless look Dan shot him, like the man needed someone to take the reins.

Grif had always been proficient in that.

"Look, it's clear you've got a problem partner in your company. Phil Brennerman's name keeps cropping up over and over again," Grif said. "And we're close, damn close to being able to expose his corruption. We've seen the financial records, but they're not enough. We need concrete proof of where the money he's been skimming from your company is going."

Grif lapsed to silence, watching Dan. He'd reached the pivot point. Either Dan would be swayed, or he'd choose now to walk away.

Dan stared into his coffee cup, his lips pursed like he might find the answers somewhere there. He tapped the side of his porcelain mug.

"I'd be an idiot to trust you again," he said, not

looking at him. The bitter tang to his tone made Grif feel like a monster of the highest order.

"Then don't trust me," Grif responded, his voice steady as stone. "Trust that if I don't expose Phil Brennerman, someone else will, and soon. From the sounds of it, we both want him to pay for his crimes. Your company's been tied to some nasty business—missing employees who wind up dead and then some."

Dan looked at him, his dark eyes cautious. "What are you proposing?"

And, hooked. Time to reel him in.

"Work with us. Control the outcome of this rather than dealing with the repercussions. We're not the only thieves who are after the blackmail information, but we are the only ones who'd be willing to work for a fee instead of playing the whole blackmail game." Grif's proposal hung in the air, the weight of his words dropping like gravel off a backhoe. He couldn't deny the spark he'd seen in Dan's eyes at their first meeting.

"You're asking me to tank my own company," Dan responded, taking another sip from his coffee. Back to that unreadable monotone. Clearly, the guy was miserable, and he was the asshole responsible.

The waitress arrived with Grif's coffee, and he lifted the scorching liquid to his mouth. He never cared about getting burned.

"Brennerman's already sentenced your company. We'll give you the chance to rewrite the narrative and make sure the blame and punishment rests on his shoulders alone. If there's any heat in the process, which there's a high chance of, we're trained and experienced in handling that." Grif didn't hide the heat in his voice. He wasn't lying. An innocent in the upper echelons of corporate dealings was rare, and he especially didn't want Dan taking the fall for scum like Phil Brennerman.

"And what do you get from this?" Dan asked. "If you dive into my company's accounts, I'm not going to let you lift the money and run away clean." His brow furrowed, and he scanned his palms, which had flattened onto the counter. "However, if I'm entertaining this insanity at all… I suppose Torres Industries could afford your retainer fee for the information." He glanced up to him. "If I agree to this, we would bring Brennerman to justice but make sure he's the one who falls, rather than the company as a whole. But I'm going to need some time to think it over."

"Now you're catching my drift," Grif said, leaning in closer to Dan. The whiff of his lime and coconut fragrance triggered memories of their time in his condo. He reached out and skimmed his fingers across Dan's hand to draw his attention. He'd be lying if he said Dan pulling away from his grasp wasn't a slug to the gut. Unsteadiness flickered in his eyes like the dim, trembling lights of the L. Not like he could blame the man.

"When did you have the extraction planned?" Dan asked.

Grif tipped back his coffee, letting the liquid burn away his discomfort. "Monday. So if you're in this, come to my place tomorrow night and you can meet the crew." He snagged a card and jotted down his address, passing it over to Dan the same way the CEO of Torres Industries had done at the fateful lunch.

Dan hesitated, but he reached out and took it, slipping it into his pocket.

"I'll think about it" was all he offered. Doubt flickered in his eyes, and Grif's stomach twisted tight. Until tomorrow night, he wouldn't know for sure if he'd sentenced the Outlaws or saved them.

EIGHTEEN

Dan wanted to hate him so badly.

Greg, or Grif Blackmore as he turned out to be, had lied. He'd approached him under false pretenses, hoodwinked him into believing in his fake company, all while he'd planned to expose the corruption within Torres Industries. Dan swallowed back the cayenne burn of his anger.

Except, that's what Dan had been trying to do this whole time. He'd shown up at the diner, terrified to see the steadiness in those ice-blue eyes change to something loathsome, to see the conviction disappear, like Grif was just another circling shark.

Yet, Grif Blackmore, for all he'd lied about his motives and his name, hadn't lied about his cause. From the moment he'd met the man, he'd admired the resolute conviction to oust corruption and how the man walked the same path he did.

This would be far simpler if he could hate him.

Instead, the man sat before him in the small vinyl booth, his big body crammed in, looking all sorts of gorgeous with his hair slicked back and a sex-on-a-stick leather jacket that didn't hope to hide his washboard abs. The man's body looked so good it should be criminal—though, apparently it was.

"I've got this," Grif said, grabbing the check and placing some bills out. "Let me walk you to your car."

"Planning on knocking me off somewhere private?" Dan shot back, unable to help himself. His skin prickled, and his battered heart squeezed tight. Today hurt more than Uncle Felix's slurs about queers whenever he was around. It hurt more than his father's avoidance any time his mother asked about his dating life. And it hurt more than losing his college boyfriend and his twelve-year-old cat all in the same week. He ached worse than he had in a long time, enough to suffocate the paltry attempts hope made to crack the door open again.

"I deserve that," Grif responded, his voice heartbreakingly steady. "But if it makes you feel better, I know your friend's watching in the booth three down, and I know he'd call the cops on me the moment I tried anything." His fingers twitched like he might attempt to reach out, but he stopped, resting them on the table. Dan's gaze trailed to Leo, who'd come as backup tonight. He met his best friend's eyes and offered a short nod.

"Fine, let's get out of here," Dan said. Before the scent of amber and leather clouded his senses anymore. Before he dreamed up any more fantasies of what the mournful look in Grif's blues might mean. Everyone had turned on him today, but Grif offered the one chance he might get to stop Brennerman. To keep him from not only tanking his father's company, but also outing him publicly.

At least he didn't have to worry about disappointing Neo-National. He was disappointed in them all on his own.

He pushed from his seat. He needed time to simmer with all of this, time he wouldn't have, considering they planned this extraction in mere days. By meeting Grif here, he'd confirmed one thing—even if everything else between them had been a lie, the chemistry wasn't.

They strode out of the diner, leaving the scents of Windex, bacon grease, and hamburgers behind. Once he stepped outside, he wished he'd brought his jacket. A bracing wind swept through, causing his skin to pebble. They reached the end of the ramp to the side of the building before Grif turned to face him.

The shadows sharpened his features, deepening his scars, the proud curve of his lips, and the dramatic arch of his nose. Those eyes held all the intensity of a derecho, whiplash winds and torrential downpours that would sweep him away.

"Look, I lied about everything from the moment we met, so I don't expect you to believe me. Fuck, I wouldn't believe me. But, right now, I'm being real with you. If you were anyone else, there's a high chance I'd find a quick way to dispose of you. This offer wouldn't even be on the table."

"Good to know you're a murderer on top of being a thief," Dan responded, his voice abrasive. His fingers numbed, and he couldn't fathom why he was even considering any of this in the first place.

"I won't apologize for that," Grif responded, his cobalt eyes gleaming in the sallow exterior lights. "You don't know my past or the lengths I've gone to survive. However, if you let assholes like Brennerman run free, you might find out."

Too late. He let out an irritated sigh before looking up. "Then why bother?"

The ragged edge to Grif's words and the heat behind them made his knees weak. The way this man turned him upside-down was so, so dangerous, and Dan knew he played with fire, guaranteed to end in burns.

Grif's eyes flashed, and he closed the space between until inches separated them. He leaned in close, his hand slamming into the wall behind him.

Dan should've been terrified at being crowded by this dangerous man who had lied to him, and yet he met his gaze, unrelenting. No matter what veneer Grif had presented, Dan wasn't the only one unraveling.

"Because I can't get you out of my goddamn head," Grif growled, his voice echoing in the chilled air. His eyes flashed with a furious amount of emotion, more than he'd ever seen from the placid man. The kind he'd lose his mind and soul trying to chase. "Because the mere thought of a moment with you has me breaking all my rules. Because you've got this softness the world hasn't managed to beat out of you yet, and I'm going insane trying to shove it out of my system."

Grif's shoulders heaved in exertion as he lapsed to silence. Dan sucked in a sharp breath. He couldn't look away from him if he tried, even though the anger had reached a melting point, burning incandescent in his chest. Those lips so close scrambled his mind, and his body warred with the temptation to either crumble against his firm chest or sling a punch. Except falling into this man's arms was how he'd gotten cornered by Brennerman in the first place. Grif goddamn Blackmore. For all his pretty words, he'd come in like the thief he was, all lies and charm.

"Pretty sure the softness has been beaten out of me now," he whispered, his voice cracking in the process. His heart was trapped in a vise, and beneath the surface lay deep shame that he'd been so stupid in the first place. Even now, he drowned in Grif's intense presence and didn't want to come up for breath.

Grif reached forward and skimmed his thumb along Dan's chin, nudging it up until their eyes locked again.

"Bullshit," he responded, his mesmerizing mouth an inch away. "I can still see it in your eyes."

The flash of yearning in Grif's gaze grew so strong Dan's breath lodged in his throat. Not fucking fair. He couldn't upend his world and stand here dropping dulcet lines that made his body respond even as his heart rioted. The gentle way his thumb smoothed against his skin was so opposite the teeming power looming in front of him.

"Flip the mirror back around," Dan responded, unable to keep the scrape of frustration from his voice. "Don't go searching for what you already have."

He reached up to place a hand on Grif's shoulder. The light push was all he needed. Grif backed away at once, and shame flickered across his features, along with a self-loathing he didn't think possible on that handsome face. For a moment, he thought he glimpsed something vulnerable creeping in his eyes, but he couldn't dwell. Not now. He needed to get home and process all of this away from this man he found impossible to resist, even after everything was shattered between them.

Dan focused on one step in front of the other as he strode past Grif Blackmore, the con man, the thief, the liar.

The man who might just have convinced him to infiltrate his own company. The one he'd placed his position on the line for without even thinking. The one he'd jeopardized not just his future for, but his company's. He focused on his Audi that lay feet away. He needed to get home—away from all of this.

All Dan knew was he'd hit rock bottom, and Grif Blackmore happened to be the one person offering him a hand up. Which tangled the circuits in his mind even more.

***

The entire drive back to his condo, Dan's heart hadn't stopped racing.

He couldn't slam the door shut on Grif's words, ones that clanged in his mind like a fire alarm. He'd thought the intense attraction would've died when he found out the man had deceived him. What sort of fucked-up was he that this magnetism hadn't faded?

The steps creaked under his heavy tread as he made his way to the third floor. Leo was minutes behind him—he owed him a full briefing of how their situation may have taken a surprise left turn.

He slipped his key into the knob, but the door was already open. Dan's eyebrows drew together as he pushed the door open and stepped inside.

Vanessa lay on his couch, curled up with a Nora Roberts novel. She kept her legs tucked beneath her, and her full concentration was zoned in on the page, like he'd found her a million times in the past. Reading had always been his sister's escape.

"What makes you think we're good right now?" Dan asked, not bothering to gentle his tone, which bled exhaustion and bitterness. He shut the door behind him and headed into the living room. After all her promises that she was on his side, Vanessa had turned on him when he needed her and then avoided him the rest of the workday. Granted, the board meeting felt like it had happened to a different person after his rendezvous with the leader of the Outlaws.

Vanessa closed her book and set it on the coffee table before she looked at him. Her eyes brimmed with a seriousness that made him want to stop in his tracks and cut a quick retreat. The amount of bullshit from today would tide him over for the next century.

"You have every right to be pissed, Danny," she said, smoothing the fabric of her skirt. "I made a promise, and I didn't pull through for you when you needed me the most. But I couldn't talk at work—it's not safe there."

Dan crashed onto the couch beside her, melting into the cushion. He toed off his shoes and just stared at the ceiling as the room spun around him while their silence percolated.

"All right, Nessa," he said at last, running a hand through his hair. "Lay it on me. Why the sudden turnaround?"

"My car rolled into traffic this morning." Her tone was perfunctory, clipped, but her eyes blazed with fear.

Dan's head whipped toward her. "Is your car okay? Did you go to the hospital?" His fingers numbed like he'd plunged them into a snowbank.

Vanessa arched an eyebrow as she shot him a look. "I got lucky, or I wouldn't have been in the office today. Hell, really lucky, because if I'd been two seconds later, I might not be here having this conversation with you. Someone cut my brakes."

Dan's hand balled into a fist even as his internal temperature plummeted. He let her continue without interruption. The pit in his stomach heralded the truth. There was no doubt in his mind who had been behind the sabotage.

"Brennerman was my last meeting of the day yesterday. We'd gotten heated, and he'd warned me against voting for your proposal. I knew the man was dangerous, but I didn't realize he would stoop to those depths. I don't think it's coincidence former employees of ours wind up dead."

Dan caught the tremble of her hands, the quiet shake that rolled through her entire body. Vanessa was the strong one, the one who'd shout loud at Dad when necessary, who didn't back down from ballbusting an executive. She'd been the sister who plunged into the deep side of the lake and held her breath as long as she could, who had never been afraid of heading down into the basement at night, even when they both heard creaking sounds.

And this monster well and truly scared her.

Her eyes watered as she looked at him, her normally perfect hair tumbling in soft curls around her shoulders. "I'm sorry, Danny. I know I let you down."

He placed his hand over hers. He'd been numb for most of the day, but this resurrected flame from embers he thought had doused. A deep, deep rage bloomed within, threatening to consume.

"We've got to stop with the digging and the hard pushes," she murmured, the concern lowering her voice. "This is way beyond anything we could've fathomed."

She could've died.

Dan opened his arms, and Vanessa closed the space between them to sink against his chest, smelling like vanilla and hazelnut. She'd done the same for him too many times to count after dates gone wrong or when Dad or Uncle Felix went on their usual homophobic, slur-laden tirade that ate him up inside. Vanessa had just held him, stroking his hair as they watched something mindless on TV.

"Okay, Nessa," he said, rubbing circles over her back in an attempt to stop her shaking. In an attempt to settle their soles back on the ground. "I'll take some steps back."

She couldn't be a part of this any longer. Phil Brennerman was the sort of dangerous he couldn't face alone, but Vanessa or Leo couldn't take the risk any longer. Interfering might mean their lives. Not that his sister would listen. She was so stubborn that given time to shake off the fear, she'd be shouting at Brennerman in the board meetings and researching the company history, even at the risk of her own life.

However, one man was dangerous enough to give Brennerman a run for his money.

The Outlaws might be criminals, liars, and thieves, but they were the only people who might stand a chance at bringing Phil Brennerman down. They also might be the only ones who could keep Vanessa safe.

His phone buzzed, and he slipped it out of his pocket. Greg—or, Grif—had sent a text.

I'm glad you know.

NINETEEN

Breakfast had been miserable this morning.

John burned the bacon. On purpose. Knowing how annoyed he'd been, he probably spit on the toast too.

Every one of his Outlaws were pissed, and understandably so. Their continued existence depended on knocking out this heist in mere nights, and he'd brought their mark in on the mission. Truth be told, he wouldn't know if he'd made the right call until tonight. Dan hadn't responded to his text last night, so either he showed and became part of the operation, or he became an enemy they'd have to avoid or eliminate.

He paced in the living room, the tangerine lamp casting a mellow glow against the cream walls. Chicago's skyline lit up outside the window against a velvet night sky, like the city's neon attempted to compete with the stars. His chest had been tight all day, not the normal cloudless-sky-serene that descended before a heist. Danilo-fucking-Torres had infested his thoughts, and he seemed to see through Grif's fronts without even trying.

"All the back and forth doesn't look a lot like faith he'll show," Alanna said from her yoga mat on the floor. She leaned forward to stretch out her leg, bringing her arm up and over to wrap around her foot. She and Tuck both shared this routine, stretching and strength training for whatever climbs and runs they'd need to do on the heist. Not like Tuck would be operating at full speed with the wound he'd gained the other night. Still, the ex-carnie sat on the floor beside Alanna, forcing himself through sit-ups.

"He'll show," Grif responded, dropping to the ground to launch into push-ups beside Tuck. The excess energy percolating through his veins told him otherwise, but he'd survived this long by following his gut, not his fears. And his gut told him Dan Torres was the real prize, genuine and honest in a way few rarely were in this misanthropic age. Too good for the likes of him. He continued pumping against the ground, his muscles flexing like pistons on a machine as he channeled everything into the movements.

"And if he doesn't, we'll take care of him," John

called over from the chair he leaned back in, laptop resting on his thighs. "Even if you can't."

Tuck grunted as he lifted from another sit-up. Sweat dripped down his forehead, causing those thick curls to plaster against his skin. "If he's anything like the rest of us, he'll show even as he's cursing you here and back." He offered a half smile, his dark eyes crinkling with amusement. Grif's lips pressed tight. He preferred the insults any day. He deserved the insults.

He pushed off from the ground and let out a low breath. "I'm grabbing a drink. Anyone need anything?"

"Yeah, a new job," Alanna mouthed off. "And PTO, or I'll unionize."

"Good luck on that one," Grif said as he wandered toward the kitchen. The pressure tightening his shoulders hadn't abandoned him, and it increased with every passing minute. Out of every plan he'd rolled through, this one contained the biggest risks—but it was also the only one that didn't end with Dan Torres maimed. At the end of the day though, no matter what sparks flew between him and the CEO of Torres Industries, his loyalty lay with the Outlaws.

When Grif stepped into the kitchen, Scarlet looked up from his laptop. He chewed on the end of a pen, and a steno pad lay on the counter, filled with scribbles. Grif strode past, and Scarlet held out the empty coffee cup resting by his side at the table. He snagged the mug on the way and filled up from the half-empty pot they'd brewed an hour ago. Coffee, Jack Daniel's, and bacon were three things that never lasted long in this house.

Grif strode over with an unopened bottle of Jameson and Scarlet's coffee. He placed it on the table, and silence spread between them as he unscrewed the cap and tilted the bottle back. The liquid splashed on his tongue, but the burn didn't come close to cleansing away his issues.

Scarlet's fingers flew across the keyboard, the clack, clack, clack echoing through the room as he took a sip of coffee.

Grif's self-loathing reached a dull roar inside him, and the whiskey wasn't erasing those feelings, just giving them a pat on the ass.

"Lay it on me, Scar." Grif broke the silence, not able to take the tension any longer. "How fucked are we?"

Scarlet arched his delicate eyebrow and pursed his lips. "I know you're a masochist, but that's not my kink, babe. You know how fucked we are if Dan Torres doesn't show tonight, just like you knew the set of problems when you chose to bring him in on our operation."

Grif gripped the bottle of Jameson tighter. Scarlet was right. He knew better, on all of this.

Scarlet closed his laptop and blew a couple of

strands of his chocolate hair from his forehead. "Listen up."

Grif sat a little straighter. Scarlet never closed his laptop.

"Some of this fuckup is your fault. You were sloppy, getting involved with a mark. However, the Sunset Ruby mishap? Luka selling our job to Doncaster? Dan having some super-hacker on his side who managed to track us down? You couldn't have predicted any of that, and you're not omniscient."

"But I'm in charge," he reminded Scarlet. He bore the weight every day, from the moment he recruited each of his Outlaws and they started running jobs together. "At the end of the day, it's my crew and my responsibility."

Scarlet flattened his palms over his laptop and leveled a look at him, one part caring and another part withering. "Grif Blackmore, I know you hate to hear it, but you're human, a right mess of contradictions. For all the front you swagger around with like you're impervious to emotions, you've got plenty. We don't follow you because we expect a perfect leader. We love you because you give a damn, and for some of us, you're the first person who has."

Grif swallowed hard and took a swig from the Jameson. Except Scarlet wasn't stopping.

"I've known you from the beginning," Scarlet reminded him, his dark eyes knowing. "My parents had kicked me out, and I was hacking from terminals, as homeless as they come. You were the one who noticed my regular library visits, who asked me to dinner, which ended up being an invitation to your crew. I don't expect a perfect plan from you, because I trust your instincts. You don't let people in easy, but once they're yours, you'll believe in them more than they believe in themselves. And it's been clear from the moment you met Dan that he worked his way into your system, same as we all did."

Grif leaned back in his seat, stretching his legs out under the table. Scarlet's words worked better than any shot of whiskey, the warmth pooling in his chest. He remembered watching her library visits—he'd been looking to assemble his Outlaws and someone had pointed him in her direction. Once he sat Scarlet down and talked to her, he'd known, a gut feeling he couldn't shake.

The exact same one he felt the moment he met Dan.

Scarlet tipped back his cup of coffee, chugging the liquid like it wasn't steaming. He offered a wry smile that crinkled his eyes, a quiet, warm presence Grif couldn't imagine life without. "For all your posturing as the bitterest bastard at the ball, you're an idealist, Griffy."

"Ugh, not that name," he groaned. "Anything but that name."

Scarlet's gaze pinned him down. "I see how you soften when you mention Dan. And don't worry, I won't bring up the dreaded *c* word, but finding folks who soften our sharp edges are rare. They're worth holding on to."

"I'd like to hold on to something else of his," Grif drawled, unable to admit how Scarlet's words affected him. His Outlaws knew him better than he did himself on most days. A flush crawled across his skin at the honest assessment, at kindness he would never feel like he deserved.

Scarlet arched an eyebrow. "Cute. I said my piece, so now it's up to you to get your head in the game, bossman."

"You're the best person I've ever known, Wylie Raven," he murmured, using Scarlet's real name.

"I know I am," he said with a smirk. "Someone's got to keep this chaos grounded."

The buzzer sounded, and Grif almost lunged from the table to press the button for entry.

Scarlet snickered. "No, you're way too cool to care. Go get 'em, tiger."

Grif reached out and skimmed his hand through Scarlet's styled hair, earning him a middle finger in response as he strode out of the kitchen. He passed through the hallway and entered the foyer of their penthouse, trying to ignore the swirl of adrenaline eddying through his veins. Every damn time with this man, the thrill of seeing him was more intoxicating than a free rappel off the side of a building. He balled his hand into a fist, then flexed his fingers again. With their streak of luck, Dan wouldn't be at the door. It would be Nevarra's cronies, here to shoot him in the fucking face.

He stroked the handle of the pistol tucked into his waistband as he reached for the knob. Grif tugged the door open.

Dan Torres stood there in a forest green button-down and black slacks, looking as gorgeous as the day they met. The guy had no casual setting. He'd slicked his hair back, not a strand out of place, and his dark eyes burned with curiosity. Even so, those full lips that had tilted in easy smiles before remained firm.

"Don't shoot me." A voice came from behind Dan, a lanky guy who wore a beat-up Star Wars T-shirt and jeans. He lifted his hands in defense with easy, smiling eyes and a somewhat distracted tone. "I'm just here as backup."

Grif leaned against the doorframe, crossing his arms as he took in the new guy who he'd spotted back at the diner. Dan watched him, his gaze saturated in a caution that hadn't existed before. The thick glasses, graphic tee, and twitches tipped Grif off. "You're the hacker who managed to figure out Scarlet's work."

"He's my best friend," Dan clarified. "And he's ignored my every attempt to keep him out of this."

Grif nodded. While the crew wouldn't be happy about another new face, a man tenacious enough to track them down and show up deserved the welcome. He stood mere inches away from Dan, and already his body reacted, like he'd lit a bunch of sparklers on Fourth of July. And he wasn't the only one. He didn't miss the glide of Dan's gaze as the guy soaked him in top to bottom, or the heat that still dwelled there even as it ducked behind worry.

He crooked his finger at Dan, snaring his gaze. "Well then, let's get you guys inside. Hope you're ready to meet the Outlaws."

TWENTY

Dan had been nervous up to the minute Grif opened the door.

A thousand and one doubts rolled through his head, only several voiced aloud to Leo, who'd reached rambling frequency. Yet once Grif appeared in the doorway of his penthouse, the nerves, the doubts, and the fears evaporated. The bedroom eyes Grif flashed him didn't hurt, but what swayed him was the sheer strength radiating off the man.

He'd made the decision to follow through last night when Vanessa ended up crashing on his couch. And after spending a day dealing with recalcitrant board members in the offices he'd come to loathe the most, Grif's offer to team up had become his save point before a boss fight, the one hope he seized onto. The email he'd gotten from Scarlet hadn't hurt either.

Welcome to the team —*Scarlet* was all it said, but the hacker had attached dozens of articles all linked to corrupt politicians, CEOs, and business owners getting hauled in for their crimes. Scarlet included clippings of mystery donations to activist organizations, to individuals who'd been wronged—most of which matched with the timelines of these companies going under. It seemed like amid the chaos of the takedown, the Outlaws hacked into accounts and found their own ways to get paid. He understood the message they sent him—this was the work the Outlaws had done and the proof he had been needing to make the leap.

They strode through a posh penthouse that somehow looked model-home gorgeous and lived-in all in one sweep. The broad floor-to-ceiling windows cast his favorite city in full view, and the fixtures were modern, chrome and angular, similar to his own place. Yet homey details snagged his gaze everywhere he went, from the sci-fi and fantasy books haphazardly stacked on shelves to the random quarterstaffs leaning against the wall, and a stack of electronic wires pouring like tentacles from several milk crates.

He should be buzzing with nerves right now, but as Grif led him through the penthouse, a serene calm trickled over him, along with a brush of interest at this brand-new world he entered.

"Can I get you something to drink?" Grif asked as

he led them through a hallway. "A beer? A cup of watered-down sugar?" The teasing note in his voice curled in Dan's stomach, remembering the ribbing he'd gotten for the way he doctored his coffee.

"I'll take the cup of sugar, thanks," Dan responded, surprised at how easy their interchange flowed. "But I probably need the beer more." He should've been guarded after the revelation yesterday, but instead it felt like a veneer had been peeled back. This was the real man he'd known existed there all along.

"I'll have a beer as long as it's not poisoned," Leo responded. Dan snorted—the man's paranoia buzzed at an all-time high, even with one of his idols in this house.

Grif rolled his eyes. "No worries, I keep all the poisoned beer in the back of the fridge. We invited you here. We're not going to kill you."

They stepped into the kitchen, where a guy sat at his laptop, the screen's glow reflected by his thick glasses. The man was unreasonably pretty, with expressive brown eyes and carved lips, and Dan wrestled with an irrational surge of jealousy. Leo's jaw dropped and he strode straight over to the chrome laptop with a mess of stickers plastered on the casing.

"That's a beaut," Leo said, skimming his fingertip along the table by the laptop as he scanned it over.

The other guy watched him with an amused look

dancing in his eyes. "I take it you're Polonius? I thought I caught the signature on the files when we hacked into your system."

Leo offered a bow, gesturing forward. "I learned from the best, Scarlet." Ah, so that was the hacker who had won his best friend's endless admiration. After the way Scarlet had reached out this morning, Dan couldn't help but like him.

Grif approached with two porters in hand, passing one over to him.

Dan accepted, trying to ignore the spark as their fingers brushed together.

"So, your friend's a fan?" Grif said, tipping the bottle back. Dan couldn't help but watch how the liquid coated those lush lips, and the desire to taste them flared to life like it never left.

"My god, you should've heard how excited he was when he found out Scarlet had hacked into our systems. Like our company wasn't at Defcon one." Dan drank from the bottle, the smooth liquid gliding down his throat. The kitchen, with all its glossy obsidian surfaces and nickel accents, emanated a bright friendliness he hadn't expected. The entire place felt less like a secret lair and more like a home.

"Hackers are a weird breed," Grif responded, his casual grin making Dan's pulse stutter. Here, he appeared at ease, comfortable in a way the predator never seemed in public.

"I heard that," Scarlet said, hopping up from his seat. The guy wore a similar style to him, a neat button-down and tailored slacks, nothing like Leo's levels of casual or Grif's athletic store raid. "Why don't we introduce you guys to the rest of the crew?"

Dan found himself following before he realized he'd begun to move. Leo trailed close behind Scarlet, an infectious excitement in his eyes. Grif strode right beside him, his leather and amber scent as alluring as it had been the other night. They'd almost kissed, again, because whenever he was around the man, he couldn't seem to hope for self-control.

They entered the living room, which featured another perfect view of the Chicago skyline. The corduroy navy couches offset the cream carpeting covered by three or four bright purple yoga mats. A short, intense woman with stubborn lips and a mousey nose twisted and turned on the floor. She didn't bother to look at them as she launched into another stretch, her ponytail whipping with the movement. Another guy with heavy curls and softer features grunted while he launched into another rep of sit-ups.

Dan recognized John at once and offered a nod. Grif's fingers skimmed over his shoulder. The slight touch sparked his synapses, a reminder of just how good the man felt pressed against him. Grif guided him to the biggest couch and then took a seat next to him, as if staking a claim. Even though his mind grew tangled with shoulds, the last few days had been such a waking nightmare he'd cling to any reprieve he could find.

Grif's presence happened to be one of those things.

"Guys, meet Dan and Leo," Grif said, hunching forward as he jerked a thumb in their directions.

The girl on the floor arched an eyebrow, the pendulum of judgement swinging clear in her gaze. "So, this is the piece of ass you lost your mind over?" Her eyes settled on him, and she shrugged. "He's damn pretty, I'll give you that. Watch out, Scar. This guy looks like he primps as much as you do."

Dan opened his mouth, her bluntness slamming into him like a brick to the forehead.

Grif let out a weary sigh, scrubbing his face with his palms. "That's Alanna. Don't wait for an apology —you're not going to get one. She and Tuck are our stealth crew."

The guy who'd been doing sit-ups pushed up from the ground and offered a nod, smoothing back his curls. "Welcome to the Outlaws," he said before heading over to the loveseat where Leo perched and slumping in beside him. When Tuck pulled off his black tank top to reveal a glistening six-pack and mop off the sweat, Dan didn't miss the hungry way Leo scanned him over. Not like Dan could blame him. If he wasn't sitting next to Grif Blackmore, he might be looking at the attractive, athletic guy like that too.

However, when Grif entered his periphery, all other men ceased to exist.

Dan had fucked gorgeous guys before, and he'd dated charmers, but he'd never felt this draw to anyone before. Being around Grif was like standing in the middle of an open field in the middle of a thunderstorm, the wind whipping leaves around, the air tense enough to drink, and the sky purpling like a fresh bruise as he waited for the lightning to strike.

"And you've already met John," Grif said. "He's the only one who never goes under a fake alias."

"John Smith's your real name?" Dan couldn't help but ask. Knowing the truth like he did now, Dan couldn't imagine ever thinking of them as up-and-coming recruiters for their fake company. Even so, they'd hoodwinked him.

John shrugged, more casual in his jeans and Henley combo than Dan had seen him yet. "Why come up with a fake name when you can blend into the most common one?"

"Let's get down to business to defeat the Huns," Scarlet said as he leaned back in the chair he'd claimed. "Or Phil Brennerman, in this case."

"What can I do to help?" Dan asked, sweat pricking on his palms at the mention of the job. "I'm assuming you need access to the building after hours."

He should feel dirty at letting thieves into his family's business, but from the moment he'd stepped into the role of CEO there, this place hadn't felt like his family's at all. And since Brennerman strong-armed him with the footage he'd captured and then almost killed his sister, Dan didn't just detest his workplace—he feared it.

"Count me in too," Leo said, catching Dan's gaze from across the room. Dan's chest tightened with relief at having his friend by his side. If anyone had earned loyalty for life, it was Leo Barnes.

Grif stretched his legs out, but the way he brushed against Dan felt intentional, especially paired with how his blue eyes heated. Dan didn't move away, letting the touch ground him.

"Alanna, Scarlet, and I will be pulling the extraction. John, you're going to be our home guy for this one," Grif said, clasping his arms behind his head. The man's scars grew even deeper in the dim peach lighting of this room, nicks in his cheek and corded lines around his arms. "Tuck, will you be okay for Doncaster patrol?"

Tuck nodded. "You know I'm not sitting this one out." He lifted his leg and flexed. "A little bullet wound won't stop me. Besides, I owe them."

"Where do you want me?" Dan asked, his voice deepening with the question. The idea of letting a group of thieves infiltrate his own company was so foreign to him he couldn't even imagine it, nor did he know what he'd be good at.

Grif crooked an eyebrow, the wolfish grin widening with suggestion.

Dan's lips flattened as he shot him a pointed look back. "I'm not sitting out while you lot invade the company I'm supposed to be running," he argued, ignoring the amused looks Alanna and Scarlet exchanged.

Grif pursed his lips, scanning him over with a serious look for once. Like this, he could see the man's genius flash in those Arctic eyes. "You can back up Tuck on Doncaster patrol, on one condition. The moment they're spotted, you need to run. They'll be slinging pistols, and unless you're holding out on me with some secret field experience, if you stick around to fight, you'll end up dead."

"What's Doncaster patrol?" Dan asked, so many terms thrown around he could barely keep up.

"You interviewed one of them," Grif said. "It's one of the groups interested in blackmailing your company. You'll be their just to alert if they show up, nothing more."

Tuck offered a crooked grin. "Hell, I barely stick around to fight. Don't like the sight of blood."

"Leo, would you want to play around on one of my laptops?" Scarlet asked, tapping the side of his glasses. "I could have you run point from the penthouse with John. Once I hack the computer on-site, I'll be able to send the information to you."

"Are you trying to give me a hard-on?" Leo responded. "Because that about did it."

Tuck smirked as he glanced down to Leo's snug jeans for confirmation. "That all it takes for you, computer boy?"

"You should see how easy it is to get my pants off," Leo cracked, his grin wide enough to display dimples. The man couldn't do anything but flirt. Tuck crooked a defined eyebrow at him, returning the smile. Dan shook his head, unable to restrain his amusement even as he tried to keep his lips pressed tight. Not like he had any room to talk. From the moment he met Grif, his mind had been a one-track lane that got dirtier the farther he drove.

"The plan's a simple one," Grif said, clapping his palm on the coffee table in front of him to get every-one's attention. "We get the direct access to Brenner-man's computer that we've been missing and extract the information, which Torres Industries is kind enough to be sponsoring. Plus, we're breaking into the safe. Once the job's done and the payment's in the bank, we can settle our debts. If Doncaster and Kirklees try anything, we'll be there to stop them. Unlike us, they've got to infiltrate their way into the building. We're getting an easy ride courtesy of the CEO."

For fuck's sake, everything out of the man's mouth sounded like a come-on. If he needed proof their one-night stand hadn't gotten him out of his system, Dan simply needed to sit beside him.

"Fate hates simple plans," John mentioned, tapping his fingers on the end of the chair arm. "Guaranteed, we're overlooking something massive. Or Dan here's going to turn on us at the last minute. No offense," he said with a shrug.

Dan heaved a sigh. "Let's be straight here, I don't trust you, and you don't trust me. But we don't need that currency, right? Because Phil Brennerman is the real threat here."

"He's not wrong," Alanna said, pushing up from her yoga mat. "This is what we do, anyway, take out corporate assholes."

"And we agreed on fifty grand for the job, yes?" Dan asked. He and Grif had hashed the number out before, but he wanted to hear the confirmation in front of the team.

"Sounds good to me." Scarlet offered a reassuring grin.

"What are you going to arm up with on Monday?" Grif asked, looking at him in with enough intensity that he didn't just feel seen, but exposed.

Dan's eyebrows drew together. "You mean my doe eyes won't pull me through on this one?"

"God, go flirt in another room," Alanna called out

while she headed in the direction of the kitchen. Scarlet hopped up from his seat and approached Leo with his laptop, settling on the arm of the couch.

Dan tilted back the bottle of porter he gripped tight to, and he savored the taste of the sweet, dark liquid. The condensation printed on his palms, and his pulse quickened. Grif's gaze still honed in on him.

"Let's get you some equipment," Grif said, pushing off from his couch. Dan cast a quick glance to Leo, who was occupied by both Scarlet and Tuck. Grif offered a hand up, and Dan took it, the scrape of those calluses sending a shiver down his spine. Grif Blackmore could never have been anyone as simple as a recruiter for a small-time business. Somehow, the sight of him like this, as the leader of a criminal organization, felt right in a way he hadn't expected.

When Grif let go of his hand, Dan slipped it back in his pocket. The hurt and betrayal that had shocked him so severely yesterday had dissipated more and more with every article he'd scoured over on the Outlaws' work. Their methods weren't pure, but from what he'd witnessed, their hearts were. And having been on the receiving end of monsters like Brenner-man, he understood far too well the helplessness and fear.

Grif led him through the hallway lined with closed doors that must've been bedrooms. He reached the very end and rested his hand on the knob. Grif glanced at him. "I'm going to arm you with a couple of knives and a few grenades to drop in a worst-case scenario. But I'm being serious when I say the minute Tuck catches sight of any of Doncaster's guys, just run."

"You did warn me you weren't the only one casing the company," Dan murmured, a sharp twinge in his chest. Each revealed truth smoothed the ragged edges of pain that had emerged when he'd found out the guy he'd come close to falling for had been lying to him. "Though they didn't go so far as to try to get in my pants over the job."

Grif pushed open the door and tilted his head to follow. He flicked on the light. "Sorry, my bedroom's a mess," he murmured, leading the way inside.

Dan's throat dried with desire he shouldn't have. Except when it came to Grif, he wanted. He was greedy for every drop of truth the man offered.

He couldn't help the grin that rose to his face when he soaked in the man's bedroom. Most people said those words as a courtesy, but Grif hadn't been joking. A stack of World War Two history books teetered on the edge of the bed, several poetry books —Keats, Tennyson, and Eliot—scattered across it, and weapons lay haphazardly around the floor. Spent cigarettes littered an ashtray on the dresser, along with several empty mugs. The mess made Dan's skin itch, but when he caught Grif's inquisitive glance, he couldn't help the yearning at this secret glimpse of him.

Grif slipped around the piles of clothes, kicking a couple of crumpled shirts out of the way as he headed to the opposite side of the room, where a sliding glass door led to his balcony. Grif pushed the door open with a soft click, and Dan found himself moving unbidden again as he stepped out to join Grif on the overlook.

Even though the icy breeze slithered across his bare arms and the open collar of his shirt, that wasn't what made him shiver. Grif leaned forward, resting his forearms on the railing as he stared out at the Chicago skyline. Dan's tongue traced his lips at the sight of the massive man in stark relief, the shadows carving into his defined features, drawing out the sharp longing and sadness he'd kept hidden. Even in his jogging pants and thin gray tee, Grif exuded a nobility he didn't think existed in this world.

"Sleeping with you was never part of the plan, you know," he murmured, gazing out at the city.

Dan stepped beside him, resting his palms on the railing, even though the cold metal bit into his skin. "Just a perk of the job, then?" He pushed, sure, but the minute the news had broken yesterday, he needed to know. Screw being coy. "I'm a big boy, Blackmore. If this—whatever this is—between us was part of the job, or a way to sway me to your side, then at least be honest."

Grif's gaze darkened. "Do you genuinely think I do this sort of thing? Sleep with my marks, risk my Outlaws over a cheap thrill? I pride myself on control, Torres, but from the moment we met, I've been losing mine."

Dan swallowed, trying to ignore how his heart thundered. If he wasn't careful, they'd dive into depths he couldn't swim out from. He tugged at the ends of his sleeves, pinching the fabric as if the motion might reassemble his brain.

"Brennerman had a camera installed in the boardroom," Dan said, the admission slipping out. "He happened to catch our interlude on film."

A growl ripped from Grif's lips, the feral sort that reflected the wild look in his eyes. "Let me guess, he's blackmailing you with it."

Dan scratched his nape, ducking his head. "Considering I'm not out with my conservative-as-Christmas father's company, yeah, he is."

"Oh, fuck," Grif said, reaching forward to place a hand over his, the heavy weight pinning him down from floating out to the atmosphere. "I'm sorry."

"You mean that, don't you?" Dan said, unable to hide the wonder from his voice. "You're a thief who lied to me from the moment I met you, and yet I can't help but feel like I've known you from the start."

Dan couldn't voice the rest—how their texts had been a lifeline, how his loneliness had grown so deafening lately he could barely get through each day let alone those aching nights. How good it felt to tell someone he'd had a shitty day and for them to listen and understand without expectation.

"That's why you do this, isn't it?" he continued. "Because Brennerman is one of far too many who push people into corners, who threaten lives and families while they speed off in Porsches and go golfing on the weekends."

Grif stepped closer until only an inch separated them. Dan stared into his eyes, unafraid of the brawny man looming over him. One who had fought for years and bore dozens of scars to prove it.

"My parents were murdered by Robert Davies, someone with enough wealth and power accumulated to become completely untouchable. They headed their own company, and when they refused to acquiesce to Davies's offer, he had them killed. Untraceable, of course, because men with money hire others to commit their dirty work, and the cops quickly let the trail go cold. He has too many folks in his pocket to be bothered by consequences."

Dan's heart twisted tight. After Vanessa had gotten threatened, he could only glimpse into the agony Grif must've gone through at losing both his parents in a single stroke.

Grif reached out and traced his jaw with a featherlight touch that made him melt inside. "And when my parents died, I was so alone. So fucking helpless. I never want anyone to feel that helpless again. So I took the trust fund I was left with and used it to form the Outlaws." His breath caught in his throat, and his Adam's apple bobbed as he glanced away, pulling his hand back to settle on the rail. "Look, I don't talk about this stuff, not even with my Outlaws. Though, the nosy bastards have all pulled it out of me at this point. This thing between us—it was never about the job."

Dan's heart squeezed tight at the admission. The idea of the ferocious man ever being a scared kid made him swallow hard. He reached forward to rest his palm over Grif's. They both stared out at the city splayed before them, the winking and static lights all different shades of lavender and silver. In the distance, Lake Michigan stretched out, an inkspill on a canvas he both loathed and loved.

When Grif turned to look at him, Dan was done waiting.

Dan closed the distance between them and leaned in to kiss Grif.

TWENTY-ONE

GRIF restrained his moan of relief when DAN closed the distance and kissed him hard. Ever since the truth slipped out, he'd peeled back layers until the raw, exposed bits left him wincing.

He hadn't mentioned that time or those memories out loud in years, yet when Dan looked at him with that intense longing and the flash of distance he recognized for bone-deep loneliness, the words just slipped out.

Dan tasted darkly sweet, the porter still on his lips, and Grif couldn't get enough. He wove his fingers through Dan's hair, tugging at the strands if only to muss it up. He wanted this man flushed and panting beneath him. He needed to soothe the pain he'd caused and needed to show him the truth his mind only dared entertain in whispers. Desire rushed through him in a heady swirl, and Grif leaned against the railing of his balcony. He wound a hand around Dan's hip to drag him closer. The cool metal bit into his body, and Grif savored the way the shock grounded him.

So much pressure percolated inside, enough he could explode. Yet with the heated way Dan's mouth met his again and again, he had the same sort of stress relief in mind. Dan's hands slipped beneath his tee, roaming across his chest. Grif was packing a steel pipe in his pants, a fact he'd made Dan well aware of with the way their hips nudged together. Dan's erection brushed against his thigh, and he bit down hard on the pouty lower lip to hear him moan.

He grazed his teeth across the man's neck and sucked on his ear, devouring every inch of his smooth skin. "You know," he murmured in between bites along Dan's neck, "I was just bringing you in to grab some weapons."

"Liar." Dan's mouth curved in a sinful smile.

Gratitude swept over him, at the forgiveness for the false charade, at the way Dan pushed through to talk to him, at how he listened and didn't pity him, reaching out to touch instead.

Scarlet was right.

"I knew you were one of mine," he murmured against Dan's mouth.

Dan sucked in a breath, his umber eyes widening.

Then he pressed a kiss to Grif's lips again, a tender sweep that revved him up more. "So, you're telling me you've done this tango with all your Outlaws?"

Grif's eyebrows tugged together, but as he pressed his mouth to Dan's again, he could feel his smile. He ran his hand through Dan's hair, gripping tight as he let loose a low growl. "You're a brat, you know?" Not like that didn't charm him even more. Grif stole another kiss before he whispered against his lips, "You're the only guy I've ever brought to my room."

The second the words left his lips, Dan kissed him with a bruising force, hard enough to leave him gasping for breath. The teasing air vanished in the wake of his admission, and he sank into the heady depth of the current racing between them. This was more than a one-night stand, more than a casual fuck. He could feel it in the desperate way Dan kissed. His grip tightened around Dan's hips, the jut of the bones pressing into his palms like he'd never let go.

A trembling sigh puffed against his lips before he dove in for more, eager to devour this man. He circled his hands around to grab him by the ass, dragging him forward until he pressed flush against him. Dan's erection brushed along his thigh, lust jolting through him with the strength of a Taser. His cock throbbed to the point of pain from the sheer need to bury himself inside that stunning ass.

He met his lips again, drinking in deep with the

kiss. The scent of Dan's cologne wrapped around him, the sweet citrus making him want to suck and bite this man from head to toe. Dan's hands roamed everywhere, gliding along his arms, his back, his neck, the exploring sweeps setting his body on fire.

Grif's fingers landed on the waist of Dan's dress pants, and in seconds, the snick of the belt coming undone followed. Next, the zipper traveling down echoed in the night air. Grif slipped his hand in past his boxer briefs to glide his palm against Dan's cock, the sleek feel making him salivate. Dan let out a groan as he fumbled for the waistband of Grif's sweats. The sound in his ear and the heat of Dan's body tore at Grif's composure. He wanted—no, needed—to flip this man over and drive him into his bed.

Grif's thumb brushed against the head of Dan's cock, which leaked precum in anticipation. The man was so responsive, and the moans shot straight to his erection. Dan ground into his palm like a wanton thing, and hell if that didn't bring him close to blowing his load.

The second Dan's fingers skimmed against his hard-as-fuck cock, the remaining thread of composure snapped.

"Bed. Now," Grif commanded, grabbing Dan's wrist and dragging him forward.

"Anyone ever tell you that you're bossy?" Dan murmured, his eyes flashing with mischief. The wry grin on his lips was one Grif wanted to capture with his mouth.

"I'll spank your ass for that one," Grif muttered, closing the distance to the balcony door in a couple of quick strides.

"Promises, promises," Dan responded. His tongue traced his lips in a slow, sensual way that made Grif want to slam him against a wall and take him out here.

The moment they stepped into his room, heat prickled across his skin, a harsh contrast to the cool breeze of the Chicago night. Not like he needed to stoke the flames to this growing inferno. By the time they reached the bed, Dan had finished unbuttoning his dress shirt, revealing his slim, toned chest. Grif tugged the fabric off him, and then yanked his under-shirt up and over. Before Dan's hands reached his pants, Grif's moved there to help him shuck them too.

Dan had one of those bodies Grif couldn't stop drinking in. The man stood bare before him, all satin copper skin and lithe muscles. He was slender in a way Grif would never be, and this time he soaked in every detail, from the definition between his abs to the pronounced jut of his hipbones, and rock-hard calves he wanted to sink his teeth into. Dan's cock was painfully erect, veins and ridges on full display, and the tip glistened with precum.

Dan's cheeks flushed, and he ducked his head.

Grif closed the space between them, his finger skimming the bottom of his chin to bring those lips to his.

"You're fucking stunning," he murmured against Dan's mouth.

Grif tugged his shirt off, tossing it onto the growing pile of clothes on the floor. He pressed his bare chest against Dan's, the smooth surface pure seduction as he dragged the man flush to him. His pert nipples brushed across bare skin, enhancing the sensation, and Dan's erection nudged against him again. Dan's hands settled on his waistband, and he let the man drag the fabric down his thighs.

Dan sank with it, and by the eager way he licked his lips, Grif knew what he planned. His cock throbbed in response at the thought of that hot, wet mouth wrapped around his length.

"I said, bed," Grif repeated, reaching to pull Dan back up. He swatted his ass as Dan crossed to the bed. Grif didn't wait for him to slide onto it; he pushed him down with a thud and loomed over that lithe and beautiful body, his arms and legs crowding Dan on either side. The sheer need in Dan's eyes struck him square in the solar plexus.

"God, I want to taste this pretty cock," he murmured as he pushed off from his crouch above Dan. "On your hands and knees."

Grif didn't bother waiting to see if he followed suit—he rolled off the side of his bed to snag the bottle of lube and condoms from his dresser drawer. By the time he turned back, Dan was in position and looked positively fuckable. He caught Dan's eyes when the man looked back and nudged him so he could slip beneath. Grif slid up on his back between Dan's thighs until his lips hovered at the end of his cock.

His tongue slipped out, and as he licked the slit, Dan let out a low moan. Grif wrapped his hands around the man's hips, gripping them hard enough to bruise. He trailed the edge of his tongue along Dan's shaft, enjoying how he shuddered above him. He savored all of it, the musky scent, his skin warm and wanting, and the steel length he proceeded to devour. With the way Grif braced Dan, he maintained full control as he sucked his cock, long and drawn out strokes that made the man's arms tremble within minutes.

Grif popped the top of the lube open and got the cool liquid on the tip of his finger as he continued to deep throat Dan.

He reached around with the tip of his finger to trace the rim of Dan's asshole. The moment he touched the sensitive area, Dan's hips bucked forward, and his cock hit the back of Grif's throat.

"Fuck, that feels good," Dan moaned.

Damn, the responsive way this man reacted to everything turned him on. His cock had become so hard he could bat an inning with it, yet he focused on gliding his finger inside the tight hole he'd fucked the other night.

He drove his finger in time with Dan's helpless thrusts inside his mouth. Sweat beaded on Dan's skin, and based on the way his thighs trembled, he was close. Hell, Grif was too. If the man even whispered against his cock, he'd blow.

Grif thrust his finger deeper and deeper until he hit the prostate. Dan's whole body seized, and a second later, the hot, salty jets of his release flowed into Grif's mouth. He swallowed it down and slipped his finger out, squeezing that sexy ass as he went. Dan shifted his cock out of Grif's mouth, and Grif slid up beneath him to find the man's mouth and press a kiss to his lips.

Dan sank into the kiss, the bliss of satiation gleaming in his eyes. Grif claimed his lips with a hunger that grew. His hard length pressed between them, and even the rub of Dan's chest against his length brought him close.

"Holy hell, Grif," Dan murmured between gasping, swollen kisses.

Grif couldn't help the grin at hearing his real name on Dan's lips. Something about that felt so right. "You know I'm not done with you, right?"

"I hope not," Dan said before he dipped down to press his lips against Grif's neck, leaving a trail of fevered kisses and bites. Each one keyed up his need until he was buzzing. "I want you to fuck me with that massive cock."

Grif let out a groan. "Babe, if you keep talking like that, I might not make it there."

Dan wrapped his arms around Grif's neck and looked at him, his dark eyes serious. "Hey, are you negative?"

"Little late for that conversation," Grif joked as he brushed his lips over Dan's forehead, his cheeks, memorizing his features with each sweep of his mouth. "But yeah, I get tested regularly."

"I am too," Dan said with a glance to the condoms lying by the bottle of lube. "So, if you wanted…."

Heaven and hell. Grif's mouth dried with how much he wanted. A growl escaped his lips as he grabbed Dan by the arms and flipped him onto his back. Dan's soft grin in response did something stupid to his heart, making it lurch forward like a rickety carnival ride. Grif's cock throbbed with how badly he needed to tunnel into his tight ass. Bare. He couldn't remember the last time he'd been bare with any of the guys he'd taken to bed. Shit, he couldn't even remember the last time he'd had repeat sex with anyone. Life as a con man and thief didn't allow for people to get to know him.

Not like this.

Grif locked eyes with Dan and gave him a slow

nod. The words wouldn't come to explain how much that meant to him. This wasn't like their first encounter, a hot, fumbling fling. Dan knew who he was, not just in name, but the details he'd shared with him… well, Scar and Tuck had needed to pry them out of him with a crowbar. For some reason, those secrets dropped like coins at a casino every time he was around Dan.

Grif grabbed the lube and dripped the cool liquid between Dan's cheeks, and then applied a liberal coating to his cock. Even the thought of sliding into his gorgeous ass bare had him hard to the point of pain, the precum dribbling off the tip.

Dan propped himself up by his elbows, watching as Grif settled between his thighs.

Grif nudged the tip of his cock into Dan's entrance, and a sharp exhale came from him. Dan licked his lips, tilting his hips up to accept more. Even though he'd just come, the guy already sported a semi. Grif pushed in deeper, the feel of Dan's tight grip around him pure ecstasy. Dan let out a moan as his head dropped back and his elbows slid down, bringing his back flush to the mattress. Grif groaned at the snug fit as he thrust in all the way. The skin-to-skin contact grew into a heady rush, almost too much.

He grabbed Dan's legs, bringing them over his shoulders until his hips tilted at the perfect angle. Once Grif began to move inside him, Dan clutched fistfuls of the sheets on either side, and his eyes rolled back in bliss. Already, the shuddering waves of an orgasm neared, the bliss shooting sparks through him as the edges of his senses grew hazier. Grif gritted his teeth and forced himself back from the brink, willing himself to last.

He needed this time between them, and he couldn't bear the idea of it ending.

Grif thrust in deep, the tight clench of Dan's ass around his cock pure perfection. This was the high of punches landing in a brawl, the thrill of bullets flying and a narrow escape. This was speeding through the city like it owed him money, windows rolled down and his hair whipping around with a force that stung his cheeks. Grif couldn't have looked away from Dan's gaze if he wanted to, their eyes locked as they both waited for each other's surrender.

His chest clenched with something deep, something true, and his strokes increased in fury and force until their skin slapped together. Until he basked in the delicious sting of their collision. Until Dan writhed beneath him, his erection stiffening between them.

Dan's heels dug into his back as he rammed inside him again and again with a mounting wildness. Fuck, the bare glide into him felt so damn good, the barriers between them completely gone. Dan's steady gaze burrowed into him, one that held no expectations, no weight to toss onto his shoulders—those eyes that simply wanted.

Grif thrust in deep, until the pounding pulse of his need throbbed so loud, he couldn't hear anything else. Droplets of sweat trickled down his forehead, his back, and he could still taste the salt of Dan's release on his lips.

A snarl ripped from his lips as he picked up the pace, ramming into him like there was no tomorrow—in his line of work, there might not be. He thrust into him, chasing the edge with all his might until at last, he cracked wide open and tumbled on over.

Grif's release poured into Dan, his cock throbbing as that tight ass milked him dry. Dan's legs slid from his shoulders, and as they hit the bed, Grif braced himself over the man. His hands pressed into the bed on either side of Dan, his sweaty palms sticking to the sheets. Dan stroked his own cock, once, twice, until bliss radiated across his features and a moment later, the sticky heat of his semen splattered against his chest, dripping between them.

Dan reached up for his neck, and Grif let the man guide him down until their lips pressed together. He slumped against him, ignoring the mess they'd made of themselves and his bed. Grif luxuriated in the feel of Dan pressed against him, of the lazy, stoked heat, the soft glow of a candle that flickered in his chest, and the vulnerability he'd never been allowed to keep.

Grif's lips brushed against the hollow of Dan's neck, against his earlobe, and against the curve of his chin. Even now, he couldn't get enough of the man.

"We should get cleaned up," Dan said, biting his lip. "Don't suppose you've got a private shower tucked away in this room."

Grif's laugh rumbled through his chest. "I mean we could take the easy route, or we could do our walk of shame across the hall to one of the shared bathrooms." He cast his gaze across Dan, scanning the man beneath him. "I call dibs on washing down this gorgeous body."

"You're making some wild assumptions that I can even stand," Dan murmured back, the grin clear by the gleam of his eyes. Grif paused to stare into his face, unable to help himself. He wanted to memorize everything about this moment, the strands of Dan's thick black hair plastered to his forehead, the healthy flush across his cheeks. The way Dan stared at him unafraid, like he'd plunged right through years of defenses to some battered part of him he'd buried years ago.

"I've got you," Grif said, pulling out of Dan with some reluctance. A moment later, his feet settled on the hardwood, and he scooped the lithe man up with ease. His heart thundered in his chest, because he meant those words.

Dan wasn't just one of his. This thing between

them meant something more, and Grif didn't want to share that with anyone. He couldn't put a name on it, or else this incandescent feeling might burn out like a bad bulb, but he wanted to follow this path as far as it could take him.

TWENTY-TWO

DAN HAD ALWAYS FELT LIKE AN INTERLOPER IN THE business that should've been his, but today, the feeling became a reality.

He'd strode through the glass doors like normal, greeting Dolores and Ken on the way in. Dan offered his hellos while he went, flashed his empty smiles like the click-click of a camera, and settled behind his desk the same way he did every morning.

Nerves rushed through him, a hefty dose of adrenaline that left him floating, like he coasted beyond the loathing, the worries, and the doubts that always crept in when he sat behind this desk. Dan's fingers tapped a heavy beat on the surface. Despite the fact he now collaborated with thieves who planned on excising the tumor from his company, Dan had never felt more supported. After all, he'd been trying to douse Torres Industries' corruption in turpentine until all the ugliness stripped away.

Because of Grif Blackmore, he stood a chance.

A knock sounded on his door, snagging his attention.

Leo strolled in without waiting for a response, and Dan's shoulders dropped with relief.

"Close the door behind you," Dan said, wanting the privacy. After the incident in the boardroom, Leo had scoured his entire office from top to bottom to make sure no similar bugs or cameras were installed.

"We've got to stop meeting like this," Leo said with a wink as he perched on the side of Dan's desk. He flexed his fingers and stared at his nails. "Unfortunately, we've got a throbbing tumor of a problem tonight."

Dan's brow furrowed, and he almost shot up from his seat. The entire plan would go down tonight: the infiltration, the extraction, and the upheaval of Phil Brennerman.

"A company is coming in to do a massive upgrade of our systems on Wednesday to a newer model." Leo's sharp eyebrows tilted with his obvious distaste. "They're arriving after-hours tonight to go over the hardware we work with."

"Aren't you the head of the IT department?" Dan asked, his pulse speeding like he'd stepped onto a raceway. How the hell were unsupervised individuals allowed into his company? If he'd ever needed confirmation of the belief everyone in his company worked around him, this was proof positive. "Anyway, shouldn't you have access to his network as part of Torres Industries? Maybe we just tap the files today and avoid this whole mess."

"No, the higher ups were granted their privacy back when your father ran the company. Your computer, for example, isn't a part of the shared network, and instead is on a local one blocked from network access, which is the reason the Outlaws need to come on site. While I could and have hacked into board emails before, I can't access the files on their computer without sitting behind the desk. And our favorite CFO went over my head to arrange this update with the board. I have the feeling that by Wednesday, any files we're searching for are going to be wiped off the map." Leo let out a huff of breath. The man rarely got ruffled, but this foul breeze slammed both of them.

Dan swallowed, hard. Every time he tried to move his rook forward, Brennerman already had three moves planned to knock him out. "Do you think he knows about the Outlaws?" He kept his voice low, even though they'd cleaned the room. After Brennerman had gotten footage of him and Grif and dared to use that as leverage, even breathing the air felt like it required permission.

Leo shook his head. "I don't know of anyone who could've leaked. My only guess is all your probing and challenges lately have him nervous. You know he's bugged the place in the past, and he's covering his ass in case you decide the blackmail he's got on you isn't enough to keep your obedience."

"Guaranteed, if I try to delay this, he'll just wave that blackmail in my face," Dan muttered. "He's got me completely cornered with it, because if he outs me publicly, that won't just tank my family relations. Most of the business partners we work with are homophobic bigots. I won't be able to do anything here."

Leo gripped the side of the desk harder. "I wish I had access to his local files. I'd scrub it if I could. But all the higher ups lock their offices when they leave them and guard their privacy like bulldogs. Brennerman's working late tonight to supervise the initial foray with the company."

Dan swiped a hand through his hair, the gel keeping it slicked in place. "So, the one chance we have of pulling this off is tomorrow night?"

Leo nodded, stroking his chin as he stared out the window at the skyline stretched before them. "I might not have the clearance to stop this machine midmotion, but I can make sure tomorrow night is clear. If not, I guarantee Brennerman is going to wipe any proof of his indiscretions from existence, where no hacker, however good, can find them."

"And there's no way I can put a stop order to this?" Dan asked, a little helpless, because he already knew the answer. The moment he tried to stonewall Brennerman, the man would release the video of him and Grif. Not only would he lose his position on the spot, but he'd be outed publicly—undeniably. The quiet avoidance he'd kept with his father would shatter, and the bond would break for good.

Dan let out a shaky sigh. Of late, he'd begun questioning how vital the bond was in the wake of all the hardship he'd been shouldering. Yet the idea of no more family dinners with his mother's adobo and lumpia, the lack of his father's solid clap on the shoulder, and no more crinkle of warmth in his mother's eyes—all of that caused the floor to open beneath him. However, no matter how much he'd miss all of that, some things were more important. Stopping Brennerman was more important.

Leo gave him an "it's in your court" look, one he deserved.

Dan gritted his teeth. "Tomorrow. We'll go for tomorrow." He stared at the wood grain of his desk as if he might etch into the surface. "However, if we fail tomorrow, or if we need another try, I'll stop the company from the server upgrade on Wednesday. No matter the cost."

Another knock sounded at his door, this time

causing them both to start. Leo hopped up from his desk.

"See you at the condo tonight?" he asked, an undeniable glimmer of excitement in his gaze.

"You just can't wait to see Scarlet again," Dan shot back, his lips quirking with a grin. "Or was it Tuck who'd caught your attention there?"

"I'm shocked you noticed anything while your lover boy was in the room," Leo responded, his tone dry as sun-bleached bone. "With those moon eyes you guys were giving each other, we were all about to evacuate to avoid the sight of the two of you dry humping."

"There was a lot more than that." A private grin reached his lips as the first hint of warmth suffused through the panic gripping his chest.

Leo crooked an eyebrow. "And to think, you called me a slut."

"Bro, you earned that one," Dan responded. "I'll see you tonight."

The door swung open, because no one respected his space today. Vanessa strode in, and her eyebrows tugged together. She cast them a suspicious glance, her heels thumping against the carpet.

Leo tipped his fingers in her direction. "Bye, Ness."

The moment the door clicked shut and Leo exited, Vanessa whirled around to face Dan.

"What's he doing here?" she asked, not bothering to hide the accusatory tone in her voice. "I thought you said you were dropping this?"

Dan pushed himself up from his desk. He needed to walk off the nerves buzzing through him. "Leo was catching me up about the IT department. He's one of the few people I trust here."

Vanessa cast a sharp look his way, her lips forming a thin line as she crossed her arms over her chest. She didn't have to believe him, but he'd continue to avoid the truth with her. After the sabotage Brennerman pulled on her brakes, Dan wouldn't risk his sister.

"I hate this," she said, breaking the silence. Her features softened. "He's got all the power here, and I'm terrified to try and stop him. Part of me wants to walk away, but this is the work I've always wanted to do. And besides, it's supposed to be our family company."

Dan reached out and slipped his hand in hers. "I hate this too."

Little did she know, something would be done about Phil Brennerman before the end of the week.

When Dan stepped to the front door of the Outlaws' condo, his heart thumped in his chest so hard, the sound reverberated in his ears. Nerves or anticipation? It was a coin toss when approaching a criminal organization. Not like his heart knew the difference every time he caught a glimpse of Grif.

He pressed the ringer for the doorbell and slipped his hands into his pockets while he waited. Once he'd gotten out of work, he'd texted Grif he was on his way over. He'd rather explain the complication in person.

The door swung open, and Dan just about forgot everything he'd come to say. Grif loomed in the frame, tall enough to fill the space. His golden locks were slicked back, and the undershirt he wore glued to his skin with a film of sweat. A couple of drops beaded his temples, and his shoulders heaved like he'd been in the middle of a workout. The moment the scent swirled around him, all heady amber and sweat, Dan got rock-hard.

He had a problem, and his name was Grif Blackmore.

Grif licked his lips as he closed the space between them. "Funny meeting you here."

Before Dan could respond, Grif's hot palm slipped behind his neck. Grif's lips descended on his, and every thought in his head vanished. His tongue snaked into his mouth, the kisses fast turning incendiary as he leaned in against Grif's hard muscle, the solace in this man's arms fast becoming an obsession. Grif kissed like he wanted to possess, like he wanted to devour, with a hungry strength Dan had been drawn to from the start.

Grif pulled away after what felt like an eternity and a second, and Dan stood there reeling.

Dan ran a hand through his hair, trying to right himself after the way the kiss had knocked him off-kilter. "Well, that's one hell of a greeting. Miss me?"

Grif grinned, those stormy blues lightening for a heartbeat. "Maybe a little. Come on. The gang's all waiting inside, so we can talk about tonight. Apparently, it pays to have a man on the inside."

Dan didn't miss the suggestive tone in his voice, and he lifted an eyebrow. "Does your mind ever leave the gutter?"

Grif let out a bark of a laugh. "Permanent resident there, babe." He ushered Dan inside and closed the door behind them. Dan stepped into the foyer, where yesterday he hadn't been sure if he'd get offed. Yet in the span of twenty-four hours, he worked alongside these thieves better than he did his own employees.

"So, what's the news?" Grif asked as they wandered past the empty foyer and living space where a large console overlooked the wide windows featuring Chicago's skyline. The peaks of the Sears Tower and Aon Center competed for attention, both trying to brush the indigo sky. "Is Brennerman planning on staying late tonight?"

Dan blew out a breath. "I wish it was that simple."

They headed into the kitchen, where Scarlet sat perched in front of his laptop and Alanna stirred her coffee so ferociously she was a step away from breaking the cup. John sauntered into the room a moment later and plucked the spoon from Alanna's hand. Alanna snapped her jaw at him in response.

Scarlet looked up from his laptop. "You've got some new intel, Torres?"

Dan hunched over the kitchen island, spreading his palms flat on the counter. "We've got a problem. Brennerman and the board hired outside technical help to rework our systems, and they're laying the groundwork tonight. Apparently this had been on the pipeline for a while and the rest of the company failed to mention it to me. I don't know if he's been tipped off, or if the way I was sniffing around has him unnerved, but they're going to be completing the job on Wednesday night. Tuesday is our one window."

Grif stiffened beside him, and Alanna and Scarlet cast their boss furtive glances. John avoided his gaze.

Dan's brow creased as he tried to gauge the reaction, like he'd dropped a frag grenade into the room. "Look, I know one night to pull this off isn't ideal, but I can at least make sure the office is cleared tomorrow."

"We've come this far, G," John said, crossing his

arms as he stared him down. "I'll sub in if you're not willing to."

Grif's hands balled into fists, and his eyes turned to thunderheads, a scowl spreading on his face. He couldn't tell what he'd said to set him off, but something in his news had tripped Grif's wire.

"Aren't you the CEO of the company?" Scarlet asked, arching an eyebrow. "Can't you just wave a hand and put a stop to this?"

Dan sucked in a sharp breath as his cheeks flushed. "Brennerman has blackmail on me, so if I don't play by his rules, he'll use it. If we're backed into a corner though, I guess I could."

"No," Grif said, his voice ringing through the room with the force of his command. His eyes flashed as they met Dan's.

"Yeah, but last time we did a gig on a Tuesday, we landed in this shit," Alanna said, zeroing in on Grif with her hands on her hips. "There's a reason we avoid them like the plague. They're damn bad luck, and we're already filled up on old Romani curses."

Oh. The only day they could swing this was Tuesday, and for some reason, that meant something to Grif. Pressure built in Dan's head like he might burst. Maybe he'd have to challenge Brennerman after all. The idea of the video hitting the public and having his privacy stripped from him like that made the room spin.

"Well, you've got to make the call, Grif," John said, leaning against the kitchen counter.

"Fucking hell," Grif spat, heading over to stride across the tiled floor. Dan watched how he buzzed, how he didn't just pace, he prowled.

"We could try swinging the job tonight, even later," Scarlet volunteered. "Maybe we can station someone there to watch for when the business clears out."

Before Dan could point out the hired company was coming in late tonight, and Brennerman would be there to supervise, Alanna jumped in again.

"Or we do it tomorrow and we're fucked anyway. Especially if John subs in." Alanna grabbed her cup of coffee and began to chug it down.

"Thanks for the vote of confidence, doll," he responded, strolling past them to crack open the fridge. "None of this matters if the boss doesn't make the damn call."

Grif remained quiet, the storm in his gaze building force. Any moment, he would snap.

"Break time," Dan said, crossing the distance over to Grif and grabbing him by the hand. When Grif froze, Dan almost stepped back. The man was like a right hook begging for a jaw to snap, positively buzzing. Dan tilted his head and started off in the direction they'd taken the other night, down the hall toward his bedroom. All the Outlaws expected answers, but he could tell the weight of the situation smashed into Grif like a truck on the freeway.

Whatever boldness gripped Dan in the moment ebbed once he stepped in front of Grif's bedroom. Grif reached past him to push the door open, but Dan ducked inside first. He didn't bother with talk—that's not what Grif needed right now. Dan turned to face Grif, and his hands descended to the button of his jeans. The snick of the zipper echoed through the room, but by the time Dan brought it down, he'd dropped to his knees.

Dan ran his hand along Grif's length, which had already begun to stiffen under his touch. The storms in his eyes hadn't lessened, but Dan didn't mind him like this, all wild and raw. He understood more than most the pressure of leading, when everyone expected you to make a call you couldn't and how much it pounded at the walls until you wanted to just scream and scream and scream.

He leaned forward and slipped his lips around Grif's cock. The firm length grew even harder inside his mouth as he began to suck, and the earthy scent made Dan's own pants tent. He couldn't help but unzip even as he continued to deep throat Grif. Dan took himself in hand, enjoying the sensation of that massive cock in his mouth.

Grif's fingers combed through his hair, once, twice, until he gripped it tight. He thrust in time with

Dan's mouth, his erection hitting the back of his throat. Dan's hand moved faster and faster along his own cock as he continued to suck Grif's. Sheer power brimmed in the way Grif's hips bucked, in the ferocity of his thrusts as he fucked his face, and the tight hold he kept on his hair, as if he owned every inch of him.

Dan surrendered to the hurricane force, closing his eyes as he stroked himself even quicker, as the cock stretched his limits, and as Grif rammed into him again and again. Fuck, this felt so damn right, here on his knees in front of Grif Blackmore. Dan's cock stiffened as his own release mounted. He rode the lust coursing through his veins, making him mindless with need. Grif fucked him even harder until he yanked on his hair, his hips stilling after he slammed back in.

A moment later, the hot, salty liquid spurted into Dan's mouth, and he drank every drop. The way Grif's cock pulsed and the audible sigh of relief did him in. Dan's breath hitched in his throat as his cum spilled onto the floor in front of him. Grif tugged out of him, and Dan swallowed the remainder, wiping a hand over his mouth.

Grif yanked him from the ground like he weighed nothing and dragged him in for a mind-melting kiss. Dan sagged in his arms, boneless in the wake of his orgasm and helpless against the sheer power this man whipped around. He moaned into his mouth as he circled his arms around his neck, leaning against the muscled fighter's body.

"You're fucking perfect, you know that?" Grif murmured against his lips. "How did you know?" Grif separated from Dan to bend down and snag a towel from one of the clothes piles on the ground. He offered it over, and Dan began to clean himself up.

When Grif's gaze burned into him, he glanced up and shrugged. "You looked like you were hitting overload. I've been there a lot lately and just recognized the signals."

Part of him wanted to ask Grif about the Tuesday hang-up, but with the locked-box way Grif guarded his past, either the man would volunteer the information, or he wouldn't.

"Well, shit," Grif said, sweeping a hand through his hair. "If I'd known that would help take the edge off in the middle of an argument... I'd still be screwed, since I'm not fucking any of my Outlaws. Besides, they'd prefer to squabble until they lose oxygen."

Dan clasped the front button of his pants and began smoothing the fabric. Whatever fierce instinct had taken over when he'd seen Grif's anxiety had now calmed.

"We should get back out there," Dan said, taking the first steps toward the door. Not like what they'd been up to wouldn't be clear to the others.

"Wait," Grif said, clapping a hand on his shoulder. Dan stilled, soaking in the heat from his palm.

"Tuesday is when I lost them. I've never done a job on that day."

Well, shit. Dan didn't need to ask who "they" were. He'd seen the shattered-glass pain in Grif's eyes at the mention of his murdered parents. He'd heard the battery acid edge to his tone when he talked about what had happened to them. Dan reached up to rest his hand over Grif's, and he squeezed tight. Those words, faint, exposed, and wholly real, gave his heart a violent tug. If he wasn't careful, he might tumble headfirst for this man.

"I'll tell Brennerman no dice," Dan said, even as he teetered on the edge of an abyss. "I'll make sure he moves the date."

Grif's arms wrapped around him, and Dan found himself pulled back into his chest. Grif's lips whispered against his neck.

"No, you won't. Tomorrow, we've got a heist to complete."

TWENTY-THREE

Grif Blackmore was doing a job on a Tuesday.

After all of the obstacles, all of the fucking back-stabbings, and all of the complications, they were finally going to nab their prize. Dan had given the greenlight.

Once they completed this job, they'd extract themselves from their debt to Nevarra and then distance themselves from the slimy mob bastard.

Grif readjusted the formfitting black fabric of his shirt, unused to wearing the same clingy shit his Shadows did. He patted himself down to feel the bump of his pistol tucked into a waistband holster. As for his knives, he'd slipped two into the straps inside his boots and kept more hidden along both sleeves.

On a normal job, nerves swept out like humidity after a rainstorm. Grif slid into his zone, calm, level, and so single-minded he banished spare thoughts or idle worries.

Except today, he couldn't avoid the hollow punch to his stomach, the same phantom sensation of what descended the day his parents died. Nights like this one were meant for devastating news and shattered futures.

He sucked in a sharp breath as he stared at himself in the mirror. The crease of worry smoothed from his brow, and the flicker of fear dissolved as Grif Blackmore donned his mask. Tonight, he was Locksley, the leader of the Outlaws. These were the pure moments, beyond the doubts and worries. Beyond the memories. Grif lived for the execution, the blade swinging down to claim his life, and the daring he seized as he thwarted death one more time.

He patted himself down again before he headed for the door. No matter that today was Tuesday and his traitor stomach twisted with unease—Grif Blackmore had a job to do.

He strode through the corridor, the warm murmur of voices in the living room a siren's lure. As he stepped in, six gazes bore down on him, each with the weight of expectation. Tonight, Grif welcomed it.

Alanna rocked back and forth on the floor, crouching like a restrained spring, and Tuck sat beside her, testing his wrapped foot with a series of stretches. They both wore thieves' black, their weapons, cords, and necessary equipment attached to their utility belts and tucked into pockets and holsters. While they wouldn't blend with corporate, they could move easier and reduced their chances of being seen.

Leo sat in front of Scarlet's laptop, and she leaned in behind him to point out different things on the screen. She wore basic black like the rest of them, but she kept her pixie cut stylishly spiked, and her namesake lipstick popped.

John stood in front of Dan, demonstrating the use of the pistol he prepared to hand over. Dan had showed up in a pair of running pants and a black tee so tight he could see every toned ridge of his abs. The mere sight of the man got Grif hard, which was a problem when he needed his other head in the game. Dan's gaze snagged on his, the same hunger flashing in his eyes. His heartbeat kicked up a notch, and he couldn't ignore the shift in the way he viewed Dan Torres.

One step at a time.

"All right, kids," Grif called out, hooking his thumbs through his belt loops. "We've got ourselves intel to steal."

Scarlet straightened from her crouch by Leo. "We've got this stud situated at home base."

John passed the pistol over to Dan and approached. "And I've got ground control." He pressed one of the earbuds into Grif's palm. "We'll be connected every step of the way."

Grif didn't miss the careful glance John made to Dan—he understood the risk of bringing an untested soldier to a battlefield. However, Tuck's injury prevented him from going by his lonesome without severe risk, and Grif wouldn't sign over one of his Outlaws to a death sentence.

Alanna hopped up from her crouch on the ground and strode toward the door. "Let's get this party train rolling."

"Hold up," Grif said. "Let's go through the bullet points before we go rushing off into danger."

Alanna huffed but stayed put. The woman was impatience personified.

Grif strode over to the window, feeling the press of everyone's gazes as he went. He turned around and crossed his arms over his shoulders. "Tuck and Dan, you'll be on patrol. If you catch sight of Doncaster and his men or any other fuckers who want to tank this operation, alert us and then get the hell out of there."

Dan's brow wrinkled. "What about you guys?"

"We'll be getting the hell out too, in our own way," Grif affirmed, staring him down. The idea of Dan out there in this volatile landscape they'd willingly chosen prickled under his skin, but he wanted to help, and they weren't in the position to turn assistance down. "Leo, when we arrive, we'll need you to be on task after Scarlet connects his computer to their systems. John, you're our point man. We're counting on you to make sure everyone gets out of this with their brains intact."

"With any luck, the two of you will be sitting pretty while I do all the work," Scarlet said, heading to join Alanna by the door. Like that would happen.

Grif snorted as he strolled behind them. Dan's gaze pressed into him, his worry radiating clear in the air.

Fuck it.

He whirled around and closed the distance between them. The rest of the crew might give him shit for the next century, but he'd been dealing with them for a long while. Grif gripped the back of Dan's neck and pulled the man toward him. His lips descended, pressing against Dan's soft mouth, which opened in invitation.

Dan melted against him, the heat between them incendiary. He tasted syrup sweet, and the scent of his coconut and lime cologne amplified Grif's arousal. Something powerful reached inside his chest and tugged, an old cord he remembered from long, long ago. Grif had operated by listening to gut impulses from the start, and when he had chosen each of his Outlaws, he'd followed his intuition. The same intuition told him Dan was worth holding on to.

Grif's grip around his nape tightened for a second, and he swept his tongue through to deepen the kiss before he pulled back.

"Don't take any stupid risks," Grif murmured against his mouth.

"Already did." Dan's eyes gleamed with a knowing that settled inside him, one that brushed across his skin like fresh sunlight.

Gagging noises came from behind him. "If you guys are done making out, we've got a job to do," Alanna called from the opposite end of the room.

Grif's lips quirked into a half-smile as he let go of Dan and headed for the others. When they made it through this—and they would—they needed to have a conversation. Because Dan Torres was someone he wanted to keep.

THE AON CENTER LOOMED OVERHEAD, AS FORBIDDING as ever. They'd hopped out of the taxi a couple of blocks back, the static silence in the cab enough that the driver kept glancing out the window as if he might tuck and roll.

The weight settled over him, the thrill of danger he'd been addicted to from a young age. Not like he'd expected a penchant for climbing buildings and sneaking into abandoned ones would lead to a life of crime. The air grew crisp with a bite, and the cool breezes threaded past him, whipping the ragged edges of his hair around in the process. He scanned the Aon Center, searching for a glimpse of light from the inside, any warning signs Dan's intel was off. However, from the tinted windows outside, the upstairs section where Torres Industries was located remained as pitch-dark as the surrounding night sky.

Alanna prowled ahead of him with the grace of a panther, her dark eyes burning in concentration. While she might be a loudmouth at HQ, here the woman was in her element, one of the shadows that slunk along the edge of the building or in the alleys. Scarlet strode a step or two behind him, keeping close. She hated field work, but they would need the direct extraction of hard copies to pull this heist off.

He headed toward the main entrance of the building, careful to monitor the area as he went. Any of the cars parked along the side of the road could contain their enemies, and any bystanders could become possible threats. Thanks to Dan, they might have the keys and cards to get into the building without a hitch, but any Samaritan in the street could call the cops over watching a group of "suspicious individuals" entering the building.

Grif's fingers slipped against the grip of the pistol in his waistband for the thousandth time since they'd exited the cab. The cool polymer surface was a reminder, one he needed to keep him grounded.

The terrace beside the building spread out, one he'd ducked and raced through a mere week ago. Nothing stirred from behind the trees, no shifting shadows or rustles in the bushes. Traffic zoomed on by behind them, the normal screech of tires and honks of impatient drivers a comfort.

A sleaze like Brennerman wasn't the only one who deserved payback tonight. Doncaster and his crew had caused them enough problems in the past, and he'd be damned if they stole another job from him. And Nevarra; well, the insidious bastard had earned one hell of a retribution.

Except, the universe was a petulant bitch, and chances were, the head of the mafia would evade justice yet again. He'd scam them for the money he'd maneuvered them into owing, and then continue to strong-arm other crews like theirs.

Grif's footsteps barely echoed on the pavement with the silent strides he observed. Together, their squad made their way to the glass door entrance, the darkened inside glaring out at them like a sullen void.

"I've got a line to the camera feed the security guards are looking at," Leo's voice came in loud and clear over the comms. "So, if one of you happens to take an elegant nosedive, there won't be any evidence left, but you'll still need to avoid direct view of the cameras. Once you get up to Torres Industries, I'll set a loop on their feed to avoid detection." Normally they operated with Scarlet at head of tech command either at the penthouse or a remote location, but Grif appreciated the convenience of having her in the field with them today.

"We marked all the spots out to avoid them," Grif murmured. "Tuck, are you and Dan en route?" Unlike their crew, who'd nabbed a taxi, Tuck and Dan were driving up for their patrol, so a getaway car lay somewhere in the vicinity if necessary. No rock left unturned.

"Minutes behind you, as promised," Tuck responded over the comms. "Let us know if you spot anything on the way."

Grif didn't bother answering as he approached the glass entrance of the Aon Center. Alanna and Scarlet flanked him on either side, moving like spirits in a cemetery. He cast another glance behind him, soaking in the dimly lit windows of the nearby hotel, the steady shhhrup-shhhrup of cars gliding by and the shadows that splayed from the carved shrubs like darkened teeth. No telltale shifts in the breeze, no furtive motions.

All clear.

Grif slipped past the main entryway to the side door that lay off the path painted the same pale color as the bricks. He stuck the master key Dan had given him into the lock. They could've just picked it, but given the newfound access to the building from the CEO, they took any advantage they could.

The door creaked open, and once they stepped inside, Grif snagged his night vision goggles and slipped them on. He took the second to adjust to the shades of green, white, and black before him and then strode down the corridor. This was a different entrance than he'd arrived through before, but they'd mapped out where it dumped them, which was familiar territory. Between the blueprints to the building Scarlet had scrounged up and the notes he and John had both made during their visit here, they'd learned every inch of the Aon Center.

The air conditioning buzzed with a steady hum that resonated through the building, and already, the cool blasts made his skin prickle. Grif continued to flex his fingers as he walked forward, one and two and one and two. The corridor came to an end, leading them to another metal door. This one didn't need a key, and he cracked it open to peer through.

The right side of the foyer spread before them, one which led to a set of elevators as well as the stairs. Elevators were too big a risk and too well-monitored, so they'd trained for the steps even though Torres Industries was achingly high up. None of the Outlaws were slouches though—Grif made sure of that. The beams of moonlight trickling in through the wide windows gleamed against all the metal fixtures and the glossy tile floors. The quiet permeated every pore of this place, and the vaulted ceilings ensured any noise would echo.

The orbs of the security cameras hung from the ceilings, and Grif followed the path he'd mapped out based on the blueprints. Avoiding detection from security was a game they knew better than blackjack, but like with everything in their jobs, the key was preparation.

One by one, they snuck out from the door, and he led them toward the steps. Grif clung to the far wall, watching the orb the entire time. Not like they needed any distractions from over-eager security guards before they even reached Torres Industries. Besides, Leo might be able to scrub data, but too many gaps would look suspicious. In the view of his night vision goggles, the room was a subterranean green, but they allowed him to view the foyer with the clarity of flicking the lights on. There were some low-level lights interspersed throughout the building, but he needed the visibility given their task ahead.

He measured his paces, careful to keep his movements quiet as he headed in the direction of the stairwell. Once they reached that, they'd be heading up those steps at a punishing pace.

First, they had to make it past the security office unscathed.

The room was stationed near the steps and the only one whose lights beamed bright from underneath the door. The low murmur of voices was clear, a direct contrast to this aching, bone-searing silence.

The silence crawled beneath his skin as he waited for the telltale click of footsteps from behind him or the creak of opened doors—especially from the office. Flex. Flex. Flex. He continued to flick his fingers out and back again as he strode toward the entrance of the stairs.

They passed the security office.

Grif's shoulders relaxed a fraction as he took the first steps away from the door, the windows gleaming and the blue light of monitors clear.

The creak of a door sounded behind him.

Fuck. Ahead of him lay the door to the stairs, a closer broom closet, and on the opposite side a cutout for a water fountain.

Grif's feet moved before he could make the conscious choice. He raced forward, sprinting the rest of the way to the stairs. He only hoped Alanna and Scarlet picked up the memo. He reached out for the knob and turned, hurling himself inside.

He stepped out of the way as first Alanna dove through the entrance, and then Scarlet, who quietly closed the door behind her. The slight sound echoed in the pregnant air.

Grif's heart slammed in his chest. If the guard

had caught sight of them, the whole team of Aon Center's security would be pursuing.

He stepped up to the door to peer through the square window in the center.

Two security guards stood in front of the office, wearing their uniforms and whipping their flashlights all around the darkened corridors. They weren't running their way. Grif pressed his ear to the door to try and hear what they were saying.

"Heard a sound from the corridor," one gruff, low voice said.

"Let's patrol around the entrance," the other guard suggested. The shuffle of footsteps followed, and Grif chanced another glance through the window. The silver rays of the flashlights aimed in the opposite direction as the two guards headed farther down the corridor toward the front of the building.

"Well, that keeps things lively," Grif muttered, stepping away from the door. The chill of concrete emanated all around them, even if it had been painted the same brazen white as the rest of the building. The first of the cameras lay closer to the first set of steps. Grif checked into his comm. "Leo, mind getting the security feed?"

"You've got it," Leo responded cheerfully.

"If they really wanted to give us some thrills, they could've chased us up the stairs," Alanna said, flashing a grin. "What better cardio is there?"

Grif shook his head even though he couldn't help his own smile. "All right, let's do this." He cast a glance to Alanna and Scarlet who both nodded in return. The stairs rose above them in dizzying spirals, an unending maze. Grif couldn't dwell on the enormity—he placed his foot on the first step and began to climb. One at a time. That had been his motto from the beginning when his entire life spun out of control. Those first days, he'd seized onto the smallest tasks, getting out of bed being the hardest.

They moved fast, the steps flying beneath them. Even with their quiet tread, the faint footsteps echoed, until their marching upward sounded like an army. Truth be told, that was the Outlaws in a nutshell—a small band of rebels who pulled off heists large groups like the mafia wouldn't dare touch.

The thud of the steps beneath his feet and the flex of his calves as he launched up yet another flight offered a soothing rhythm. Grif poured himself into the task, gaining the same serenity a fight in the ring or a ten-mile run offered. He lost himself to the physicality, which banished away the thoughts, fears, and worries.

By the time they'd scaled the first twenty-some floors, Scarlet's breaths had grown ragged, echoing in the stairwell. Their mechanical motions began to flag. Torres Industries wasn't at the very top, stationed beneath the observation towers in the forty to fifty range, which was still a punishing task for anyone, no matter what shape you were in. Drops of sweat beaded on his forehead, begging to fall.

Grif continued to lead the charge, until the steps blurred beneath his tread and the drops of sweat trickled down his forehead to sting his eyes. The only shadows that shifted were their own, and the sounds that echoed through this steep stairwell were their shallow breaths and the steady thump of their tread.

Nearer. They reached the fortieth floor.

"There's a car that's been circling," Dan came in on the comm. Hearing his voice over their private system brushed Grif's skin with whiskey warmth. Circling meant patrol. As long as they didn't give any tip-offs, those fuckers could keep running roundabouts all night for all he cared.

"Keep out of sight," Grif responded. "At any point, if the car stops, let me know."

His pulse thumped hard, but the jolt urged him forward up another stairwell. The steps flew under his feet until the level he'd been looking for flashed into view. Grif skidded to a halt, almost slamming into the door. After the perpetual motion of scaling the stairs, his legs pulsed like he should still be running.

Grif cracked the door open and peered past. The familiar polished marble floor and wide entryway leading to Torres Industries stretched before him.

"Are you in?" Leo asked, buzzing in.

"That's what he said," Dan fired back. Grif bit the inside of his cheek to keep from laughing.

"We're approaching the entrance," Scarlet responded, keeping her voice low. "Get ready. I'll be connecting you to his system in a matter of minutes to transfer the files."

The front doors for Torres Industries gleamed, the sign bold yet elegant, even in the greenish view of his goggles.

Grif pulled out the keycard Dan had given him. He swiped the slot beside the frame, and a moment later, a click sounded as the doors unlocked. He pushed them open without a creak. The scents of bleach and toner warred the moment he took the first steps.

"I'm inside," Grif murmured over the comms, his whisper cleaving through the quiet.

"That's also what he said," Alanna responded by his side.

"I swear to fuck," Grif muttered, even as the grin lifted his lips. Damn, he loved his Outlaws.

"Security alarms are deactivated," Leo came in over the comm. Scarlet's combination of on-site and remote abilities was unparalleled, but this guy did a damn good job of stepping into her stilettos.

Grif took one step in, then another, waiting for a scuff, a light flicker, or even a breath. Silence ached from the tiles to the darkened fluorescents of this place.

"Let's find this old bastard's office," Alanna murmured, brushing past him. She scampered ahead with a lithe fluidity he could never manage. Scarlet stepped in line with him. Even though the night vision goggles obscured her eyes, he could read her expression loud and clear with the way she chewed her lower lip.

"We just need to extract proof of his theft from the company, and we're out," Grif reminded her as they strode down the corridor.

"What if I could do more?" Scarlet asked, a cryptic edge to her voice.

"I trust you," Grif responded. "As long as Doncaster isn't slugging bullets at us, I'll back whatever play you want to try." Scarlet nodded in response.

The air tasted stale, like chewing paper, and Grif quickened his pace when they reached the hallway they'd taken to get to Dan's office. Brennerman's should be two to the right, close to the conference room where he and Dan had stolen a kiss. Alanna's hand already leapt to the handle, and she twisted the door open.

Grif's senses buzzed on high alert. He noticed the sharp pine of the polish in the air, every creak of the wind beating against the windows, and each shift of the moonbeams spilling through the broad windows at the far end of the corridor. He stepped in behind Alanna for his first view of Brennerman's office.

If Grif didn't already know the guy was a sleaze, he'd be able to tell with one glimpse into this room. No pictures decorated his desk, and while everything had the same clean, uniform look as Dan's, this one emulated its owner in hiding the expenses. The desk was top designer make, and the seat behind it belonged in a Ferrari, not in an office. The surface held some clutter—stacks of different reports, guaranteed to be inconsequential and not what they searched for.

Alanna wandered over to the bookshelves behind the desk, filled with first editions of books like *Atlas Shrugged* and *The Fountainhead*. The paperweights gleamed, and as Grif lifted them, the heft ensured they were at least gold-plated.

Scarlet settled into the ridiculous chair and leaned forward to pop on his computer. The noise of the machine starting up made Grif's muscles tense on reflex, but he strolled toward the filing cabinet on the opposite side of the room. Maybe he'd be able to find some sort of old paper trail, even though he doubted it. In this part of the job, Scarlet leapt to the fore. He and Alanna were the muscle to make sure she achieved her end.

The neon light of the screen illuminated the

room, and Grif slid the night vision goggles up. Scarlet's eyebrows drew together in concentration as her fingers flew across the keyboard, the clack-clack-clack the only sound echoing through this place.

Alanna started rooting through a filing cabinet, her fingers rapidly sweeping over file after file.

"Found a trail," Scarlet murmured in the distracted tone that meant she'd immersed into whatever she was diving into on the computer. "Let's crack this bastard wide open."

Grif crouched in front of the safe by Scarlet's side and began to work his magic. He'd been cracking safes for a long time now, and this wasn't even the latest model. He leaned in, pulled his Phoenix out and worked over the electronic keypad. It only took mere moments before he heard the solid click of the lock releasing. He tugged open the door of the safe to examine the contents inside.

"Oh… fuck," Scarlet said. One glimpse and his stomach sank. She glanced to him, her eyes widening in horror.

"What's wrong?" Alanna whipped around from the bookshelf she crouched in front of.

"I recognize this name—it's one of Nevarra's aliases." Scarlet's fingers still flew across the keyboard; if anything, the typing was coming in more furiously. The room spun.

Grif examined the safe in front of him—not filled

with cash, files, or anything he'd expected. Instead, there was a document with account information printed on the front with a deposit number with the dates included.

Brennerman was in bed with Nevarra. Of course.

He'd gamble his left nut that the safe was their go-between, and this was the account they funneled the cash through.

His gaze switched to the filing cabinet Alanna rifled through. Something flashed from inside the top drawer.

"What the hell?" Alanna cursed as she nudged around in the top drawer to reveal the flashing green light of a security alarm.

TWENTY-FOUR

THE REALITY OF DAN'S SITUATION DESCENDED THE
moment John handed him the pistol back in the
apartment. The cool steel against his palm and the
weight in the holster at his side solidified this reality
he'd stepped into. This was happening.

Engineering nerd turned CEO hadn't prepared
him for a heist in the slightest, but he showed up
anyway.

He came to a halt a few back streets away from
the Aon Center, where he snagged a parking spot
along the road. Patrolling around his own business
wasn't something he ever thought he'd be doing.
However, Brennerman had pushed him to extremes,
and Grif's confidence and passion stole him over the
rest of the way. Tuck stared out the window, his dark
curls casting deeper shadows over his eyes. He'd been

quiet the whole way over, but the man didn't seem like much of a casual talker.

"What are the chances I'll need to fire this thing?" Dan asked, trying to break the silence.

Tuck cast him an appraising glance, and he regretted opening his mouth. He'd plunged into yet another situation and fumbled, just like when he'd entered Torres Industries.

"Unless you've fired in the field before, I wouldn't," Tuck said, tapping his fingers along the side of the car door. "We're not here to get into fights —we're the lookout. With any luck, we'll be watching a whole lot of nothing while the others infiltrate."

"And if I've got the worst luck imaginable?" Dan asked, his mouth going dry.

Tuck offered him a wan smile, one that reached his eyes. "Then you're going to run, and I'll make sure you get out safe. We might flirt with danger, but I joined the Outlaws because Grif made it clear our lives are worth more than any cargo. Those kinds of leaders are rare."

He wasn't wrong. Dan couldn't deny how his heart sped at the mere mention of Grif's name. When all this ended, the idea of the leader of the Outlaws ditching his number, of them going their separate ways, made his stomach sink. Dan didn't need to be told Grif was rare—he'd spent years searching for a fraction of the spark he felt around the man.

"You ready?" Tuck asked, cracking the door open a fraction.

Dan nodded. "Let's do this."

Grif and the others had made it into Torres Industries.

He should've felt a slight sense of violation at allowing a band of outlaws into the company, but it never belonged to him. Not truly.

As he and Tuck made their thousandth loop around the Aon Center, Dan soaked in the difference of listening to the city like this. On an average night, he might down a couple of drinks at Cindy's or Columbus Tap, either by himself or with Vanessa, and then he'd grab an Uber back to his condo. Most of what he noticed was the traffic, the flash of cars driving by and the steady thrum of the normal pedestrian flow in those sections.

However, as he patrolled with Tuck, these Chicago streets took on a new life to him. The nearby scent of the river drifted his way, one the cool breezes swept away. The normal light display on the top of the Aon Center flashed, and certain floors held the dim gleam of lights kept on, yet his floors remained black as onyx. Honks and screeches sounded as cars traveled by on the still-busy street, but Dan's gaze didn't gloss over them like normal.

"How long have you been with the Outlaws?" Dan asked. His nerves demanded conversation, otherwise the shifting shadows from the headlights in constant flux would have him leaping out of his skin.

"Six years," Tuck said. "Grif plucked me from the circus, and I've been with this crew ever since."

"Does he do that often?" Dan asked, shaking his head, unable to help the grin on his face. Another slew of cars whipped by as they strolled through the pathway lined by manicured shrubs.

"Four times, to be precise," Tuck responded, flipping the knife in his hand as they walked. Dan didn't miss the way the man's eyes roved, scouring their surroundings. He emanated a slick competence like Grif's that Dan felt safer around. Tuck cast him a look. "No matter what loner bullshit the boss spews, when he brings someone into his life, it's for keeps."

Dan sucked in a sharp breath and avoided his gaze. The hope jerked hard in his chest, crystallizing into a sharp, fragmented sort of pain. He focused on the road, watching the flow of the cars. A black van looped their way. Tuck stilled beside him and stepped behind one of the taller shrubs to obscure himself from view. Dan followed suit, even as his heart thumped harder in his chest.

The van screeched to a halt in front of one of the

temporary unloading spots in the entrance area of the building.

"Think this is Doncaster?" Dan asked, his voice barely above a whisper. His calves tensed, and his hand drifted to the holster by his side, as if somehow the pistol might protect him despite having never fired one in his life.

"We'll find out," Tuck murmured in response, not exactly quieting his nerves.

The doors flew open, and at least five guys piled out of the van.

All of them wore the navy uniforms he recognized. "They're janitors in our building."

He pulled up the binoculars they'd included in his pack and took a better look. The faces were familiar ones, guys he'd seen mopping the floors in the corridors who he'd waved to over the past year. His stomach performed an aerial flip.

"Do the janitors normally clean the building this time of night?" Tuck asked, an edge to his voice suggesting the same concerns nagged at him. Tuck stopped flipping the knife, holding the grip tight.

"This is well past their scheduled time." Dan hesitated. "I know those faces though. They've been working for the business since before I arrived."

The five men approached the building in unison, heading straight to their normal side entrance where a lot of the cleaning supplies were stocked.

"Fuck," Tuck muttered. "I've got a bad feeling about this."

"Never tell me the odds," Dan responded on reflex. His cheeks heated. He hadn't meant to say that out loud.

Tuck cracked a flicker of a grin. "Nerd." He tapped the comm in his ear. "Grif, there's a group of five guys heading into the building. They're not Doncaster's men, and they've worked as janitors in this building for a while."

Dan's heart thumped harder as the guys approached. One glance over here and the crew could spot them. He edged in behind the shrub even further, the rich pine scent suffocating, and the needles prickling against his clothes.

"Brennerman has his own security system, and we just tripped it." Grif's voice came over the comms, icing-on-a-cake smooth despite the bomb he dropped.

"How the hell does he have his own alarms?" Dan blurted aloud, anger flaring through him. The man had been causing problems from the start, but Brennerman had delved far deeper into illicit activities than he could've anticipated. This went beyond skimming from company funds. If he'd hired these janitors as his own personal attack staff, the man must have connections to someone far bigger.

"More bad news, kids," Alanna came in loud over

the comms, her voice bleeding irritation. "Brennerman's working with Nevarra."

"Blood and bones, we'd be better off red lighting this plan," Tuck swore.

Dan's skin prickled. "Who's Nevarra?"

The seriousness in Tuck's eyes conveyed the impact before the words slammed into him. "The head of the Chicago mob."

Dan ran a hand through his hair. "Oh, fuck." No wonder Brennerman operated with such vicious tactics. The squad of "janitors" closed in on the entrance to the Aon Center. If they had proper access and badges, they could get in at any time of the night, since security was used to different cleaning rotations. Any moment, they'd be inside the building and traveling up, up, up.

If Brennerman had been working alongside the Chicago mob, no wonder former employees had wound up dead. Had they been people who uncovered Brennerman's secrets before or just those unlucky enough to witness the wrong thing at the wrong time?

Dan pressed on his comm. "They're heading in. You guys need to get out."

"Negative," Grif responded over the comm. "Scarlet's still got to make the extraction. How many guys?" Despite the situation, his voice never wavered, the same slick as if he sat at Polished Knives nursing a whisky.

"Five of them," Dan responded, his palms pricking with sweat. He hated this helplessness, watching the men pop the door open and enter. Whatever they'd be attempting, he could guarantee it wouldn't be good news for him or the Outlaws.

"What are they packing?" Grif asked. Dan squinted, trying to gauge through the binoculars. Not like he'd be able to tell unless they waved their pistols or knives.

"Pistols at the minimum," Tuck responded. He tilted his head in the direction of the janitors fast disappearing and mouthed "outline of the holsters" to Dan.

"Fun," Grif responded, the smile in his voice. "Lucky for them, I was just getting bored."

"All aces from ground patrol," John reported in. "Curb stomp some lackeys for me."

Dan shook his head and stared at Tuck. "You're all insane."

Even as he said it, the adrenaline bubbled up inside him, and a laugh escaped. His nerves buzzed like a live wire, and his calves twitched to run, to move, to do something besides standing frozen here watching their enemies enter the Aon Center.

"Yeah, but you knew that when you signed on to

this," Tuck said, flashing him a roguish grin. "Now, come on, we've got to keep on patrol."

The moment the janitors disappeared inside and the door clicked shut after them, Tuck pushed up from where he leaned against the shrubs. He began striding along the pathway again, heading toward the side of the building.

"Shouldn't we be keeping tabs on the group who just entered?" Dan asked, moving a little faster to keep up with Tuck. For someone who'd just gotten shot in the leg, the man strolled with natural ease, like a cheetah in the grasslands.

Tuck shook his head. "We gave Grif and the others the alert. They'll have the advantage. We're necessary on the ground to make sure if reinforcements arrive or Doncaster and his goons show up that Grif and the others get the alert to scram."

"How the hell do you guys stay sane during these jobs?" Dan said, shaking his head.

"I grew up walking the tightrope," Tuck said as they cased the side of the building. His eyes grew distant as he soaked in the surrounding city. "Chaos is going on all around you, but that's life. You keep your gaze on the next step, and all the troubles melt away."

Dan had felt like that once. The building could be burning, and if Dan was neck deep in trying to repair the thermal sensors on a machine, he would barely notice. He missed the focus that neared obsession like a limb.

Apart from the cars rushing along the roadside, Dan didn't pick up any movement closer to the building, nor did he spot any repeat vehicles. He kept his eyes on the road, just in case.

He took Tuck's advice and focused on each breath, cycling it in and out as he scanned their surroundings. Dan focused on the quick and quiet pace they maintained as they wove around to the back of the building, a hypnotic flow to the regular, careful movement. His gaze flicked to the upper levels, but they remained dark. Not like he'd hear or see anything from here, unless the sound came through the comms. The night settled over his skin, and he breathed in the shadows.

This was Grif's world, his territory. The man had done jobs like this for years, and disruptions had to be the norm.

At least, that's the comfort Dan clung to.

They continued their rotations around the building, but no new vans emerged onto the scene. There weren't hordes of janitors encroaching, or even mob enforcers, whatever they might look like. Dan's heart thumped hard in his chest. Maybe the janitors hadn't been sent to attack Grif and the others.

Maybe they headed in for a late shift packing heat. Because that made sense.

A white van slowed to a crawl along the street. Dan's senses wailed warnings like a speeding ambulance at this point, and Tuck slipped to the nearest retaining wall around the landscaping and crouched behind the brick. Dan followed him, trying to maintain the same quiet.

"Either it's backup or Doncaster's making his move," Tuck murmured.

Dan's throat squeezed tight, and he didn't respond. Grif and Alanna might be able to handle five guys, but more than that? They'd be fucked six ways from Sunday. "So, what do we do?"

Tuck lapsed into quiet again, staring at the van like he might burn holes into it with his laser gaze. A woman hopped out from the front, one Dan recognized from his brief stint interviewing. Grif had clued him in that Betty Lancaster was none other than Betty Kirklees, a part of Doncaster's gang and mortal enemies to the Outlaws. The underworld was *almost* as cutthroat as corporate politics.

Betty and three other guys exited the van, probably planning on diving in to complete the job on their own.

"We need to do something," Dan hissed. His muscles screamed "run," and his brain begged him to race away. "If another gang corners them, they'll be screwed."

Tuck nodded and pressed the comm at his ear.

"Doncaster's crew has arrived on the scene. We're going to run interference."

"Roger that," Grif responded, a bit breathless. A gunshot echoed in the background of the communication, electrifying Dan to full alert. Helplessness surged through him like a shaken Coke can. At least in pulling the new crew's attention away, he could run off some of this.

Tuck glanced his way. "I'm going to fire a warning shot at them. The moment I do, we've got to be running. You'll need to follow my lead without question. I know these streets better than most."

Dan nodded. "Trust me, I'll barely be able to do much else."

Tuck pulled out his pistol to take aim. Sweat pricked Dan's palms as Tuck honed in on the crew who exited the van. The slam of car doors echoed through the air. Betty faced the direction of the Aon Center and pointed ahead, making their trajectory clear. Dan held his breath, watching as Tuck's finger found the trigger. His muscles tensed, and he prepared to bolt.

The doors to the van closed, and the crew assembled. When they descended on the Aon Center, Grif and his crew would be fucked.

Tuck squeezed the trigger.

The bullet sailed in the direction of the van. The bark exploded in the air, and Tuck already blurred in motion. The Outlaw surged past him, heading to the pathways that wrapped around the building. Dan launched forward after him.

The breeze whistled past his ears, iced his cheeks, and stung his eyes, but Dan focused on following Tuck. They'd be leading the Doncaster crew on a merry chase, and the run for his life had begun.

TWENTY-FIVE

In any job, no matter how big or small, there was one guarantee.

The plan you spent hours outlining and setting into place would get set on fire and kicked off a hill. So, the remaining choices were either adapt or get caught. Since Grif and his Outlaws had never been caught, they'd gotten A-plus at adapting.

The little blinking light in the back of the filing cabinet was the first deviation. Nevarra's involvement with Brennerman was the second. And the crew of janitors who he could guarantee were members of the mob were the third.

Black days and bleaker times. The moment Dan and Tuck's warning came over the comm, he turned to Scarlet.

"How much longer?" he asked, the adrenaline surging like he'd never suppressed it.

She cast him a sharp glance, looking up from the computer for a flash. "I need ten more minutes if you want this done right."

The janitor crew would reach the top floor within five. Which meant he and Alanna would get to blow off some steam.

"Do I get to kick some mafia ass?" Alanna asked as she shifted from foot to foot. "Pretty please, with sugar on top?"

"Only if I don't get to them first," Grif responded, grinning as he cracked his knuckles. "The janitor squad's packing heat, which means they're showing up ready to samba."

"Leo, I'm going to start transferring over the files," Scarlet's voice broke out through the room and the comms. "Remember the dummy protocol we discussed as backup? We're going to need to bust that out."

"Running into problems?" Grif asked, walking the serrated knife's edge with the amount of bad luck that had descended on them this past month.

Scarlet offered a shrug in response. "It's only a problem if I don't have enough time to complete the set-up. Which is why you guys better keep those assholes off my back." Even as she said the words, her fingers hit the keys a little more forcefully, betraying her nerves.

"So, we're running the Ezekiel Protocol then," Grif confirmed. They'd discussed the "oh shit" maneuver just in case, but he'd hoped beyond hope they wouldn't have to try this one. However, their streak of bad luck was as vicious as a downpour midwinter. "Aces, doll. While you're at work, we'll go offer our janitor hit squad some compelling arguments on why they should head on home."

Either Scarlet got the files sent over, or she didn't, and they were fucked. At this point, they could only buy her more time. He had a lot of restless energy and rage to channel. Busting in some skulls would be the perfect outlet.

He tapped the doorframe and glanced to Scarlet one last time before he strode down the corridor. Alanna followed suit, her knives gliding out.

"I've got the protocol running, Scarlet," Leo came in over the comms. "It'll just take a minute to set up, then hack away."

Grif headed down the corridor, his nerves jangling with the whoop-whoop-whoop of a car alarm. The cool metal of his Beretta pressed against his palm, the trigger begging to be fired. He slipped the night vision goggles back over his eyes—precision was key here, and he couldn't be wasting shots in the dark.

Alanna kept pace with him, her ponytail whipping back and forth behind her. She flipped her knives as they walked toward the entrance of Torres Industries. By day, this place looked bland as paste, vacant faces behind far too many cubicles and the same stale air circulating throughout. However, at night all the mediocrity took on an insidious bent. The shadows stretched sharper, and the empty cubicles made for a minefield of blind spots.

Perfect for them.

Grif swept over to the cubicles near the door, ducking behind to gauge the best vantage point. He tested one spot, then another, while Alanna swerved to the opposite side to do the same. He crouched behind a cubicle far enough away to line up a good shot, but close enough to switch to hand-to-hand or knife if needed. Grif glanced to his watch, checking the neon numbers. They'd arrive any minute now.

Grif sank into his stance behind the cubicle, and he listened.

The quiet stretched through this place, gliding over the stacks of papers on the desks, creeping into the cracks in the ceiling panels, and settling inside him. As Grif descended into the silence, his senses opened. He heard the gentle hitch of Alanna's breaths from the other side of the room, the slight rattle of the wind outside, and the distant ding of the elevator.

The ding grew louder, and the click of those elevator doors opening echoed from beyond Torres Industries.

Grif lifted his pistol, watched, and waited.

The thump of steps echoed through the hallway, not heavy enough to be careless, but they couldn't compare with his Shadows, Tuck and Alanna. Nevarra's men approached. Go figure the asshole would find some way to make their lives difficult even when he wasn't trying. The glass doors of Torres Industries placed the hallway on clear display. Any moment, the mob cronies would step into view.

Grif's breath snagged in his throat, which had grown dry in the waiting. Scarlet needed the time, otherwise this entire enterprise would wash up like their dead bodies when Nevarra didn't get his payday. If they didn't have the funds, the Outlaws would have to go deep underground and leave the city in the hopes they could evade Nevarra.

The footsteps grew louder, and the shadowy figures stepped into view. Five men approached, all wearing the same janitor jumpsuit. Brennerman had gotten Nevarra's men into Torres Industries under this guise far before Dan Torres had ever started to work there.

The door creaked open, all five guys striding in with their pistols aimed. They flicked the lights on, and Grif and Alanna slipped their night vision goggles off.

Five to two weren't odds he'd bet on, but he had the advantage of location and surprise.

One way to flip those odds.

The moment the janitor squad made their way three steps forward, Grif squeezed the trigger.

The bark of gunfire lit the air, and a mere second later, another echoed from the opposite side. Alanna.

Feet away, Grif didn't miss. The pistol fired, and the bullet buried into the nearest guy's neck, crimson spraying out. Alanna's shot tunneled into the skull of the man closest to her side, and in the span of seconds, both men dropped. The thumps sounded, but these guys were professionals. They didn't blink.

Before the bodies ever hit the floor, the remainder had their pistols raised, circling from side to side to try and spot them while ducking and weaving between the cubicles. They took one step closer. Another.

He just needed them incapacitated while Scarlet finished the job. Grif waited until they took one more step forward, mere feet away from the cubicle he crouched behind. He needed to burn some energy. Time to get close and personal.

His calves tensed, and he slipped the pistol in the holster. The movement was liquid and hidden behind the cubicle, but the slight rustle caused the guy nearest him to tense and whip the muzzle his way.

That's when Shadow chose to move. Alanna leapt to another cubicle, further away, drawing their attention.

Grif seized the second.

He leapt from the cubicle, descending upon the three remaining guys faster than a hawk to its prey.

Grif hooked his arm around the closest guy's neck before the muzzle could whip around. Using the leverage point, he wrenched back, slamming his forearm against his neck. Without letting go, Grif swung out with a side kick. His boot thudded against the middle lackey's wrist, causing the pistol to drop from his hands. Grif whipped around, and with the force of the pivot, he hurled the guy off his feet.

The man flipped, thudding onto the ground. Grif already moved to the next target. The furthest guy kept his finger on the trigger and tried to take aim. He squeezed tight right as Grif dropped to the ground and slid the rest of the way over. The bullet soared overhead, cracking into the back wall. Grif reached for the man's leg, grabbed hold, and yanked him down.

The middle guy stretched for his pistol, feet away.

Alanna dropped into the fray.

Shadow moved like liquid, wrenching the man's hand back before he could reach the pistol. She kicked it further away.

Tuck crackled in over the comms. "Doncaster's

crew has arrived on the scene. We're going to run interference."

Well, fuck. Because they didn't have enough uninvited guests at the party, Doncaster and his cretins had to come crashing in. They'd be sans lookouts.

"Roger that," Grif responded, whipping around to face the man he'd flipped moments before.

He caught the glint of the muzzle and dropped, right before the man squeezed the trigger. The pistol barked, and a gunshot flew inches above him. It zipped past to thud into one of the nearby cubicles, sailing right through the flimsy material.

Grif didn't wait around to gawk.

He grabbed the man by the wrist to yank him forward, and then he drove his elbow in. His forearm thudded against the guy's throat, hard enough a strangled whump came from him. The man staggered back, hands to his throat and gasping for air. Grif pivoted around. The janitor he'd dropped rose to his feet and charged.

Grif crouched, waiting, waiting, waiting. He rocked on the balls of his feet.

Feet away. Inches. A knife glinted in the fucker's hand.

The knife came whipping around to promise pain upon delivery, but Grif ducked. The poor bastard let him get in close—his mistake.

Grif circled his hands around him and released his tensed legs. In one quick motion, he hefted the man into a throw. The guy soared a couple feet to smack against the ground, a whoosh of air leaving his lungs. Alanna had leapt onto the other janitor's back like a spider monkey, her arm wrapped around his neck in a chokehold. He kept scratching at the offending forearm to try and escape, but that just made Alanna cling tighter. The man had no idea how stubborn his Shadow was.

The man with the raw, red neck came rushing in, knives brandished. Too bad Grif had lost what little patience remained. The man led with the knife in his right hand, thrusting forward to try and catch him between the ribs. Grif slid to the side and grabbed him by the forearm. He thrust up with the flat of his palm to catch the guy under the chin. A mix between a gag and a gurgle came from the man's throat, and he swayed once, twice, then dropped.

Alanna's janitor let out a retching sound, and she careened down with him, extricating herself before he slumped to the ground.

The last guy standing took a look at the two of them, and his gaze darted for the door.

No damn way.

Alanna's right foot edged forward. They didn't need any verbal communication to fight in tandem.

Alanna's time in the American Ballet Theatre meant body cues were bible. After years bare-knuckle boxing in the ring, Grif operated the same way.

The man lifted his pistol to guard himself as he backed away, one pace, then another.

Alanna launched off from her leading foot, sailing through the air to close the distance. He squeezed the trigger, but the shot flew awry. Grif already prowled to close the distance as the spent bullet thudded into the plaster wall. The man tried to whip his pistol in Grif's direction—too late.

Grif ducked low and swept his leg out. His shin collided with the man's ankles hard enough to reverberate. Alanna descended from above, her arm dropping like an executioner's blade to chop the side of his neck. Grif's blow sent him teetering, but Alanna's strike did the rest of the work. The moment his head bounced against the ground, those eyes glazed over.

Grif straightened and checked his watch. Ten minutes were up. Scarlet should've completed the Ezekiel Protocol by now.

Alanna wiped her palms on her pants and stared at the five bodies littering the floor in front of them. Under the fluorescent lights, the pools of blood looked brighter than ever.

"I thought they would've given more of a workout," she commented.

Grif snorted. "Want to wake one of them up and try again?"

Before they could turn and walk away, three more janitors rushed through the front door. Heaven and hell.

Dan and Tuck had already taken off when the Doncaster patrol had arrived—these guys must've been waiting in the wings.

Grif cast Alanna a glance. They'd been too distracted by the squad of hit men to hear the others approach.

Alanna vaulted forward.

Grif let out a low curse as fingers leapt to triggers. He leapt behind one of the cubicles, and the first shots fired. One of them grazed his leg, and he winced. Grif settled behind the cubicle before tugging out his own pistol. The hollow throb of pain followed a moment later, but he'd sustained far worse than a graze to the calf. He peered out around the side.

Alanna had tucked and rolled to the L-shaped front desk and crouched behind it. The fake janitors littered the thick cherrywood with bullets, all of them lunging like a dog to bacon at the first chance to shoot their guns.

Grif aimed his pistol and fired.

His bullet tunneled into the throat of the first guy. The moment blood spurted and their fellow hitman dropped, he might as well have screamed "scatter."

They bolted forward, whipping around the desk to where Alanna hid.

No, no, no.

Grif bolted forward even though his calf protested, vaulting the distance to the remaining two. Bullets barked before he'd reached three paces forward, and his blood flash froze.

She couldn't have ducked out of the way in time.

A grunt sounded, but Alanna rolled to the far end of the desk before leaping deeper into the maze of cubicles. The breath constricted in his throat.

Grif closed the rest of the distance.

The butt of his gun whipped down on the back of the closest guy's head with a heavy thump. By the time the other two pivoted toward him, he'd already wrapped his arm around one guy's throat. He squeezed tight, restraining the fucker from lashing out as he kicked forward. His boot connected with the other janitor's wrist, and the pistol fell from his grasp.

Alanna ducked in from below, appearing like a wraith as she sliced her knife across his Achilles. The moment the guy let out a gasp of pain, Alanna delivered three strikes—solar plexus, under the chin, and temple.

Grif tugged his arm tighter until the guy in his grip stopped thrashing. The second those eyes flickered shut, Grif let the guy slump to the floor. Alanna's target had already joined the others there.

"Where did you get shot?" Grif asked, his voice a rough scrape as he faced Alanna. She crouched to the ground, tugging out supplies from the utility belt she wore.

"One of those fuckers grazed me, but I'm still standing," Alanna muttered, pulling out the patch gauze they all carried in case of emergencies. She lifted her shirt and slapped the bandage on, the sticky outside adhering to her skin.

"Technically, you're crouching," Grif retorted, taking in his first full breath since the guns went off.

"Ha, you're hilarious, assface," Alanna muttered, glancing to the door before she rose again. "Let's get back to Scar."

Alanna pivoted toward the corridor. Grif strode past her, his long legs carrying him further faster. He reached out and grabbed the edge of the doorframe, swinging into Brennerman's office. Scarlet didn't bother looking up, deep in the process of pulling off this Hail Mary pass.

"Did you have fun with your friends?" she asked, her fingers flying across the keyboard. The neon light reflected on her features, illuminating the seriousness in her eyes and the line in her brow as she concentrated. "Just need one more minute, and then we're aces."

"Bushels of fun," Grif responded. "Alanna, you guard the hallway. Since we're down our external patrol, I'm going to check out the front of the building." He knew where the best view in Torres Industries was, because he'd spent time sitting in the waiting room memorizing the details. He loped past Alanna and down the corridor. The moonlight spilled out of the broad window at the end of the hall, and the familiar chairs lined the far wall.

The lack of response on the other end of the comm unnerved him. He shouldn't have let Dan run around with Tuck below, even if the guy wanted to help. Now he'd be dodging gunfire with zero field experience to help apart from an assist from Tuck, who'd been slowed by his injury. They'd been patrolling as a precaution—Grif had hoped Doncaster and Kirklees would take a night off—but of course, their luck was fouler than Stickney Wastewater Plant.

Truth be told, he wished he and Dan had more time in the first place, separate from the heist. The man left a mark on his psyche like a tire iron, and the idea they'd go their separate ways after this twisted in his stomach. After a taste of the criminal life, it was guaranteed the guy would be scared away for good.

Grif reached the waiting room he'd been in almost a week ago, wearing his suit and a liar's smile. He strode to the window along the wall and tilted his night vision goggles up on his forehead. By the time he reached the large panes of glass, he'd extracted his foldable binoculars and brought them front and forward.

A dark van sat along the street side, but a few sedans parked behind it, their hazards blinking. The uniform look of the cars preached mafia elegance, but the people pouring out of them made for a more obvious cue. At least five from each car. They'd infest this place and surround them in mere minutes. That's if they hadn't already started infiltrating the building.

Brennerman's alarm had worked.

Nevarra wasn't just sending a hit team to protect his interests, but an army.

Grif bolted from the window. He couldn't feel his feet as he raced down the corridor at top speed. Not like he moved fast enough. They needed to be out of this building five minutes ago. He whipped into Brennerman's office, Alanna jogging to meet up with him once she caught sight from the end of the hall. The computer screen darkened, and Scarlet stepped out past the desk the moment he appeared in the doorway.

"Time to head out," Scarlet said. "We've got enough to nail Brennerman for good."

"Nevarra's squads are on their way up," he said, gripping tight to the doorway.

Alanna skidded to a halt midstride. "What's our escape plan?"

Grif's mind whirred, but in times like this, where

the world turned into a blur and the situation spiraled out of control, he followed his base instincts, the ones that had gotten him through fights he should've died in, the ones that kept him from drowning after his parents died.

"Follow me."

TWENTY-SIX

DAN WORKED OUT. HE WENT FOR A DAILY RUN AND put time in at the gym lifting weights. However, a mere five minutes into this chase, he began to realize how out of shape he was.

Even with the slight drag to Tuck's left heel, the man hurtled through these streets like the stray bullets zipping after them. His gaze didn't falter from the streets and alleys spread out like a maze before them, and barely a sheen of sweat glazed his forehead, his curls whipping around with the breeze. Dan already sweated like the survivor at the end of a horror movie, his shirt glued to his chest as they raced away from the Aon Center and further into the network of thin streets and winding alleys ahead of them.

He hadn't been lying when he told Tuck all he could focus on was one step in front of the other.

This time of night, most of the stores they raced by were closed, vacant, with darkened glass glaring at them. Streetlamps cast their feeble hues onto the asphalt, and the traffic lights flickered through their perpetual cycles as they vaulted by. Dan chanced a glance behind him. Three of Kirklees's guys raced after them at top speed, and he didn't miss the moonlight gliding over the pieces they ran with.

"Front and forward, Torres," Tuck called from ahead of him. The man's time in the circus must've made him omniscient.

Dan snapped his attention to the roads ahead of him as they passed a Starbucks and a Nordstrom, the big-ticket places all shut for the night. Tuck's shoulder twitched, the most instruction he'd get from the guy, and the Outlaw veered to the left into an alley between buildings. The darkness grew stifling here, the stench of garbage spilling out of dumpsters stagnant in the air. His shoulders scraped against the building walls, the tight space causing the breath to catch in his throat, but he didn't stop running.

His calves ached, and sweat stung his eyes as they vaulted through the alleyway. With his focus on Tuck alone, his other senses crept to the fore. Beyond the honks and screeches of traffic they'd left behind them, he heard the steady thump of pursuit. Doncaster's crew hadn't given up yet.

"Duck," Tuck barked.

Dan's mind whirled too much to do anything but listen. He hunched down as he continued to hurtle down the alley, which opened into the loading area where the reeking dumpsters lay.

The whine of a loosed bullet filled the air. The projectile zoomed mere inches above him, close enough to make his bones hum.

He'd be lying if he said he wasn't terrified. The sight of the bullet driving into the far wall dosed him with fear he hadn't felt since he broke his arm at six after falling out of a tree he'd been determined to climb. Yet, an unexpected euphoria followed in the wake, the victory chant of *survive, survive, survive*.

Tuck whipped around the corner, and Dan followed. Instead of continuing to the left where the alley dumped into another main street, Tuck bolted for the adjoining alley with a speed reserved for someone who could navigate the city in his sleep.

Dan's breaths grew shallower, each inhale scraping against his too-dry throat. Yet the march of those footsteps pounded behind them, and with the way they were outnumbered, he and Tuck couldn't afford to stop or try and make a stand. He veered down the alley after Tuck, hoping these whiplash turns would help them lose the crew following. The massive buildings glared down on him, the darkness impenetrable here.

"How far are you from here?" Grif's voice came

over the comm. It had sharpened in the interim. Not for the first time, Dan wished he fought side by side with Grif on this one, rather than running through the alleys and feeling like he was a lifetime away.

"Near Garrett," Tuck announced over the comms as he took another hard left. The scent of the popcorn lingered in the air around here, melding with the trash gumming the cracks in the pavement they leapt past. "We're still hot."

Those steps pounded behind them, unceasing, relentless. Any second, they could unload their bullets and Dan would be a goner. The breath caught in his throat as he whipped around another corner at Tuck's heels.

"Nevarra's sent an army in response." Grif's words echoed stark in the air.

Tuck, the man who'd been running like a machine, stumbled.

Ice trickled through Dan's veins until he grew colder than a Chicago winter.

"The getaway car's parked on Stetson a block away," Tuck responded, resuming his fast pace as he continued to lead them deeper into the city. "Can you reach it?"

"They're infiltrating the building now," Grif responded, a reaper's grimness in his tone. The calm emanating from him even now held the finality of a graveyard, the stillness that came with the permanence of death.

"Blood and bones," Tuck swore off comm. He flexed his hands out once, twice, but never stopped running.

Dan was going to be sick. If they didn't get out, this entire endeavor was for nothing. Brennerman, the mafia—they won. If they didn't escape now, Dan held no delusions about the six-feet-under state they'd end up in.

"Is there any way to flush them out?" Leo asked over the comm. "If they interfere with the program we set up, this is all for nothing."

Grif's breaths came in harsh as his comm turned on. Based on the thump-thump-thump, they were running too. "Not that I can see. We're too hot to attempt a climb this high, and they'll be swarming the stairs and the elevator."

"Head for the emergency exits," Dan responded, not even questioning if Grif's crew could disable them. "The one on our floor is the opposite side of the regular stairwell."

"Thanks for the reminder, Torres," Grif responded, his rough, deep tone offering the reassurance he craved right now. The man oozed competence even in the midst of a full-blown siege.

The alley ahead emptied into a broad street lined by parked cars on either side. Headlights flickered by as the night traffic raced along. Tuck swerved to the right, directing them onto the street. Dan couldn't do anything at this point but follow. His body moved automatically, his mind sailing so far away he couldn't connect.

Leo's warning stuck with him, slamming around in his head like church bells in full swing.

They needed a way to flush the mafia out of the Aon Center, to force everyone out before their work was disturbed. Before Nevarra's men wiped Brennerman's system and the man continued poisoning his father's company with his underworld connections. No fucking way. Dan was done. Done with hiding, done with bowing to bad circumstance, and he was done following anyone's orders.

Grif and the Outlaws wouldn't be happy, but this might be the one chance they got.

Dan whipped out his phone, trying to glance to the glowing screen even as he continued to hurtle after Tuck. They burst onto the street and began a game of dodge-the-pedestrian as they soared over the sidewalk.

He managed to thumb across the screen and open the app on his phone. He couldn't focus while he ran like this. Dan glanced to Tuck, a couple of feet ahead of him at his slowed pace. His legs begged him to stop at this point, but he'd already come so far. Even though the pounding of Kirklees and company's footsteps were drowned out by street noise, he knew without looking they were back there. That they were coming.

Dan brought his phone up, the screen bouncing so much he couldn't read a damn word. Not like he needed to. The big red button on the side of the screen begged to be pressed.

He'd face Grif's wrath later. He just needed him alive.

Dan's thumb wavered as it hovered over the screen. He swallowed hard. Dan pressed the button. The older guy walking toward him bolted out of the way right before he mowed him down. Dan teetered to the side before he slammed his phone back in his pocket and pressured his calves into pushing forward faster.

Dan tapped the comm in his ear. "I set off the security alert for Torres Industries. Cops will be en route, which means you've got ten minutes."

The second he turned the comm off, he picked up his phone again, his hands shaking with the pounding of his footsteps as he didn't dare break his stride.

"Nilo?" Vanessa's voice came over the other end.

"I need you to do me a favor, no questions asked."

TWENTY-SEVEN

They'd flirted with screwed, passed fucked beyond measure, and vaulted straight into dead-on-arrival territory.

Grif raced through the emergency exit door after his quick work with a magnet to disable the electro-magnetic sensor. Already, the steady pounding of foot-steps echoed from the opposite side of the building, and the ding-ding-ding of the rising elevator hitting floor after floor reverberated through the place. He, Scarlet, and Alanna raced neck and neck down these steps, more like a concrete cattle chute than a stair-case, even though they'd be as much of a nightmare as the other steps.

Ten minutes.

Ten minutes and the cops would be descending upon this building. The Aon Center would have top-of-the-line alarm systems installed—that sort of shit went off, and the police squads wouldn't be idling.

Grif wasn't sure whether he wanted to curse Dan or kiss him, but the action gave them a definite deadline. Given the fact they'd been slower on the steps and Alanna already nursed a slug to the gut, they couldn't drop the whole way down from here. They'd have to chance the elevator if they hoped to make it in time.

Grif raced down the staircase, Alanna following so close she'd almost slammed into him twice now. Scarlet trailed behind, lagging after their strenuous climb. His calves flexed, just beginning to protest. Their footsteps barely made a shummp shummp, but with the way Grif's senses grew violin-string tense, the reverberations echoed like they stomped the whole way.

They wound down one floor, then another.

That's when he caught the rat-a-tat-tat of footsteps to concrete steps below them, reverberating like gunfire.

Of course. Nevarra's men were storming the emergency exits too. Unlike his Outlaws, Nevarra had his "janitors" familiarity with the building to tap into.

"We need to chance the elevator," Grif called out, a bit breathless. He hated the idea of being enclosed in those murder boxes even for a couple of floors, but they needed to get down, fast. He glanced to his watch. Nine minutes left. They'd already reached the fortieth floor. Time to take the risk.

Grif skidded to a halt and grabbed for the door at the landing, his slick fingers almost gliding right off. He snagged his magnet to deactivate this one as well. The footsteps from below grew louder by the second. He plunged through the doorway, the scent of bleach and orange polish intensified on this level. The fortieth floor remained as dark as the rest of them, the silver moonlight reflected on the polished floors like a portal to another realm.

They couldn't waste time creeping around, not when their window of escape was creaking shut.

The clip of footsteps echoed from both stairwells, a steady whup-whup-whup like an oscillating fan. He prayed the ascending crews weren't doing sweeps through the floors. He crept toward the opposite side of the atrium where the elevators parked right next to the door for the regular stairwell. Everything about the lack of control involving elevators made his throat dry, but they'd run out of options.

He strode across the polished marble floors, passing the void entrance to another business. At this point, any remaining security guards would be heading for Torres Industries and hopefully leaving them the fuck alone, or they'd be incapacitated by Nevarra's men. The elevators beckoned at the end of the atrium, neon numbers ticking by in the overhead screens. Doubtless, Nevarra had already sent swarms of his men up to Torres Industries. The footsteps grew louder and louder from the stairwell, as if an army of thousands prepared to descend.

"Your boy toy apparently likes to flirt with danger as much as you do," Alanna muttered under her breath. A smile ghosted Grif's lips. The move had been ballsy, that was for sure.

The next eight minutes would tell if they'd survive to rob the reaper another day.

He lunged for the elevator button, the down arrow blinking to life. Grif rocked back and forth on the balls of his feet, needing to move, move, move. His gaze flickered to the door mere feet from them. The window in the center would give anyone inside a view that they needed to stay out of. And the footsteps grew louder.

The numbers ticked away on the screen above the elevator to the right, zooming their way. Not fast enough. Nevarra's men could be waiting to ambush them on the ground floor, which was why they needed to get off earlier.

Alanna planted herself in front of the elevator and jabbed at the line between the doors. Scarlet leaned against the wall, her gaze focused on those lights as her chest rose and fell with serrated breaths. Grif's eyes kept flicking to the stairwell door on the off-chance it creaked open.

Thump. Thump. Thump.

Those footsteps were so loud.

A man dodged past the stairwell door, and the breath caught in Grif's throat. The elevator was a few floors away.

Another guy flashed past the window, but this one stopped.

A pair of eyes stared at them from the opposite side of the glass.

The shout of alarm came next.

Ding. Ding. Ding. One floor away. Grif's muscles rioted, his nerves roared, and his entire being begged to hurl himself headfirst at the elevator. The door to the stairwell swung open, and one of Nevarra's men burst through.

The elevator dinged beside them, and the doors opened.

Alanna darted inside, and Grif shoved Scarlet in first. By the time he dove in after, the muzzle swung to greet him, and the man fired the pistol. The bullet sailed through the air. The shock of pain descended a second later. His right leg throbbed—the bullet must've gotten him.

He clapped his hand on the pistol in his holster, bringing it up to aim at any threats.

Alanna jammed at the button to close the doors. The guy who'd shot him surged in front of them as if he'd try to wedge himself in the center. The elevator slammed shut, and off they went.

They zipped down, the floors flashing neon on the overhead black space. Grif stood in the center with his pistol aimed, trying to ignore the throb of his thigh and the ensuing trickle of blood that gummed his pants to his skin. He spared a glance to his watch. Seven minutes.

Each time the elevator passed another floor, Grif tensed, and his finger skated the trigger. Any moment, those assholes could open the door and try to flood the car. The numbers ticked down fast, already to the twenties.

Lower. They'd hit the teens, yet no one had tried to stop them. Grif's stomach twisted with a knowing that loomed like thunderheads.

The lights flashed above him.

They blinked once, twice, and then flickered out. Black days and bleaker times. Those assholes had cut the power. The elevator car switched to the low emergency lighting.

"Oh, fuck me," Alanna cursed.

Scarlet popped her flashlight on and swung the beam toward the panel. With the power out, he wasn't sure what floor they were on. Not like it mattered. They needed to get out, even if Nevarra's men waited on the other side. If they stayed inside, those bastards could pick them off in here like ducks in a puddle. Grif loped to the elevator doors and knelt to the ground. Scarlet swung the paltry beam his way, and Grif thrust his knife into the bottom, trying to wedge his fingers on the opposite side to get a grip.

"Not my type, sweetheart," Grif responded to Alanna as he gritted his teeth, trying to wedge the doors open. She leaned in overtop him and assisted in prying the doors apart.

"Sorry I don't have a dick," Alanna grunted as she helped him push at the doors. The crack widened, gliding open. They had begun descending from a floor and halted midway, so the entrance was big enough to climb through.

"I'm sorry too," Grif said, flashing a grin before he reached forward to pull himself up and over. He crawled onto the cool tile of the floor they'd been exiting and glanced in both directions. Those footsteps echoed through the place on either side, like a never-ending drum circle determined to drive him insane.

Both stairwells. They were fucked, but they were still too high up.

"Emergency exit." Grif made the call, setting off in that direction. His thigh ached hard enough he could feel it in his teeth, but he ran faster, rushing across the tiled floor in the direction of the dim exit sign. Out of the two, it could fit fewer people per step, and the strides pounded louder from the main stairs.

His heartbeat slammed in his throat hard enough he could spit it out. A drop of sweat tickled down his forehead, the salt stinging his eyes. The glow of the neon above the emergency exit was his sole focal point as he raced forward, his grip steady on his pistol. The neon numbers of his watch glowed at his wrist. Six minutes.

He grabbed the door handle and flung it open. The alarms would sound, but the time for caution had ended. Grif didn't just enter—he vaulted inside.

Shouts sounded from floors above, followed by the rattle of the railing.

He couldn't spare the glance up. Not if they wanted to escape. Alanna darted past him, nimble as ever, and Scarlet's harsh puffs of breath sounded right behind. They descended one floor, then another, then another. This time, they didn't bother to mask their movements. Their footsteps thundered to the rafters, echoing far, far in the distance. Grif's breaths cycled sharper and more tattered, but his sole focus remained on placing one step in front of the other. Survive. Survive. Survive.

A bark erupted through the air, followed by the whiz of a bullet. It sailed about a foot away from them to thud into the concrete. And now they were getting shot at. Joy.

The numbers of the landings flickered by until they'd passed ten, nine, and then eight.

Three more shots flew through the center to clatter uselessly on the first floor.

Past the seventh floor. Fuck it. They needed to get out twenty minutes ago.

Grif skidded to a halt and grabbed the door for the sixth floor. He bolted inside, the ringing shouts from above echoing down to them. Nevarra's men jumped to their comms to give away his location. Any moment now, men would be rushing this floor to riddle them with bullets.

The hallway stretched out before them all the way to the elevators at the other side, but smaller offices bisected this one.

"Grab your lockpick," Grif called to Alanna as they raced for the nearest office, J. Rutgers Financial Holdings. On this side of the building lay the entrance they'd arrived through—they wanted the opposite. He tugged the AP hook from his belt, as well as the length of cord he kept wrapped around his belt. "Make sure your gloves are secure, crew."

Scarlet tugged at hers, and Alanna ignored him, bending over in front of the darkened door leading into one of the small offices. She slipped out her lockpick. Within a second, the knob was turning, and she bolted.

The stairwell door creaked open, and three of Nevarra's men burst through. They caught sight of him, and their shouts echoed to the vaulted ceilings.

These guys didn't hesitate. Their pistols barked, and bullets flew.

Grif barely ducked in time as one zoomed an inch overhead. His heart lodged in his throat as the other two burrowed into the wall beside him. He slammed the door shut and twisted the lock.

Grif whipped around, spotting the secretary desk to the right. In a few strides, he grabbed the chair and wedged it beneath the knob. The temporary block wouldn't hold Nevarra's men back forever—or even five minutes.

Grif raced deeper into the offices, following the patter of Scarlet's and Alanna's footsteps. He wound around one corner, then another, his stomach offering an over-easy flip at the idea they'd walled themselves into a dead end. Not like he'd researched this floor or if this office contained a window.

This was all down to gut instinct and luck. With the way things had been rolling—fifty-fifty odds.

The rattle of the doorknob echoed from behind, followed by a whump, whump, whump. Any moment, Nevarra's men would break through, and they'd be screwed.

"Grif, over here," Alanna's voice sounded. To the right. A door lay open.

Grif plunged through to find Alanna and Scarlet standing in front of one of those big bay windows like the ones in Dan's office.

"This should take us around the back of the building," Scarlet said, shooting him a nervous look. Grif strode to the conference table and tried to tip it over. The thing didn't budge. It had been bolted to the ground. Perfect. He leaned down and wound the cord around to create a noose, threading it through the AP hook as he pulled tight.

Alanna dragged one of those big-ass chairs over to the door and wedged it beneath the knob.

"We're going to drop and then jump," Grif gave the warning as he tugged the length dangling from the AP hook. He glanced out the window. The cars lit the streets like fireflies, and they stood high enough that a straight drop would be fatal. The door at the far end of the hall began to rattle. Any moment now, Nevarra's men would break it down.

Alanna tugged out her pro-level Lifeaxe hammer and struck. The glass shuddered, and a crack formed. She seized upon it, slamming hard enough the surface shattered.

"Time for some rousing heroics," she said with a smirk.

"Except, you know, we're the thieves here," Scarlet drawled, doing her best at bravado.

Grif checked his watch again. Five minutes left. "You haven't lived until you've dangled off the edge of a skyscraper in Chicago. All it took was a little mishap with the mob, a should've-been-simple heist, and a massive fuck-up to get this extravagance."

The pound of footsteps came from the corridor. Nevarra's men had already broken through. In no time, they'd be busting into this room.

Either they scaled the building in the next five minutes, or they faced one of two fates. Dead at Nevarra's hands or locked up by the cops.

Grif wasn't sure which outcome was worse.

TWENTY-EIGHT

DAN WAS PRETTY SURE HIS LUNGS WERE GOING TO explode. Pack of C-4, fuse-lit sort of burst.

The cab driver kept looking back, with the way he wheezed and sweat dripped in buckets off him, but the old, gap-toothed guy didn't say anything. That was fine, because Dan kept glancing through the back window to see if any cars tailed them or if he spotted anyone suspicious along the sidewalk. Once they'd lost sight of Kirklees and the others for at least five minutes, Tuck had made the call to head back. Dan went into the first cab, and Tuck had waited behind to snag one a couple of blocks up.

Either Kirklees and the others had tried to reroute to the swarms of cops about to descend on Aon Center, or they'd sulked on home. Both outcomes meant he and Tuck had accomplished their task.

When he wasn't staring out the back window, he glanced to his watch, counting down the minutes Grif and the others had left. He'd already cursed himself a thousand times over for the move he pulled as images of Grif hauled away in cuffs paraded through his mind.

His breaths came out ragged around the edges, and his shirt made a valiant attempt to glue itself to his skin. The sweat that had been dripping while he ran now pasted to his skin in a sticky film.

"Marathon training?" the cab driver asked, breaking the quiet.

A soft laugh escaped Dan, and he offered a thumbs-up. "Yeah, that's it."

The buildings flashed by, past the part of the city he'd grown familiar with and into the territory he'd just gotten to know. His heart squeezed tight. Even here, he could almost smell the amber, leather, and sweat.

His heart sped at the sight of the familiar towers of On the Park penthouses where he'd first met the rest of the Outlaws, and where he'd gotten to know the real Grif Blackmore.

"Right here," Dan said. The cab screeched to a halt, and he passed over a couple of crumpled bills. Dan stepped out, his legs screaming at the movement after the brief respite they'd gotten. He glanced behind him, expecting Kirklees and her cronies to come whipping around the corner. Nothing like running for your life to ramp up your paranoid tendencies.

Another cab pulled in front of him, and Dan froze midstride, his palm creeping toward the gun he probably couldn't fire. Enemy or ally—it was a coin flip who would emerge.

Tuck hopped out, a spring in his step, as if his ankle hadn't gotten grazed a few days ago and he hadn't spent the last hour running through the alleys of Chicago. The Outlaw lifted his hand in greeting, and Dan strolled over to walk in line with him. Together, they made their way to the On the Park penthouse, relief gripping his chest and waiting for release.

Dan's watch beeped, the sound echoing through the air like a gunshot. The ten minutes were up. Tuck glanced at him, worry gleaming in those chocolate eyes.

Tuck pressed the comm at his ear while they continued toward the entrance of On the Park. "Locksley, are you out?"

Dan sucked in a breath and glanced to the bruised sky, the slate clouds threatening to snuff out the stars. He didn't know what he searched for—answers, a sign, some glimmer of hope—yet only silence and stillness greeted him. The comm remained quiet, and that filled Dan with the worst sort of foreboding.

He only had himself to blame.

"I'm sorry," he said, the apology slipping out before he could help himself. They reached the back entrance, and Tuck slipped out his key card to unlock the door.

Tuck grabbed the handle, but he looked to him, meeting his gaze. "No apologies. You made the call none of us could. Grif and the others have slipped out of worse situations than this. Now come on, let's head back up to HQ."

Dan nodded, unable to voice his thanks—for the forgiveness, the reassurance. Every member of the Outlaws he'd met so far wasn't sleazy, cruel, or twisted like he'd expected criminals to be. Like Brennerman was. No, everyone here had a moral code of their own, one that mirrored Grif's. And as much as he knew they were breaking the law, he couldn't bring himself to condemn them. After all, the Outlaws dealt with the scum who blackmailed him. The one who tried to kill his sister.

They headed inside and made a beeline for the elevators.

With each step forward, the silence from the comms echoed louder and louder, until it grew deafening. They slipped into the elevator, and with a ding, the car surged up. Dan leaned against the wall, almost slumping to the floor. His legs had begun to tremble, reminding him how out of shape he was.

"So, what's the protocol while we wait? Knitting tea cozies?" Dan asked, needing to break the silence and get out of the horror show on constant rotation in his head. All he could see was the splashy headline on the news: Grif Blackmore, Caught! Or the lurch in his stomach when they found out the police hadn't nabbed him, because Nevarra's men had placed a bullet through his head. Somehow in the short time they'd known each other, the man had made a significant mark on him, and he wasn't ready to let him go.

"That's what J-man does," Tuck said, tapping his fingertips along the wall as he stared at the ceiling. "Except he crochets."

"And what do you do?" Dan asked. His one plan revolved around burying his head in his hands and trying to scour his mind clean.

"Usually pop on a video game. If you're down, we can play a couple of rounds." Tuck cast him a knowing glance.

"Yes, fucking please," Dan responded, the words whooshing out of him. The elevator binged as it settled onto the top floor, and the doors opened. "I don't know how the lot of you deal with this tension on a regular basis."

Tuck shrugged and took the lead off the elevator. They headed down the hallway to the door he'd approached last week with his palms sweating and half-sure he was going to get shot. In such a short time, everything had flipped.

"You adapt, I guess. I'd take this sort of worry over feeling helpless any day of the week. We all know the risks going in, and we fight in our own way." Tuck approached the door and placed his thumb to the square beneath the doorbell, pressing it there. A ding, ding, ding sounded inside, and a moment later the door clicked. Tuck twisted the knob and opened wide.

"Took you guys long enough," John called as he grabbed the door and dragged it open wider. "Did you stop to wine and dine Doncaster's crew?"

"Yeah," Tuck responded. "They insulted my taste in merlot and tried to skip out on the bill."

"What about Grif and the others?" Dan asked, unable to help himself. "Any word from them?"

John's lips formed a thin line, and Leo swiveled around from the rig. He looked at home behind the computer, and he stretched his arms above his head.

"We haven't heard anything," Leo said. "I've been monitoring the video feed and Brennerman's console. No one's tampered with it yet, and based on the cops I just saw flooding in through the main entrance, they won't get the chance to."

"Good," Tuck said. He snagged one of the folding chairs stacked against the wall and flipped it out and around, close to the console Leo sat behind. He leaned in against the seat and cast Dan's best friend a heavy-lidded glance. "You did good work behind the rig."

Leo tapped the side of his glasses. "Hacking for an operation was something I've always wanted to do. Not going to lie, I might need to change my pants."

"You're welcome to strip down here," Tuck commented in the same lazy tone. "No one's complaining."

Dan's feet started to carry him back and forth, but his calves fast throbbed in protest, so he found a wall to lean against and slid to the ground. He couldn't listen to Tuck and Leo flirting, not while his heart drove ninety miles down the freeway with no brakes. The scuff-scuff-scuff of John's shoes hitting the ground as he paced went at the same tempo as his nerves, and he sank into the sound.

On the desk near the console, Dan spotted a half-crocheted navy-and-white scarf. If Tuck's story was to be believed, that was John's handiwork.

He watched the feed Leo had left on the screen, of the cops running through the building. They swarmed the steps, and some of them had already reached Torres Industries. Seeing his own office building, the place he'd loathed and regardless entered daily for the past year, caused his stomach to turn. This job with the Outlaws had felt natural, like peeling off his starched shirt and pressed suit after a day at the office.

The realization hit him like a sudden summer storm, warm drops trickling through him.

He didn't have to stay at Torres Industries. If they pulled off this heist, if the cops locked up Brennerman, Dan would walk away. The company could do a complete overhaul without him. In the past month he'd been threatened, blackmailed, and shot at. All of those hurdles had hammered in the understanding that life was one wrong turn away from ending up dead in a ditch. He was done wasting away in a job he hated, and he was done hiding who he was from his parents. Either Mom and Dad would accept him, or he'd find himself a new family.

The resolution gripped him by the chest, and he grabbed at it and clutched tight. Relief still eluded him, but that wouldn't settle into his bones until the moment Grif walked through the door.

If he did.

"Want to go play some *Mortal Kombat*?" Tuck offered, even though he made no move to get up from his seat near Leo. Still, he appreciated the attempt at distraction.

Dan shook his head. "I want to be here." He let the unspoken dangle in the air. Tuck nodded, understanding flickering across his features.

"Scarlet? Dales? Locksley?" John's voice echoed over the comms. He hadn't stopped pacing, even though he emanated a terrifying sort of placid. No wonder he was their resident con man.

Silence echoed through the room.

Dan tugged the comm from his ear, unable to listen to the static in response. His gaze returned to the door. Watching. Waiting.

He hadn't spotted the cops seizing Grif and the others inside the building, but that didn't mean they couldn't have cuffed them outside. Or they lay on the floor of the Aon Center, blood pooling on the marble tiles. The thought rocked him like a boat in the storm, and Dan tasted bile.

He leaned forward and pressed his forehead to his knees. The motion didn't erase the carousel of shitty images, but it did cause some of the pressure in his head to ebb. He would offer his legs for a shower at this point with the way his clothes clung to his sticky skin, but he didn't dare leave the room. Maybe he could ask Leo to look through the video feeds for them again, to try and scan to see if they were still in the building.

Ding. Ding. Ding.

The doorbell rang, and the lock unclicked.

Dan's head shot up from the slump, and his adrenaline spiked like he still raced through the streets.

Alanna stomped inside, her shoulders heaving, and Scarlet entered after, her movements carefully composed.

"How you got here the same time as me is a mystery," Scarlet commented, shutting the door behind her. As fast as his hope had soared, it now plummeted. Grif wasn't with them. "You're the one who got the car, while I had to wait around for an Uber."

Alanna tossed a middle finger in the air. "Excuuuse me for wanting to make sure I didn't have a tail. I'll be sloppy next time and lead them right to the penthouse."

"Where's Grif?" John asked the question before he could.

A frown creased Scarlet's brow. "He's not here yet? We left about the same time."

"Locksley, you fucker, report in," Alanna said into the comms. "Oh, crap, the jump must've messed with our comms." Dan was grateful he didn't have his earpiece in anymore, because the discomfort at what he assumed was more silence grew so loud it was almost audible.

A cold sweat broke out over Dan's skin, but he sewed himself together even as he threatened to unravel at the seams.

"How did you guys escape?" Leo asked. "I saw the elevator got compromised."

Scarlet strode over to the console, scanning over Leo's handiwork. She pushed her glasses up on her elegant nose and let out a low whistle. "Not bad, newbie. We rappelled down the side of the building. Managed to sneak through an alley right as the cops peeled up to the entrance."

"All thanks to Torres," Alanna commented, her glance flicking to the door again. "We should've stopped to bind up his wound."

"He was bleeding?" Dan asked, the fear punching past the shame.

"All thanks to Torres, my handiwork is still in order," Scarlet said as she scanned over the console. "Grif got shot when we were trying to board the elevator. Stubborn fucker wouldn't have stopped for treatment if we tried."

"Can you trace him?" Dan asked. The urgency pulsed in his veins like the hummingbird thrum of his heartbeat. If his legs hadn't been dead to the world right now, he'd surge up and start patrolling the outside of the building.

"I can make an attempt, but if he isn't responding on the comms, it probably broke or is glitching too much to get a signal," Scarlet murmured, nudging Leo out of the way. He scooted his chair closer to Tuck as Scarlet crouched in front of the console, the blue light painting her pale skin and illuminating the exhaustion on her features.

The thought of Grif staggering out there alone was too much to bear. Dan swallowed his regrets of all the words left unsaid between them. Of all the potential, like stars extinguished, if Grif didn't make it back.

"You pulled off the Ezekiel Protocol?" John said, changing the subject. Dan wanted to snap at him, but at the same time he appreciated the distraction. Alanna leaned against the wall next to him in a temporary truce, her arms crossed in front of her.

Scarlet nodded. "We've got the backup files here for safekeeping too. By tomorrow morning, Phil Brennerman is fucked harder than an escort working overtime."

Dan gripped his knees harder. He should feel relief at that. The man who'd plagued him for the past year would be behind bars, where he deserved to be. However, his heart pole-vaulted into his throat every time he glanced to the door.

Ding. Ding. Ding.

This time, Dan did stand. He was striding over to the door the moment the lock clicked.

"I've got to say, the state of the L these days is positively criminal." Grif's sarcastic voice came from the doorway as he entered. Dan devoured the single glimpse of him, his windswept blond hair, the Arctic blue of his intense gaze, and the way he leaned to his side, his palm pressed over his right thigh.

John let out a sharp laugh behind him. "That's your own fault for taking the L back home."

"Use your comm next time, asshole," Alanna called.

Dan's legs carried him across the room until he stood in front of Grif. He was here, he was real, and he was safe. The relief that had been hanging over him like an errant thundercloud opened up, and the downpour threatened to wash him away.

Grif closed the door behind him with a click, but his gaze never left Dan's. The intensity there was like standing at the edge of Lake Michigan as the sun set, unable to look away from the glittering expanse that held him spellbound. He'd never felt this around anyone before, but Grif inspired it, every damn time.

Dan didn't hesitate. His hands slipped around Grif's nape, and he brought the man in close. His lips crushed to his in a fierce, breathless kiss. Grif's hands wound around his waist, bringing him in flush against him as he deepened the kiss. Heat stung Dan's eyes at the relief that ached his bones, that soothed his nerves. Each press of their lips together offered a reassurance they needed right now. Dan drank in the salt and sweat, the musk of his cologne, and he savored the taste, those scents. The thrumming in his chest stilled, and Dan sank into the quiet.

No matter how many twists and turns his life had

taken of late, Dan now understood they opened up to a path he could've never imagined, one of hope, one of thrills, and one of freedom. As he sank into Grif's embrace, he knew the man who was to blame, and he couldn't be happier.

TWENTY-NINE

Grif grew aware of three things upon waking: his right thigh ached like a bitch, he could sleep the next century and still not feel rested, and someone lay curled next to him. That got him bolting upright fast. He'd been sleeping alone in this bed from the day he bought this place.

"Grif, it's just me." Dan's voice cut through the haze, the low, sweet tone that got his blood pumping. "Given the current state of my company, I told them I got the call from the cops and I'll be heading in to talk with them first, which gives me a little time now. My phone's been blowing up nonstop since five."

He blinked the sleep out of his vision and glanced to his right. Memories of last night came crashing in on him. They'd swapped a bit of empty chatter before everyone rushed for the bathrooms to try and shower off the scum and patch up wounds. He and Dan had shared some scorching kisses under the spray of hot water before they passed the hell out. Dan sat next to him in the bed, the sheets loosely draped over his legs. With the sunlight through the blinds causing his skin to gleam like polished bronze and threading brown notes through his thick black hair, the man looked fucking delicious.

He ran a hand through his hair, not looking away from Dan Torres, who lay in his bed. He could get used to this far too fast. Yet, they hadn't even bothered to talk last night, both too exhausted to do much more than fall into bed.

"You're looking at me with scary eyes," Dan said, lifting an eyebrow. "Like you're planning how to dispose of my body in Lake Michigan."

Grif snorted. The comment eased the tension mounting inside him, somehow making what he was going to say easier. Dan had been doing that since he met him: smoothing the sharp edges before he'd even realized. The man had a calming effect on him and came at problems from a different approach, something Grif admired. He couldn't let go of him.

"So, the job's over," Grif started, and Dan flinched. He reached over to trace his finger along Dan's cheek, hating to see the pain flicker-flash across those gentle eyes. "But I'll be honest with you, I'm not ready to let go of whatever this is between us."

Dan's mouth dropped open for a moment, and he rocked closer, the bedsheet slipping and revealing more of his smooth, biteable skin. When he'd arrived through the door last night and Dan had slammed his mouth to his, any doubts and fears cleared away. The relief had filled his hollowed heart to the point he'd almost forgotten it shattered years ago. Grif had never been into relationships, but with Dan, he wanted to give the whole commitment thing a fair shake.

"Though," he continued, needing to cut through the quiet at the prickle of vulnerability that swept over him. "Things might be difficult for a while since my fake Neo-National company happened to drop a major bomb onto yours."

"Whose company?" Dan asked, a gleam in his gaze that looked brand new. "I'm going to be walking away from Torres Industries. It's about time I followed what I want rather than what my father dictates."

Grif leaned forward and stole a kiss, those silken lips melting against his. Dan let out a moan of frustration and pulled away.

"I'll never manage this conversation if we start down that road," Dan murmured against his mouth. "You're too damn tempting." He pulled back and sprawled on his bed like an invitation. The scent of his lime and ginger cologne already had Grif hard.

Dan blew out a breath. "I was terrified you were going to tell me we were quits. Sorry I didn't give an immediate response, but I was bracing myself for the worst." He reached out and threaded his fingers through Grif's, the motion so tender it speared right through his heart. "I want this, and I know you're not the picket fence sort, but hey, I'll settle for a penthouse."

The grin tugged across his lips before he even realized how wide he smiled, like a complete idiot. He squeezed Dan's hand tight and then tugged him in to wrap his arm around his shoulders. Dan leaned against his chest. Grif wanted to memorize the soft puffs of his breath against his skin, the addictive scent, and the way strands of his hair stuck straight up, tousled from sleep.

"You're something spectacular, you know that?" he murmured into his hair. "If your father can't deal with you following your own path, then fuck him."

Dan traced his fingers along his thigh, the tease traveling perilously close to his cock. "That'd be awkward," Dan joked, and then he squeezed Grif's thigh before looking up at him. "Especially since I hope you'll be meeting them sometime in the near future. At the very least, you'll meet my sister. Hope you like Filipino food."

Grif swallowed, hard. While he'd formed his own family after his parents passed away, this was the first time he'd be meeting any significant other's. "Are you sure they won't take one look at me and run screaming the other way?" Dan's earlier words clicked in his head. "I thought you said your dad isn't a fan of your 'lifestyle.'"

Dan bit his lip, the vulnerable look in his eyes causing Grif's heart to tumble headfirst. "It's about time I told him. Like I said, I'm done hiding who I am. I want you to be a part of my life, and I'm willing to take the risk."

He had been in every facet. Grif couldn't have imagined when he first met the sharp-dressed CEO of Torres Industries that this sweet, clever man could've maneuvered past all his defenses to witness his truth—and still want him. The thought hit harder than any punch he'd received in the ring.

"Damn, Torres, keep sweet-talking me like that and I might find myself falling." Before he could let those words settle inside, he slid to the edge of the bed and rested his feet on the ground. "We'd better get out there for breakfast before the other Outlaws skin us alive. Or Leo—with the way Scarlet and Tuck were eyeing him up, I'm worried for your friend."

"The slut would probably eat it up," Dan muttered, running a hand over his face. "Let's break up the orgy before it starts." Dan climbed out of bed, his muscles sore, and began tugging on his pair of sweats from the night before.

"Let me get you a clean pair," Grif said, striding

over to his dresser. He grabbed two and handed the navy ones over to Dan.

"I'll be swimming in these," Dan grumbled, even as he tugged them on and pulled the drawstring tighter. Grif grabbed one of his undershirts and tossed Dan one too.

Dan lifted his eyebrow. "You're massive. I look like a toddler wearing adult clothing in these."

"Not like you were complaining about my size the other night," Grif teased, the sight warming his chest. Dan wasn't wrong, but he looked fucking adorable, and if he were being honest, he liked the look of his boyfriend with sleep-mussed hair and wearing his clothes.

Fuck, that word would take some getting used to.

"Yes, you've got a massive cock I've been fixated on from the day we met," Dan said with a yawn, waving his hand in front of his face. "But you mentioned breakfast, and I have a severe need for coffee."

Grif laughed and clapped a hand on Dan's shoulder, leading him out from the room. The moment they stepped into the corridor, the sounds of the rest of the crew echoed his way. Today was starting out to be a damned good day. When they stepped into the kitchen, five pairs of eyes honed in on them.

"What's this sleeping in nonsense?" John called

over to him. "Don't tell me a measly bullet wound has you lagging in your old age."

Scarlet pushed his glasses up on his nose and slapped the table. "It's about time, pay attention."

Scarlet had brought the flat-screen into the kitchen this morning and set it on the opposite end of the table. Tuck slumped into his plate, half-awake, while Leo fingered a piece of bacon on his plate before breaking the slice into smaller pieces. Alanna clanged the dishes at the stovetop and tossed the spatula as she raced over to join them.

"I've got to see this." Alanna elbowed John in the side as she took the seat next to him. He reached over to flick her on the nose, grunting when she slammed her fist into his ribs seconds later.

"Kids, stop fighting," Scarlet reprimanded as he leaned against the edge of the table. He wore a pressed button-down and linen pants as if he hadn't been running around with them last night. The fucker looked way too refreshed. Scarlet met his gaze. Ah, the news they were waiting for.

He guided Dan over to snag a plate and some bacon and eggs before they joined the rest at squeezing on the one side of the table. Everyone's elbows jabbed into each other, but no one gave a damn, focused on the breaking story.

Torres Industries had been infiltrated last night, and while the police cleared out the intruders they found some damning evidence on the CFO's desk of illegal activity, an account listed with deposit amounts, which was enough to obtain a warrant for his computer. Once they did, the cops discovered a lump sum of fifty thousand dollars of the company's funds deposited into a shell corporation, Renmark Industries. This was one of many irregularities found on his desktop, leading to years of mishandled funds between him and Renmark. He'd be facing criminal charges.

"A round of applause to the brilliant Dan Torres who had his own sister phone in an anonymous tip to the cops that someone had been trying to steal files from Brennerman's computer," Grif announced, clapping a hand on Dan's shoulder. Pride warmed his chest at the stroke of brilliance. "If he hadn't, we might be waiting a bit longer before they uncovered Brennerman's dirty deals."

Scarlet and Alanna lifted their cups of coffee in tribute.

"Here, here," John called out. Dan blushed furiously and stared harder at his plate. The man was too adorable.

The picture of a red-faced, blustering Phil Brennerman getting led off in cuffs was one of the triumphs of Grif's morning. One of many, matched only by the moment he showed up to Nevarra's to deliver the funds owed.

"Wait, fifty thousand was the amount I planned on paying you guys as a finder's fee for exposing him…" Dan trailed off. He glanced to Grif, who couldn't resist a smile.

"When Scarlet got to the files, he needed to make some adjustments," Grif said, passing a knowing glance to Scarlet. He had his gloating expression on, the cocky one that he donned whenever he pulled off something tricky.

"The Ezekiel Protocol is a maneuver we prepared to make sure we'd get paid either way. Brennerman had enough to tag him in his files, but we had a far better opportunity in our grasp," Scarlet explained, his arms crossed. "So, I took an advance on the funds you were going to give us."

"He deposited those funds into a dummy account Leo set up, one that brought down Renmark Industries in the process, a shell company of Marco Nevarra's," Grif finished the explanation, his finger tap-tap-tapping on the table. "Not only is Brennerman going to get locked up, but we delivered a hefty fuck-you to Nevarra and his cronies, yet we can claim immunity since their partnership wasn't public knowledge. *We* were just doing a job."

"Damn, so that's why you pulled the maneuver?" Leo said, shaking his head in admiration.

"You clever, clever bastards," Dan murmured, wonder gleaming in his eyes. "What about your own take in the heist though? Didn't you need the money to pay Nevarra back?"

"That's where our Scarlet pulled out all the stops," Alanna jumped in, stabbing the eggs on her plate. "He might've rerouted our original take into Brennerman's accounts, but the excess funds the old asshole squatted on in one of his other accounts? That got siphoned into ours. A whopping five hundred thousand to be exact. Meanwhile, Scar covered our tracks entirely."

Dan let out a low whistle. "I knew he was bad news from the day I started at the company. Good goddamn riddance."

John clapped. "Bravo, Scarlet. A job well done."

Scarlet winked and swept his arm forward as he bowed.

Grif chewed on a piece of bacon, the salt exploding across his tongue. "We got paid, but we also got payback." Dan's leg brushed against his under the table, bringing a grin to his lips again.

"Ugh, are you two playing footsie now?" Alanna complained. "You just hit my toe. Stop being so disgusting."

"I'll second that," John responded with a teasing glint in his eyes. "I'm two steps away from puking up my eggs."

Grif lifted his middle finger, waving it at both of

them. "You're lucky we're not fucking on the table. You can handle a little PDA, assholes."

Dan almost choked on his coffee, a couple of drops flecking onto the tabletop. His cheeks turned ruddy. He'd get used to their lively breakfast conversations and fast.

"Taking the day off, Torres?" John asked. "Unless you're planning on heading in late to rally the troops."

"I've already set up appointments to talk to the police later today," Dan responded. "I'll head in tomorrow to begin tying up loose ends, but I think I'm going into early retirement after my short stint as CEO. I still have contacts at the university to see if I can pick up where I left off on my studies."

An offer leapt to Grif's lips, but he chewed it back. Too much had happened over the past couple of weeks, and he wanted to see where this thing between him and Dan Torres headed.

"Well, shit," Leo said. "If you're leaving the company, I'm bailing out too."

"Had a taste of the criminal life and can't go back?" Tuck teased.

Leo's lips tilted in a smirk. "What's to say I haven't been there for a while now? Hacking's only fun if you're breaking the law."

Grif reached under the table to settle his palm on Dan's thigh. Dan looked at him, his expression unadulterated sunshine as his eyes crinkled around the corners. Grif lifted his mug of coffee with his other hand. "A toast," he said, drawing the attention of everyone at the table. "To new friends, regular breakfasts, and robbing the reaper one more time."

Alanna, John, Scarlet, and Tuck raised their respective glasses. "To robbing the reaper one more time."

Dan and Leo lifted their mugs. "To new friends."

Grif settled into his seat, watching the table before him as his Outlaws dissolved into their normal bickering while Leo and Dan joined in. Sun streamed in through the slats in the windows, the rays glinting off the chrome surfaces in the kitchen and the slick surface of their kitchen table. Dust mites floated through the air like fairy lights, and he drew in a deep inhale of the salty bacon, the rich coffee, and the lingering scent of antiseptic from the bullet wounds they'd dressed last night.

They'd survived to fight again, and they'd taken down yet another corrupt asshole, this time getting a twofer with screwing over Nevarra. Moreover, he'd completed a heist on a Tuesday and hadn't burst into flames.

No knocks on his door the morning after, delivering the nightmarish news. Some taut thread inside him loosened at last.

Instead, he sat at the kitchen table eating breakfast with his family. They might've taken a different shape from the one he knew as a kid, but he treasured each of these individuals just as much. And beyond his Outlaws, he'd found something rare in Dan. He spotted it from the moment he met the man, even if he hadn't been able to place what he'd sensed.

What he felt for Dan Torres wasn't any tame camaraderie or connection. The attraction between them was a volatile, explosive thing, the sort that would either destroy or remake them. Yet they'd stepped through the fire together, and on the other side he saw all their potential spread out before him. It was blinding.

Dan placed his palm over Grif's and squeezed. The day he lost his parents, he'd convinced himself he'd forever be alone, but somehow, Grif Blackmore had cultivated a community of his own and met a man willing to brave his chaos to chase after something real.

THIRTY

The bright lights were blinding, and the constant flashes irritated Dan about five minutes into this press conference. Even the suit felt restrictive after he'd returned to wearing the jeans and flannel from his graduate studies days. Dan adjusted his cuff links, hoping the reporters had gotten their fill from the relentless stream of questions he'd been answering.

Three weeks had passed since they'd executed the heist. Grif and the Outlaws had paid Nevarra back the very next day. He no longer had any hold on them —or any concrete proof they were the ones who'd screwed his shell company over. Doncaster and Kirklees hadn't cropped back up again, but Grif had assured him the longtime rivals were roaches who'd reappear at the next opportunity.

Phil Brennerman would face trial, and Dan was

well-prepared to testify against him. His father was on edge from the investigations, even though they'd managed to focus the attention on Brennerman and Nevarra's dealings through everything. Dan had shown up to Torres Industries increasingly less, and when he broke the news to his father that he was leaving at the first Sunday dinner, Dad raged.

Dan left.

At least, until Mom calmed him down, and he returned at her request to hash things out like adults. Either his dad accepted him as he was at this point, or he would move forward without him.

The solution they'd come up with was perfect.

"In summary, due to the indiscretions that our CFO committed under my watch, I feel it best I step away from the company," Dan spoke, barely able to see the reporters and others sitting in the stands with the glare of the spotlights. "I think our employees will find the new CEO a suitable choice."

A few reporters tried to cut him off, but Dan lifted a hand. "I'll ask you to wait. Any further questions will be fielded to Vanessa Torres, the new CEO of Torres Industries."

Nessa stepped up, looking every inch the cutthroat businesswoman in her Ralph Lauren business suit and Harpy Red lipstick. Her black curls were pinned back, and she gave him a grateful look. Dan didn't need the thanks. His sister had been born for this role—she'd been wanting the job for years now, and he was happy to hand it over at last.

Nessa had been true to her word and never asked about what he'd asked her to do, though she cast quite a few more scrutinizing glances at him. Someday they might crack open that tome, but they both had far too much going on to delve in now.

Dan clapped a hand on Nessa's shoulder and squeezed. "Go get 'em," he mouthed before striding off the stage. He stepped through the back to avoid the clusters of reporters and TV stations trying to capture the news. He'd been fielding questions for weeks, and he hadn't been lying when he said he was ecstatic to hand the reins over to his sister. Ever since he'd made the decision to quit Torres Industries, Dan could breathe again.

He strode out into the late afternoon sun, and a gunmetal grey Bugatti zoomed across the back lot. The tires screeched as it whipped around to a halt, and the passenger window rolled down.

"Hey sexy, want a ride?" Grif called, his eyes gleaming in amusement. The man's long blond hair brushed across his forehead, threaded with gold under the sunlight, and the jeans, white T-shirt, and leather jacket combo highlighted the man's stunning body. Dan's lips quirked. He headed for the sleek, powerful car and the sleek, powerful man inside.

"I'm not supposed to accept rides from strangers,"

Dan said as he clicked the door open and slid inside. "But what the hell. Apparently, I'm more addicted to danger than I thought."

Grif leaned in and grabbed him by the nape to draw him closer. His lips crushed against his, and Dan sank into the kiss at once, letting out a sigh of relief. The man's touch melted him every time. Grif pulled away and stepped on the gas, the car peeling across the asphalt, away from this place.

"How'd you survive the vultures?" he asked, casting him a glance.

"I can't wait to be out of this thing," Dan said, peeling off his blazer and tossing it into the back seat. He rolled up his sleeves to the elbow and settled against the leather seats, drawing in the scent that dosed him with comfort.

"Not fair," Grif drawled. "I'm supposed to be the one undressing you." A couple of weeks in, and Dan may as well have been living at the Outlaws' penthouse with the amount of time he spent over there. For someone who had been so averse to sharing his space, Dan was starting to see that when Grif went in, he went all in. The man was beyond attentive, more affectionate than he would've ever expected, and the more late-night balcony conversations they had, the more the glacial expression in his eyes thawed.

"Where are you heading?" he asked, watching the

turns Grif made, different than the roads he would've taken to head back to the penthouse.

"We're making a quick pit stop," Grif said, whipping around corners with a liquid smoothness that defied Chicago traffic. "It's too gorgeous of a day to be cooped in HQ, and I want to go on a walk with my boyfriend."

Dan still flushed every time the word was said out loud. He'd been longing for something real, a seed that could grow into an oak tree with time. With Grif, he might get the chance.

Within minutes, Grant Park stretched before them, the manicured, violent shocks of green standing out against all the asphalt and concrete. Grif pulled into the parking lot and flipped the engine off.

"Let's go stretch our legs," Grif said, hopping out of the car.

Dan slipped out after him, jogging to catch up since Grif had already started walking. "Anyone ever tell you that you're bossy?"

Grif flashed him a heartbreaker smile. "That's why I'm the boss, gorgeous."

The sky was a sapphire blue with smears of pastel clouds scattered throughout. The wind brought the crisp scent of water traveling his way, and Grif threaded his fingers through his as they strolled down the walking path. Up ahead, the Buckingham Fountain spurted jets high into the sky, the pale green statues chalky under the intense rays. The water glittered.

Any remaining tension from the press conference leaked out of him while they walked along. The closer they got to the fountain, the louder the burbles grew, a soothing sound. Grif guided him closer until he reached the fencing and found a spot to lean on.

"I've been meaning to ask you this the past couple of weeks, and I couldn't find the right time," Grif started. The edge to his voice made Dan's nerves flare to attention, but he remained quiet, listening. "This isn't a dealbreaker, but it's something important to me. These past few weeks we've been together, I've felt closer to you than I have with anyone in a long, long time. And if I thought you weren't a good fit, I'd still want to try to make things work between us. In no way am I asking you to give up your studies either."

Grif sucked in a sharp breath. He tugged at the leather jacket he wore as he stared at the sky. Dan's stomach flipped, but he let him continue.

"You're smart, you keep me in check, and your knowledge with machines and sensors from your degree is something we could use in the field. I formed the Outlaws to take down corrupt corporations, and Brennerman was one of many. We have a lot of work to do, and I'd like you to be a part of it."

Dan's eyebrows drew together. The beginning of the speech had sounded a whole lot like a breakup, and he'd already gripped onto the fence to brace himself, the cool metal imprinting in his palm. "Wait, are you asking me to join the Outlaws?"

Grif pressed his lips together and nodded, avoiding eye contact. Like this, he bled a vulnerability he only let out around Dan. "Yeah, I'd love to have you on the team."

The breath rushed out of him. Relief crashed in next. Dan let out a shaky laugh and shook his head. "You need to work on your pitch, babe. I was pretty sure this was a breakup speech."

Grif slid his fingers through his hair. "Look, I can throw speeches all day long when it doesn't matter. Spinning lies comes easily. This sort of shit, I'm terrible at."

"You mean shit like telling the truth?" Dan teased, loving the fact that Grif tried in the first place with him. He leaned against the fencing and mulled over the question for a moment. Being a part of the Outlaws. In all honesty, part of him had been waiting, hoping, Grif would ask. As terrifying as the night of the heist had been, the thrill infected him like a virus he hadn't been able to shake.

And he'd be able to apply his engineering work in a whole different way with the Outlaws. Grif wasn't asking him to give up his dreams—he offered to enhance them. Dan had been longing for change, silently screaming inside his prison at Torres Industries, and Grif had come in like a summer squall and overturned the trees at the roots. Being a part of the Outlaws was the exact adventure he'd been searching for.

Dan nodded—until he realized Grif still squinted at the sky, trying to act unaffected. His chest warmed at the sight as he rested his hand over Grif's. "I'm all in, Blackmore. I want everything."

Despite the vibrant green leaves surrounding them, the gorgeous fountain in the distance, and the picturesque view of the skyscrapers looming over Grant Park, Dan's focus was on one thing.

Grif looked at him at last, and the breath caught in Dan's throat. The look in those blue eyes was dizzying, like standing at the edge of the shore to watch the sun rise. His hair glinted like gold, and Dan memorized the raised skin of the scars decorating his arms, the nick on his cheek, the one above his eyebrow. This time, Dan closed the distance between them.

He pressed his lips to Grif's and sank into the connection threatening to engulf him every time. Steady palms encircled his waist, and he melted against him. The scent of amber, of leather, and of crisp water flooded his senses. Grif's power wasn't just from his presence alone or the words he spun. The man inspired the people he held dear to become greater versions of themselves, to fight, so they'd never feel helpless again.

As they deepened their kiss, the spark flared between them, the connection that had blazed bright when they'd first met and matured into a deep and lingering promise waiting to be explored.

Together, they'd take the first hesitant steps down that path.

***

Looking for more LGBTQI+ romances, check out Katherine's ***Confined Desires***.

ACKNOWLEDGMENTS

Many, many thanks to Rebecca, Rob, Ember, and Landra for the insightful critiques and letting me bounce ideas off you. This book had a lot of moving parts and was a tough balance between the heist and the romance elements, and I wouldn't have been able to pull it off without you.

Thank you to my amazing editors for pushing me to make this manuscript the best it can be and to Hot Tree Publishing for taking a chance on this story.

Also, I want to shout out to Tom, who happened to send a random meme on the right day to get my gears turning.

ABOUT THE AUTHOR

Katherine McIntyre is a feisty chick with a big attitude despite her short stature. She writes stories featuring snarky women, ragtag crews, and men with bad attitudes—and there's an equally high chance for a passionate speech thrown into the mix. As an eternal geek and tomboy who's always stepped to her own beat, she's made it her mission to write stories that represent the broad spectrum of people out there, from different cultures and races to all varieties of men and women.

Website: http://www.katherine-mcintyre.com

Newsletter sign-up: http://eepurl.com/duIScb

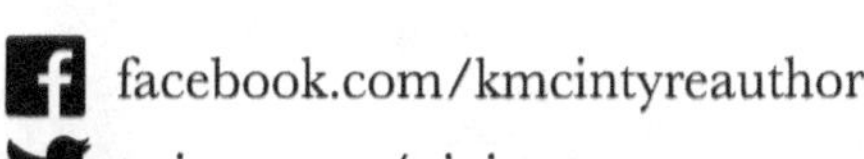

facebook.com/kmcintyreauthor

twitter.com/pixierants

instagram.com/authorkmcintyre

bookbub.com/profile/katherine-mcintyre

ABOUT THE PUBLISHER

Hot Tree Publishing opened its doors in 2015 with an aspiration to bring quality fiction to the world of readers. With the initial focus on romance and a wide spread of romance subgenres, Hot Tree Publishing has since opened their first imprint, Tangled Tree Publishing, specializing in crime, mystery, suspense, and thriller.

Firmly seated in the industry as a leading editing provider to independent authors and small publishing houses, Hot Tree Publishing is the sister company to Hot Tree Editing, founded in 2012. Having established in-house editing and promotions, plus having a well-respected market presence, Hot Tree Publishing endeavors to be a leader in bringing quality stories to the world of readers.

Interested in discovering more amazing reads brought to you by Hot Tree Publishing? Head over to the website for information:

www.hottreepublishing.com

facebook.com/hottreepublishing

twitter.com/hottreepubs

instagram.com/hottreepublishing